SWIMMING
UPSTREAM

RUTH MANCINI

Booktrope Editions
Seattle, WA 2013

Cover Design by Loretta Matson

Edited by Christine Lawson

This is a work of fiction. Names, characters, places, brands, media, and incidents are either the product of the author's imagination or are used fictitiously. Any resemblance to similarly named places or to persons living or deceased is unintentional.

PRINT ISBN 978-1-62015-192-1

EPUB ISBN 978-1-62015-288-1

Library of Congress Control Number: 2013922389

For Tracey and Clare, with love

ACKNOWLEDGMENTS

Huge thanks to Christine Lawson at Oxford Editing Services Freelance Press for copy editing and commenting on numerous drafts of this novel. My thanks go also to Oxford Literary Consultancy for their extensive editorial and marketing advice. I'm very grateful to my fantastic team at Booktrope; I'd particularly like to thank my book manager, Sárka-Jonae Miller, and proofreader, Jennifer Gracen (she of the laser eyes. She even picked up on the incorrect spelling of Jimi Hendrix's name!), as well as Loretta Matson, for the amazingly beautiful cover design. Thanks also to Dominic at Redgraphite Design for producing the original cover artwork and for sourcing the face that has become the hallmark of this book.

My heartfelt thanks go to my lovely friends Catherine Scammell, Tracey Wood and Angela Ridley and also to Lesley Scammell, Clare McDonnell, and everyone else who read and commented on earlier drafts of *Swimming Upstream*. Many thanks also to fellow author Catherine Amey for her editorial and marketing advice and to Clare Mac for the insight into radio journalism. A special thank you to Estelle Jobson for her funny story about the talking stars…

I remain indebted to Jaimie Cahlil (my "Uncle Silbert") for his love, support, and words of wisdom, and to my dear friend Lucy Bagourd for her wonderful descriptions of Eaubonne.

Finally, thanks to my husband, Mark, for contributing the odd word or phrase here and there, and for making me laugh, most days.

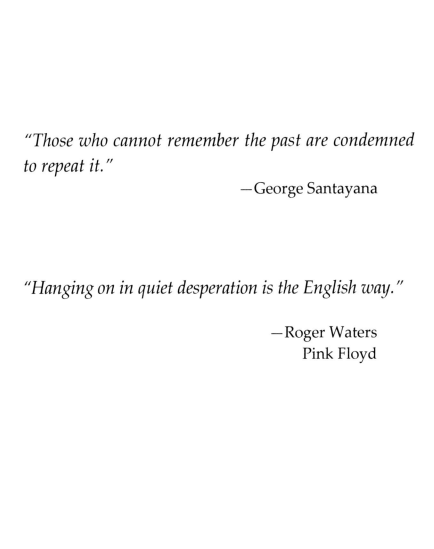

"Those who cannot remember the past are condemned to repeat it."

—George Santayana

"Hanging on in quiet desperation is the English way."

—Roger Waters
Pink Floyd

1

I ONCE READ that the end of a relationship is like being involved in a road traffic accident. Which is quite fitting really, given what happened. Only you'd probably think of an accident as something sudden, out of the blue, and I suppose breaking up is like that for some people. For me, though, the road had been rocky for some time, and I could see all too clearly what was about to happen: a multi-car pileup. People screaming and car horns blaring. And here we were, me and Larsen, gliding towards it, the wheels beneath us slipping and spinning out of control.

It was Spring 1992, a typical blustery April afternoon. The streets of Cambridge were gloomy, the pavements wet, and the turrets and spires of the city in the distance were lost in a sepia haze. A strong gust of wind and a smattering of chilly raindrops assaulted me as I jogged across Parker's Piece, and crossed the road at Gonville Place to cut through to the red and grey brick building on the corner that housed the College of Arts. Even after over seven years of living in Cambridge, it still surprised me that such an ancient and architecturally stunning city could be cocooned within the boundaries of what was, on the outer fringes, a perfectly modest late twentieth century town. But this very building, of course, was where it all started for me; this was what had brought me here, to Larsen's home, and into his life. It suddenly seemed a very long time ago.

I cut through the cemetery behind the college and paused for breath, ignoring the droplets of rain that were dribbling over my forehead. I looked back again at the brick and glass building behind me and the strangest of feelings washed over me, something that I could only describe as homesickness. But for what? I had my own home — a pretty two-bedroomed Victorian terraced house in Vinery Road — and a stable life with Larsen. I had friends. I had a budding career in broadcasting. My life was full and busy and I had no reason to feel insecure. And yet, something was missing.

I shifted my swimming bag on my shoulder and set off again down Coldham's Lane, breaking into a jog, and a few minutes later I pushed through the revolving door into the swimming pools complex. I was met by a welcome wall of heat and the familiar scent of chlorine. I picked up my ticket and walked into the changing room, hot steam from the showers rising up to greet me. I didn't in fact much feel like taking off all my clothes and immersing myself in cold water; I was wet and cold enough already. There was also a knot in my stomach and a heaviness in my chest that was more than the predictable outcome of having drunk the best part of a bottle of wine by myself and smoked numerous cigarettes the night before. I knew that I should have talked to Larsen long ago about the way I was feeling, about the thing that had come between us. But I couldn't name it; I didn't know what it was. So I carried on as if nothing was wrong. Because even thinking that I could lose him made me hold my breath until it stopped short in my lungs and nothing came back out again. Because saying it would make it real for both of us and I didn't know how or why it had come to this.

My heart sank even further as I exited the changing rooms onto the pool side; there were no lap lanes marked off. The pool was packed full of dive-bombing eleven-year-olds and elderly people doing widths. ("You're going the wrong way!" I always wanted to shout.) It wasn't the tranquil haven I had expected; it was one big wet free-for-all. I sighed, pulled on my goggles, took a deep breath, and plunged in, fighting my way in a frustrated crawl down to the shallow end. A girl on her back clipped me on the right ear as she meandered past me in an aimless kind of circle, then carried on regardless, while I wobbled around in her slipstream. I could feel the tension creeping up my shoulder blades and setting into my jaw. A length and a half later, there was a huge splash to my left and an elbow jabbed painfully into my hip. I was in mid stroke. I swallowed a large mouthful of water, choked and gasped for breath. My goggles filled up with water. I shot an angry and waterlogged glance around me and grabbed for the edge of the pool.

A face appeared. "You okay?"

I pulled off my goggles and hauled myself up onto the edge. "It's supposed to be lengths," I said, making no attempt to mask my irritation. "Two 'til four."

"Sorry, love," said the lifeguard. "Not in school holidays. Different timetable."

"So where's that advertised? How is anyone supposed to know that?" I was simultaneously angry and ashamed at the tone of my voice. I seemed to have been speaking like this to people a lot lately. I pulled the elastic back on the strap of my goggles. They pinged out of my hands and landed at the lifeguard's feet.

"There's a new timetable in reception." The lifeguard bent down beside me and, seated on his haunches, picked up my goggles and began adjusting the strap. I watched him with a confusing combination of irritation and gratitude. I knew how to fix my own goggles, for Christ's sake. But then, despite what Larsen thought, I didn't always enjoy doing everything myself. I just never seemed to have had much choice.

"There you go," said the lifeguard, rubbing at the plastic lenses with his t-shirt, and handing my goggles back to me.

"Thanks." I looked at him more closely. He was tall, well over six feet, with thick sandy-coloured hair, hazel eyes, and, I noticed, eyebrows that met slightly in the middle. "Never trust anyone whose eyebrows meet in the middle," Larsen had told me once. I had forgotten to ask him why. I smiled involuntarily at this thought, and the lifeguard smiled back. His eyes met mine and I turned away, embarrassed.

"So, do you come here often?" he asked. I looked back at him, incredulously. Was he really trying to chat me up? "I just mean… you're a strong swimmer," he added. "Your technique's good. I was wondering if you had ever competed?"

"I used to," I said. "County level. The ASA. It was a while ago."

"You should give it another go."

"I don't know. I haven't got time for that amount of training."

"Well, if you change your mind… I do a bit of coaching. I've got time for a few private lessons, if you're interested?" There was something suggestive in the way that he said this and he backed it up with a raising of his eyebrows and a smile.

"I'll think about it. Anyway… must get on," I muttered, embarrassed at his attentions and feeling disloyal to Larsen. I stood up to dive back in but became suddenly very conscious of the slippery tightness of my Speedo, which was more than a little chlorine-worn round the chest area. I had been meaning to buy a new one. I lowered myself back down again and glanced back over my shoulder. The lifeguard was still smiling at me.

"Hey," he said. "What's your name?"

"Lizzie."

"See you again, Lizzie?"

I nodded without meaning to. "Maybe," I added, then turned and plunged awkwardly into the water.

At precisely twenty-nine lengths, I went through the pain barrier, the lifeguard was forgotten, and the kids went home for tea. As my body grew lighter and my strokes became effortless and even, my thoughts drifted back to Larsen. The ephemeral nature of everything scared me. Why did nothing last? I couldn't bear the thought of failure, of losing him, of giving up. And yet I wasn't happy. I just didn't know why. Was it me? Was I congenitally dissatisfied? And if so, what did it matter whether I was with Larsen or… or that lifeguard, for instance? How could I be sure that I would not arrive back here again in another seven years' time, in this fog of unhappiness, the pain of yet another break-up looming up ahead in the distance? This is what scared me the most: how could I be sure that I would ever be happy again?

I showered and dressed. In the foyer, I spotted the lifeguard, still in his shorts and flip flops, leaning with one leg up against a wall and chatting with a young woman in a pink neon leotard and Spandex tights, who had clearly just come out of the dance studio. She had long blonde hair and, I noticed, an exceptionally tiny waist. I watched as he appeared about to place one hand on her arm, but then he looked up and saw me and took his hand quickly away. He smiled at me and I smiled back briefly as I passed. What a flirt *he* is, I thought. I knew the type: good looking and knows it. And chases anything in Spandex. Or a see-through Speedo. I fed some coins into the vending machine and pressed the buttons. My cereal bar wiggled a little and went through the motions of dispensing itself but had barely moved by the time the metal robot arm came back and captured it again. I glanced up to look for an assistant and saw the lifeguard coming towards me. The woman in Spandex was nowhere to be seen.

"Having trouble?" he said.

"This happens every time. I don't get it. F6. I pushed F6. This machine never works properly."

"You have to let the money drop down fully first. Otherwise it gets confused. You just need to wait a minute before you make your selection," he said. He smiled and looked me straight in the eye. "Although, of course, sometimes that's difficult when you know straight away exactly what it is that you want."

"That was *really* corny," I said, shaking my head.

The lifeguard just laughed and shrugged his shoulders, as if he didn't really need to try that hard. He waved his hand at a junior member of staff and clicked his fingers, beckoning him over. The young lad appeared beside him, blinking vaguely.

"*Keys*, Sean," he said. "Hurry up. Off you go." Sean glanced up at him and rushed off at a pace.

"So," said the lifeguard. "What are you doing now? I finish my shift in a minute. Do you fancy a coffee somewhere?"

I shook my head. "Sorry. I need to get home. I've got work in the morning."

"Come off it," he said. "It's only four o'clock!"

"Yes, but I've got an early start. *Really* early."

"Why, what do you do?"

"Radio. I'm a presenter."

He raised his eyebrows. "I'm impressed. Which station?"

"Oh God, only local. You know. GCFM. I'm normally on the lunchtime programme, but it's my first shot at Breakfast tomorrow. I need to be up bright and early."

"So you are... Lizzie... Lizzie..." He clicked his fingers again, making a good show of searching for my not-so-very famous name.

"...Taylor," I finished for him.

"That's it. I know the name. Though I can't say I've ever listened. But I will now. Definitely will now. Ah, I've just realised. You're Elizabeth Taylor. Ha ha. That's funny."

"No. It's not."

"You've heard that before, I suppose?"

"Just a few times," I sighed.

Sean came back with the keys to the machine. I watched uncomfortably as he fiddled around putting different keys in the lock, trying to find the right one to open it. I could tell that the lifeguard was getting impatient.

"Hurry up Sean, the lady's waiting," he said. And then, "Oh, for God's sake, give them here!" He snatched the bunch of keys from Sean, opened the glass door and released my cereal bar. He handed the keys back to Sean and steered him back in the direction he'd just come from, giving him a little push as he walked away.

"You just can't get the staff," he commented tragically. He handed me my snack. "So. I suppose I am just going to have to settle for hearing your voice, then. On the radio. For now, at least."

"Yes," I said. "I think you are."

Outside, the rain had stopped. I walked up Coldham's Lane, my hair still wet and tangled, the late afternoon sun barely warming my numb ears. I'd buy tuna and pasta and salad for dinner, I decided, and a bottle of sparkling water. No wine tonight. And no fags. And only one more night without Larsen. He was away on tour with his band, due back tomorrow. One more night to try and figure out what it was that I actually wanted from him. Or, more to the point, from myself.

I stood at the edge of the road, waiting for a gap in the traffic. The dual carriageway was busy; it was the beginning of the rush hour. I shouldn't really cross there, I knew. There was a pedestrian crossing further up the road near the traffic lights, but that would mean an extra couple of hundred yards' walk up the road, and the same back down again on the other side if I wanted to get off the road and cut through the park. I watched for several moments until the traffic slowed for the lights up ahead and then stepped out, putting a hand up and smiling at the driver of the car in front of me who nodded and slowed to let me cross. But then, as I ran across the next lane towards the crash barrier, I saw a car heading straight towards me.

I heard a voice scream from a distance, amid a squealing of brakes. I tried to pull myself back but it was too late. My ankle twisted painfully and I stumbled in the road. The car in front of me screeched to a halt. I felt the bumper hit my leg and then I found myself sprawled, face down, my hands and chin bouncing against the hot metal of the bonnet. For a brief moment I lay prostrate, almost nose to nose with the startled driver who was staring into my face through the windscreen. And then I was thrown into the air.

I hit the ground with a thud. It felt as though my heart had stopped.

A young woman rushed over and kneeled down beside me. "Are you okay?"

I nodded. I could hear car doors slamming and people talking nearby. The woman leaned forward and put her arms around me. She was wearing a black fake fur duffle coat. I tasted fake fur and everything went black. The woman sat back up and the sky reappeared above me.

"I think we'd better get out of the road," I mumbled. My heart was beating like crazy. I felt really scared for some reason I couldn't fathom. I could sense that a small crowd was gathering round, but all I could see was a pale yellow sky, and the clouds moving eerily above me, as if I were somewhere else, stuck in a parallel universe, or in some horror movie.

"No! You mustn't move!" The woman's voice sounded familiar. She leaned forward again and I squinted up at her pale face and her long dark hair, which was hanging over me, tickling my chin.

She gasped. "Lizzie? Lizzie Taylor! I don't believe it!"

"Catherine?" I breathed, recognising her as an old school friend I hadn't seen for years.

She bent down and kissed me. "Oh Lizzie, it's so good to see you. You're going to be alright, darling. Don't worry. But you mustn't move."

I couldn't move at all, in fact. It felt like Catherine and her big black coat were still pinning me down, but at the same time I could see her standing up and talking to the driver of the car that had hit me. I heard her say, "Never mind whose fault it was! Has anyone called an ambulance?"

An irrational ice-cold knot of terror tightened in my gut. "I don't need an ambulance," I protested, but my words were lost in the stream of traffic, which was now moving again in the next lane. I could feel the back of my head becoming heavier, and then everything really did go black. From somewhere nearby a voice bellowed out, "She just walked out in front of me!" but I was zipping through the air by then. When I glanced down, I could see the road below me; but instead of a busy dual carriageway, it had turned into an empty tree-lined avenue, a quiet street with a lone little girl with auburn hair and a pink dress, dancing on the pavement in front of a gate, crying. The silence was suddenly shattered by an ambulance, turning into the street, its siren blaring.

I zoomed back down into the blackness and into the road again. Catherine was leaning over me and calling my name. Her voice became a man's voice and she was wearing a green uniform.

"Lizzie?" said the voice again. "Can you hear me?"

I realised that this was not Catherine but a paramedic. "Oh God," I groaned. "I'm not going to be doing Breakfast tomorrow, am I?"

"That's the last thing you want to be worrying about right now, my love," said the paramedic. "Anyway, let them get their own. Do them good."

Catherine was sitting on my bed. I lifted back the curtain that surrounded us and looked out of my cubicle. Casualty was full, wall to wall with broken legs and noses.

"I'm so sorry," I said. "You don't have to wait with me."

"Don't be silly," said Catherine gently. She gave my hand a squeeze. "I don't mind. I wouldn't leave you like this. Anyway, it'll give us a chance to catch up." She lifted her hand to display a diamond-encrusted fourth finger.

"You're getting married?"

Catherine nodded, smiling and arching her eyebrows expectantly.

"Congratulations," I added.

"So," said Catherine, "How did you end up here? In Cambridge, I mean, not here!" She laughed and waved her arm round expansively.

"I came here to study. And then I met someone. So I stayed." I told Catherine about Larsen, from the beginning, but leaving out the end, because I didn't know what the end was.

"So. You're shacked up with a pop star. How cool is that? And he sounds gorgeous," said Catherine when I'd finished.

"He is. Gorgeous," I repeated.

"But?" said Catherine perceptively, and I realised how much I needed to talk to someone. I realised suddenly that I didn't have any friends, after all. Not *real* friends, friends that I could talk to about how I was feeling. All I had was Larsen's friends, the friends I had inherited the day that I met him. The friends that had always been Larsen's friends before mine.

A nurse came in with my X-rays. "Well, nothing broken," she said.

"Really?"

The nurse started to bandage up my foot. "It's badly sprained. You've torn a few ligaments. Don't expect to be running a marathon any time soon." Or swimming, I was guessing. She disappeared again.

"So, what about you?" I asked Catherine, not wanting to bring her down with my problems. "What have you been doing since I saw you last? And who's the lucky man?"

"I went to drama school, luvvie. Four years at the Central School of Speech and Drama. London. Swiss Cottage. Then I met Martin when I was performing at the Arts Centre here in Cambridge. A fringe thing. Some play one of my classmates had written. It was awful actually," she laughed. "Martin knew her, so he came along… and the rest is history, as they say. I moved to Cambridge to be with him."

"What are we like?" I smiled.

"What do you mean?" asked Catherine.

"Following men around."

Catherine looked puzzled. She smiled faintly and pulled back the curtain. An elderly registrar arrived. He handed me my prescription and a pair of crutches.

"Watch where you're going in the future, young lady," he told me. "How are you getting home?"

"Home? I can go home?"

"You've been lucky. No real damage done. Your observations are all good. Blood pressure's on the low side, but I understand that's normal for you."

"Yes."

"That will account for the temporary loss of consciousness. Nothing to worry about. And the sprain will heal in its own time. So, is there anyone who can take you home?"

"My fiancé," said Catherine. "He's coming to collect me. Us. We'll take her."

The registrar nodded and disappeared.

"You don't have to do this!" I protested. "I can get a cab."

"Don't be silly. He won't mind."

"Are you sure?"

By way of reply, Catherine took me by the arm and hoisted me off the bed. We hobbled together down the corridor towards the reception area. Outside, I pulled a pack of cigarettes out of my bag and hastily lit one. Catherine took one crutch for me and I leaned on the other one and breathed in deeply while Catherine glanced round the car park.

"There he is!" Catherine pointed towards a black BMW Three Series, which was parked up just outside the entrance. "He's here already."

"Nice car," I said. I stubbed out my cigarette.

"It's old," said Catherine modestly. "Not as flash as it looks."

"So what does he do?" I asked her, trying to show some enthusiasm for her good fortune in the wake of my own despair.

"Do?"

"Martin. For a living."

"Oh!" she laughed. "He works at the pools complex. That's where I was heading when I saw you doing your kamikaze act in the road. I was on my way to meet him from work. To surprise him."

"He works at the pool?"

"He's a lifeguard," she explained.

At that moment the door of the black BMW opened and out stepped Martin, still in his shorts and flip flops. I recognised him instantly and could see that he recognised me.

2

WHAT WAS IT LIKE, the beginning, with Larsen? Magical, heady, scary. A chance to forget anything bad that had ever happened to me. And to discover that love really does conquer all. Well, for a time, at least.

Cambridge was beautiful, but I didn't belong. My first term at the College of Arts was like being part of a big, new, interesting jigsaw puzzle, only I was the piece that didn't seem to fit. I was studying French, and trying to make friends was harder than I'd thought. I'd sit in the canteen and try to join in the chat with my classmates, but somehow there was never a connection, and that just made me feel insecure. Their background, their frame of reference, was so different from my own — their conversation, their experiences did not fit with my own thoughts, my own reality. Not only that, but everyone spoke better French than I did. And although we'd all started the course at exactly the same time, it felt as though they had all been here, studied, and met and forged their friendships long before I came on the scene. I wandered by myself from tutorial group to lecture hall, feeling more and more isolated as the weeks went by. I discovered that being alone in a crowd is the worst kind of lonely.

Then, in early December, I got chatting in the launderette to a girl called Karen, who told me they were advertising for bar staff at the club where she worked. Before long I was working there too, in the evenings and at weekends. It was just over the Romsey bridge, off Mill Road, but far enough from both the red brick of the Tech and the gothic splendour and tended lawns of the University to feel as if it could have been the street that I grew up in. Immediately my mood lifted and I began to feel as if I belonged in Cambridge. Everything made more sense at the club. Everyone seemed more real to me. And it wasn't long before I spotted Larsen, up on the small stage with his band.

"Who's that?" I asked Karen, the first time I saw him.

"Larsen Tyler," she said. "He's *the* local talent."

Larsen was a natural performer. I watched him, constantly, every chance I got, every time he played. I watched him longingly, but quickly averted my gaze whenever he seemed to be looking my way. He seemed at home in his body in a way that I never had been with mine. He stood on stage, his legs splayed, his head bent over his guitar, his shoulder-length blond hair flopping forward and covering his face as he strummed. He would throw his head back and smile as he sang, his eyes working their way round the room and locking briefly with everyone in his field of vision. When the song ended he would whip his guitar strap off his shoulder and leap onto the piano seat, his fingers moving gently over the keys to a slower melody, while the rest of the band fell into time. After the set finished, he would disappear into the back room with the manager of the club and the rest of the band, where I knew they were drinking until late. Occasionally, I would see him chatting to some girls at the back of the bar and would feel an irrational knot of jealousy tighten in my stomach. But he never looked my way.

Once or twice he came to the bar, but Karen always served him and chatted away easily with him while I hovered nearby self-consciously, smiling and nodding in agreement as she complimented him on the set. Once or twice he smiled back at me, but we never spoke.

Then, late one Sunday evening, when the club was all but empty and we were near to closing, he appeared out of nowhere, standing at the bar. I pushed shut the till, turned and looked up to find him looking straight into my eyes. His were a deep blue-grey, with laughter lines in the corners. When he smiled you could see all his teeth. It looked as if he still had all his baby teeth, like Peter Pan.

"So, what are you drinking?" he asked, fishing in his jeans pocket for his wallet. I gazed back at him, and cleared my throat softly. "Me? Oh, well… a pint of Harp, please," I said in a voice that didn't sound like mine.

"You don't wanna drink that gnat's piddle," he replied, leaning over the bar towards me. His blond hair flopped forwards. I glanced down at his muscled forearms, which were resting on the sticky bar top. "How about a pint of Kronenbourg?"

"Okay then," I agreed. Larsen watched me closely as I moved down the bar to the tap.

"So, what's your name, then?" he asked.

"Lizzie. Lizzie Taylor." I waited for him to give me the "Not *the* Elizabeth Taylor" line, like most people did, but he didn't.

"Lizzie Taylor," he repeated, as if it meant something really special.

I felt myself flushing. It felt really intimate, him saying my name like that. I thought it would sound false and stupid if I asked him his, but "I know who you are" would sound even worse, so I didn't say anything, except "Cheers."

"Cheers," said Larsen, clinking glasses with me. "Nice to meet you at last. So, you're a student, right?"

"Isn't everybody?" I was still reeling from the "at last" comment. Did this mean that he had been watching me, after all, like I had been watching him?

"Nope. I'm not. I *was*. At the College of Arts."

"That's where I am!" A person to whom I didn't have to explain, "It's not the University". "So, what happened?"

"I packed it in. Failed my first year exams. Never looked back."

"Really?" I said, hope rising inside me. I wasn't alone. Larsen had trodden this path before me, and survived. "I think I'm going to fail mine. It's really hard. It seems like a big leap between sixth form and studying for a degree. For me, anyway. Everyone else seems to get it. It's just me. I don't seem to fit in." I stopped abruptly. I had surprised myself with my confession. But Larsen was already nodding, as if he understood.

"Leave, then," he said simply. "It's an elitist institution anyway."

I laughed. "Well, you could argue that the Tech is the institution of the underclass, since it's not part of the University."

"Right. So, how many poverty stricken students from working class backgrounds are there on your course?"

I smiled. "Point taken. So what are you doing now then? Apart from…" I waved my arm in the direction of the stage.

"Apart from wasting my time playing music?" Larsen smiled and raised his eyebrows.

"I don't think that at all. I think you're brilliant."

Larsen looked at me for a moment, then in one swift movement placed his hands onto the bar, vaulted up, leaned over, and kissed me on the lips. I was so stunned that I couldn't speak. I glanced around the near-empty bar, but no-one appeared to have noticed. Karen was busy playing on the Mad Planets machine.

"I work for the council," Larsen continued, as if nothing had happened. "Ents. The Entertainments Department, that is. It's a good job. And we have a laugh."

"That's Entertainment," I said.

Larsen laughed. "You're funny. You know what that song is about?"

"No," I admitted.

"Listen to the lyrics," said Larsen. "If you get it, you're working class. It's the true definition."

"Well, I don't know if I am working class," I said. "I just don't seem to be truly middle class either. Are there any classes anymore?"

"It's like saying, 'How old are you?'" said Larsen. "Everyone says you're as old as you feel. I think it's the same with class."

"How old do you feel?" I asked him.

"Ageless," smiled Larsen.

I smiled back. "So why do you live here, surrounded by all the students, if you don't like them?"

"I was born here," said Larsen, simply. "It's my home. I'm town, not gown. Hey, do you know about the Rock against Racism gig on Midsummer Common?"

"That's next month, isn't it?"

"Yup. I'm organising it. It's a great line-up. We're playing. You should come. It's going to be mega."

"Sounds great."

Karen appeared. It was time to close up.

"I need to change the barrels," I told Larsen. "Ready for tomorrow."

"Need a hand?"

"I can do it. It's okay." Idiot, I told myself and added, "I do need another crate of cokes though."

Larsen followed me down the steps into the cellar. Unnerved, I tripped on the second step and Larsen caught me.

"Steady!" He put his arms round me. "You okay?" he asked, stepping back and surveying me, his hands still round my waist.

"I'm okay," I smiled. "Now."

He held me a little longer than necessary, looked at me for a moment then said, "Tell you what, do you fancy coming back to my place? There are a few people coming back, a bit of a party? Karen's coming," he added, as if I needed persuading. "It's only about five minutes from here."

I nodded. "That would be great."

"Good," said Larsen. "You get and close up while I pack up my gear. Then we can grab a few beers and head back."

I washed glasses and Karen dried them while Larsen turned off the stage lights, shut down the PA desk, boxed up microphones and wound up leads. All the while I felt my heart thumping in my chest with excitement, feeling somehow that this short time — which included all three of us, together inside the empty building, calling out and laughing as we worked — was a joyous prelude to something momentous that was about to happen in my life; an end to the isolation of my student world. Karen and I turned the plastic chairs upside down on the tables and pulled down the shutters. Once all the glasses had been stacked neatly on the shelves and the ashtrays emptied, I picked up my coat and Larsen set the alarm and locked the door while Karen and I stood outside shivering, our breath making foggy clouds in the cold night air.

"Poor Larsen," whispered Karen. "He needs a bit of cheering up. He's just split up with his girlfriend."

"Really?" I asked, hope rising up inside me.

The party was in full swing when we arrived and I felt heady as the wall of heat and smoke rose to greet us in the hallway. Music was blaring from the living room. I followed Larsen and Karen into the kitchen. The floor was sticky and the soles of one of my shoes had picked up a fag end. I lifted my foot and pulled it off.

"Larsen, man, you made it," said a huge dark-haired guy wearing a checked shirt and jeans. He took a beer out of Larsen's hand, stuck his fingers up at him, and took the top off with his teeth. He turned to look at me with friendly curiosity.

"Of course I made it, I live here, you fool," said Larsen and put an arm round his shoulders.

"Doug, this is Lizzie. Lizzie, Doug."

Doug took my hand and kissed it.

A girl appeared in the doorway. She was tall, with light brown shoulder-length hair and green glassy eyes, oval-shaped and slanted in the corners like a cat's. I thought she looked sophisticated, even though she was casually dressed in a baggy black jumper and jeans. I looked at Larsen, who was taking off his leather jacket, and felt suddenly overdressed in my mini skirt and tight-fitting jumper.

"Tyler, you're here," said the girl, accusingly, as if someone should have told her. She looked straight through me, bounced up to Larsen and flung her arms round his neck. He caught her with one arm as he swung round.

"Jude, meet Lizzie," he said brightly.

I smiled. Jude responded with a vague nod and, tossing her hair, disappeared back into the crowd. Doug and Larsen exchanged a furtive glance.

"Come on," said Larsen, and we all trooped into the living room.

The guy beside me passed me a joint. His name was Jeff. He had something of a cross between a Mohican and a footballer's haircut going on; short at the front, long at the back and shaved at the sides over his ears. He talked interminably about music, reeling off the names of various obscure bands that I guessed I was supposed to have heard of, while I sat and nodded at him in silence. All I could think about was Larsen, who was leaning up against the wall next to Jude, deep in conversation.

"Don't get back together," I pleaded at them inside my head, feeling hopeless. I wondered why I cared that much. After all, I barely knew him. I must be crazy. I wondered if I should go home, but knew I wouldn't, not yet.

I looked around the room. It was unmistakably a student pad — minimalist, quirky. A chipboard table and chairs were pushed into one corner, and a stolen road sign "No U-turns" — took pride of place near the door. Underneath the window opposite me was a sagging green sofa, with lots of people I didn't know spilling off its edges. There were several interesting-looking pictures on the wall which I would have liked to get up and contemplate, but I was sitting on the floor in a bean bag and not at all sure that I could get up without drawing huge amounts of attention to myself. I was suddenly feeling very stoned.

"What about Jellybelly?" asked Jeff; at least that's what it sounded like.

"What?" I turned my head slowly. The rest of the room did a lightning dash to catch up with me.

"Jellybelly," Jeff persisted, leaning against the bean bag and wedging me even more deeply into its contours. My forehead felt cold and prickly. "You must have heard of Jellybelly."

He turned to Karen, who had sat down in front of us with a bottle of vodka.

"She hasn't heard of Jellybelly," he said.

"Stop it," I stammered faintly.

"Stop what?" said Jeff, looking confused.

"Saying Jellybelly. Please." With a concerted effort, I lurched up out of the beanbag and stumbled into the hall, past Jude and Larsen, and up the stairs. Larsen watched me go and looked as though he was about to say something, but Jude was talking to him, her mouth pressed up against his ear.

I stood at the washbasin, squinting under the bright light at my reflection in the mirror. I looked a mess. There were dark rings of eyeliner under each eye. I licked my finger and wiped at them, but it only made it worse. Then my mascara started coming off as well. I turned the tap on and splashed cold water onto my cheeks.

Someone banged on the door. I opened it and a tiny girl with short blonde hair shot in, hoisted up her raincoat, and pulled down her knickers.

"Sorry. I'm busting." She stared at me from the loo. "Are you all right?"

"I think so." I smiled, steadying myself against the sink.

"I like your hair," she commented. "Red's my favourite colour."

"Thank you," I said. "I prefer to call it auburn."

She grinned at me. She had a tiny elfin face, with big blue eyes, a turned up nose, and a pointy chin.

"You look like a pixie," I observed. I was still feeling very stoned. I sat down on the edge of the bath. Her eyes twinkled, amusedly. She flushed the chain and squeezed past me to the sink. "Although I have to say you're not dressed like a pixie," I continued, looking down at the black stockings and shoes under her navy raincoat. "I'd say you were... a traffic warden?" I guessed.

"Not quite right," she said, turning round and opening her coat with soapy hands, to reveal a light blue uniform. "A nurse."

"This isn't fancy dress," I pointed out.

"I know," she said, and winked at me. "Got a kinky boyfriend, that's all."

"You're kidding? He makes you wear that to parties?"

The girl in the raincoat laughed. "It was a joke. I am actually a nurse. I work at Addenbrookes. I've just finished my shift."

I put my head in my hands. "I'm so gullible. What an idiot."

"Hey, hey, hey," said the girl. "I am the queen of gullible. I used to think that the stars could talk."

I lifted my head up. "The stars? As in the ones in the sky?"

"Yes. I was told that by the matron at the... the home. I was brought up in a children's home. Out in the countryside, near Saffron Walden. In the middle of nowhere, it was. And at night I couldn't sleep for all the... well, the noise. There was always this noise going on outside the windows, crickets, I think, and I don't know what else. I told Matron and she said it was just the stars chattering."

"That's kind of cute." I smiled.

"Not when you're sixteen, it isn't."

"What?"

"I was sixteen before anyone told me that the stars can't talk. I was kissing my boyfriend under the moonlight and I said, 'Aren't the stars quiet tonight?' He looked at me like I was crazy. Then he dumped me."

"That's harsh," I said.

The girl in the raincoat nodded. "So, who are you? I've not seen you before. Are you a friend of Jude's?"

"I don't think so," I said. "I think we've established that."

"Oh, right. Don't take it personally. If you're not a friend of Jude's, then you're not a friend of Jude's. The Girlfriends' Club, well, they're all a bit cliquey. Anyway, I'm Zara," she said, and held out her tiny hand. I took it.

"I'm Lizzie," I told her before I lost my balance and slipped backwards into the bath, still clinging onto her hand. Zara tried to pull me back, but she was taken by surprise, and she flew forward and landed on top of me. We both cracked up laughing so hard that neither of us could stop.

"Zara?" called a voice from outside the door.

"In here!" Zara called.

The door opened and Doug's head appeared. He smiled affectionately at the pair of us, laying sprawled in the empty bath, then helped us out one by one. Zara followed him out to the landing. He smiled and put his hand on her arm, then turned and looked at me warily, as I came out behind her. Standing next to him, she looked even tinier. She could barely have been five feet tall. She swung from side to side on her black stockinged heel and they both watched as Larsen came running up the stairs.

"There you are," he said to me. "Hello, Zara."

"Hi," said Zara, who seemed to be moving backwards, with Doug behind her.

"Are you okay?" asked Larsen, looking deeply into my eyes, his face racked with concern. A door slammed behind us and we were alone.

"I have to go."

"Why? Don't go," he pleaded. "Aren't you feeling well?"

"Not really."

"Come on, you need to lie down," said Larsen, and before I could protest he took my arm and manoeuvred me into one of the bedrooms.

The room was dark. Larsen eased me down onto a mattress on the floor, took off my shoes and sat beside me. I could feel the vibrations of the music thumping underneath me. Moonlight streamed through the bare window, which had no curtains, and my eyes adjusted slowly. Up on the ceiling above me, a number of glow-in-the-dark stars twinkled down, reminding me of my conversation with Zara. To my left, beside my head, a stack of vinyl albums stretched the width of the room. An acoustic guitar was propped in the corner next to a raggedy-edged poster of Jimi Hendrix. The room smelled vaguely of old cigarette butts.

"Is this your room?" I asked.

Larsen nodded.

I sat up uncomfortably. "What's your girlfriend going to say if she comes up and finds me in here?"

"My girlfriend? What are you talking about?" Larsen frowned and my heart leaped. "Ah, you mean Jude?" He laughed. "You didn't think…? Jude's not my girlfriend. She lives here, that's all. She shares the room downstairs with Bri."

"Bri," I echoed, and lay back down again.

"Brian. Her boyfriend. They're both artists — those are their paintings downstairs, his and hers. Only he's not here; he's at a lock-in in the Jugglers Arms, which is why she's pissed off. She's okay, though. She's gone round Marion's."

"Marion?" I added the name to my mental register.

"Doug's girlfriend. Her and Jude are best buddies."

I was confused. "But—"

"Marion doesn't like parties," said Larsen. He shifted on the mattress beside me. "Now enough about Jude and Marion. Let's talk about something more interesting, like… you and me."

I looked up into his eyes and he looked back into mine. He was so beautiful. He was the most handsome man I had ever laid eyes on. But more than that, there was something familiar about him. It was as if I knew him already.

Larsen lit two cigarettes and passed me one.

"So why did you drop out of College?" I asked him.

"Failed my exams. Like I said."

"You didn't think of re-sits?"

"Nah." Larsen shrugged. "What's the point? That's just going backwards. I believe in going forwards."

"No U-turns," I smiled.

"Precisely." Larsen smiled back and kissed me on the cheek. I felt a shiver of excitement running up my back. He took a puff of his cigarette. "Besides, that was the old man's dream for me, not mine. Get a degree. Become a teacher."

"A teacher?"

"Yeah. They're both teachers. Academics. They both lecture at the University."

"And that wasn't for you?"

"No. My dream was always to play music."

"Let me guess. They don't approve?"

"My dad thinks I'm wasting my time."

"And your mum?"

"She doesn't even acknowledge that this is what I do. Her eyes glaze over if I mention music. Unless it's Mahler. Or Mozart. Or Mendelssohn. She's German," he added. "She's fluent in five languages. But she pretends not to understand if you say anything she doesn't want to hear."

"Do all her composers have to begin with 'M'?" I smiled.

Larsen grinned. "Something like that."

"So you're a closet academic. And middle class to boot," I teased.

"Like I said, it's how you feel, not the family you were born to." Larsen sounded defensive, and I regretted what I'd said.

"It's a shame about your degree, though," I said. "A degree can get you a long way."

"I thought you were packing it in?" Larsen challenged me.

"Well, I didn't say that. I mean, it's early days. I don't think it's come to that yet."

"Your call," said Larsen, and shrugged. I sensed he wanted to hear me say that I was leaving college, and I wondered why he cared. I was strangely and secretly glad that he did.

I looked up at him. "Karen said you had just broken up with someone."

"Karen told you that?"

I nodded.

"Yeah. I have. It's been dead in the water for a long time now, though."

"How long were you with her?"

"A few years. Five, maybe."

"That's a long time." I paused, and then asked, "Is there any chance of you getting back together?"

Larsen looked at me as if I were mad. "I told you. I never go back, to anything," he said. "Once it's over, it's over."

There was an awkward silence.

"It doesn't matter," I said, uncertainly. "I'm sorry I asked."

"Time for another drink," he said, and he jumped up and headed out of the room.

I could hear people milling around on the landing, and someone called out "Hey, Tyler" as he passed them on the stairs. I lay and watched the shadows cast on the ceiling by the passing traffic, while the music throbbed below. After ten minutes had passed, it started to dawn on me that maybe he wasn't going to come back. Of course he would, eventually, since this was his bedroom, but I couldn't just stay there, not for much longer, not if he didn't want me there. I wondered if Jude had come back from Marion's and was once again crying on his shoulder over the elusive Brian.

I turned over and buried my face in the pillow. It smelled sweet and musky, an indefinable aroma of sleep and shampoo and sweat, of Larsen. I inhaled deeply, breathing him in. Five more minutes, I kept telling myself. Five more minutes, then I'll go. But every five minutes was followed by another. Eventually, I sat up and felt around on the floor for my shoes. I was about to get up when the door opened and Larsen stepped into the room, holding the remains of a bottle of vodka and two paper cups.

"Why, oh why, oh why," he said, "do people bring brown ale to parties?"

"Because it's cheap and no-one likes it," I said, almost laughing with relief. "And they'll still have something to drink when they've drunk what everyone else has brought."

"Spot on. Bloody scroungers." He looked at me. "And where do you think you're going?"

"Nowhere," I smiled and lay down on the bed again.

"Look, I got this. Took me a while to find it." Larsen kneeled down on the floor beside me, poured two generous measures of vodka into the paper cups, and handed one to me. "So," he said. "Where were we?"

Several hours later, I became aware that the music had stopped and that the house had fallen silent.

Larsen leaned over, pushed my hair away from my forehead and kissed me gently on the lips. His breath was sweet and warm.

"What time is it?" I asked.

"I dunno, three or four."

"Do you think everyone's gone?"

"Yep. Or crashed out."

I propped myself up on one elbow and peered around the room, blinking and trying to focus in the dark. The moon had shifted. All I could see were darkened shapes and Larsen's silhouette above me.

"Do you think I should go home?" I asked.

"No," he said. "I think you should stay here, with me."

There had been many times in my life when I had been indecisive, many times I'd felt ambivalent about things and unsure of what I really wanted (especially when I got it). But I knew beyond a shadow of a doubt that I wanted Larsen, more than I'd ever wanted anything or anyone in my life.

Larsen sat up with his back to me while he unlaced his trainers. I could just about see his shoulder muscles moving up and down inside his t-shirt. With a deep-seated sense of foreboding, I wondered if I was going to have to pay for this at some point in the future, if the Gods would get jealous, as the saying went; but I didn't care.

"How're you doing, are you okay?" Larsen was leaning over me again.

"I'm okay," I said. "I have to admit, horizontal is good."

"It's good for me too," he confided, as he slid under the covers and covered my body with his own.

3

MARTIN STOOD BY THE CAR in silence and held the back door open.

"Uh uh, sprained ankles in the front," said Catherine, tugging at the passenger door and helping me inside. She climbed into the back seat with my crutches.

Martin got into the driver's seat beside me and started the engine. He drove silently out of the hospital gates and out onto the ringroad. Once or twice I caught him glancing in my direction. When I glanced back at him, he looked back at the road ahead of him and smiled. I was a little taken aback at his cheek. Here he was, engaged to be married, and yet he was chatting up strange women at the swimming pool and inviting them for coffee. Surely he must at least be wondering if I was going to tell Catherine? The tension between the two of us was palpable. Catherine, however, didn't seem to notice anything and talked all the way back about school, telling various anecdotes about the two of us for Martin's benefit.

The strange thing was that I barely remembered any of the events that Catherine was talking about.

"Do you remember that time I came over to your house?" asked Catherine, as we stopped at the traffic lights on Hills Road. I noticed that Martin was going the wrong way back, or at least taking a longer route than necessary, but I didn't like to comment. "We must have been ten or eleven. Your dad threw your bike onto the neighbour's skip because you had left it on the path outside?"

"No," I said, surprised. "I really don't."

"Go, on, you must remember. You promised to put it away in the future, but he wouldn't let you have it back. We sneaked out later to see if we could rescue it, but it was gone."

"I don't remember, Catherine, honest. I don't even remember ever having a bike."

"Well, I guess you didn't after that," said Catherine, quietly.

I turned back and smiled at her. "It's not you, it's me. There's loads of stuff I seem to have forgotten."

"Me too," said Catherine, cheerfully. "Mind you, I did miss a lot of school. Glandular fever. I had it every summer. And bronchitis in the winter."

"Sticky mattress more like," said Martin, speaking for the first time. "Your parents were too soft on you."

I felt Catherine tensing behind me.

"You caught up, though," I said quickly. "You didn't fall behind. That was amazing."

"I was good at exams, that's all. I knew the formula. How to give the examiners what they wanted. I wasn't naturally brainy like you. Lizzie was the clever one," she said to Martin. "She got five A's in her first year report and she was Student of the Year. I was so envious."

"Hmm," I sighed. "Now that I *do* remember. The girls in my class buried me in the materials box during needlework and took turns to sit on me."

Martin let out a short snort of laughter. "Sorry," he added.

"That's okay," I smiled. "I'm over it."

We turned right off Gonville Place into Mill Road. The house would be empty and in darkness, of course, but since we had left the hospital, I realised I'd been harbouring a small and selfish hope that maybe the tour would have finished early and that Larsen would be here. I really missed him, I realised that now. Maybe we could talk things through, be honest with one another, discover what was wrong and fix it — find a new bright way forward, together. Telling Catherine about him at the hospital, talking about how we had met, had reminded me of the passion between us, of how much he had meant to me, and still did. It had reminded me of exactly how much I had to lose.

"Which street is it, then?" asked Martin.

"Sorry, sorry. Just here, turn left," I apologised.

Martin pulled up outside the house. I thanked him for the lift. He shrugged by way of reply and nodded at the house. "No one home?"

"No," I said. "My boyfriend's away. Due back tomorrow."

"Pity," he said quietly as Catherine got out of the car to help me out.

I turned to look at him. What was a pity? That I was on my own tonight? Or that I had a boyfriend who was coming back tomorrow? Martin just looked back at me and smiled.

Catherine opened my door. She handed me my crutches and helped me out of the car.

"Can you manage?" she asked. "We can help you inside if you like?"

"It's okay. I'm going to have to get used to these things sometime."

Catherine stared up at the house. "Are you sure you'll be all right on your own? I don't like to leave you."

"I'll be fine. Honest," I smiled.

She held me steady while I hooked my swimming bag over my shoulders and fished around in the side pocket for a pen. I wrote my telephone number down on the back of her hand.

"I'll call you," she smiled. "I really want to stay in touch."

"Me too," I said, pleased.

We hugged and said goodbye.

I pushed open the front door and walked into the living room, hoping irrationally for the habitually irritating sight of Larsen's jacket dumped on the stairs and his trainers under the coffee table. But nothing. The room was empty and the magnolia and fawn-flecked carpet stretched ahead, unspoilt. I poked my head round the door to the kitchen. Instead of the usual sink full of plates and cups and the crumby work surfaces I'd been half expecting, the sink was empty and every surface still gleamed and sparkled, just as I'd left it that morning. I checked the answering machine. There were no messages from Larsen.

I shrugged off my coat and began to heave myself shakily up the stairs. Halfway up I became afraid I was going to fall back down. I decided it would be easier to leave the crutches behind and go up backwards on my bottom. Once or twice my foot thudded against the stair and a spasm of pain shot through me, causing me to squeal and stop and gasp for breath. At last I reached the top and, hauling myself up with the aid of the banister, I hopped heavily and slowly into the bedroom. I would have to get in to work somehow in the morning, I decided. Grab a taxi. I really didn't want to miss my first chance at presenting on prime-time radio. In any event, it was too late now to call and line up someone else. I shrugged my bag off my shoulders, set my alarm for three A.M., and pulled out the bottle of painkillers they'd given me at the hospital. The label said I should take one or two, with food. I swallowed three, undressed, and crawled under the duvet, where I lay cold and dejected until sleep overcame me.

When I woke it was daylight, and the sun was streaming in through the window. I felt a fleeting, random burst of happiness; then I tried to move my legs and the gentle throbbing started up again. The memory of last night's events crept over me. With a start, I remembered that it wasn't supposed to be daylight; it was supposed to be three A.M. I reached out and pulled my alarm clock from off the bedside table. I groaned, and flopped back down onto the pillow. It was ten past eleven on Tuesday, as far as I could tell. I had slept through the Breakfast Programme. Not only had I missed my moment of glory, I was going to be in big trouble with my boss.

I lay motionless on my back for a few moments. My arms and legs felt like lead weights. Eventually, I lifted my head. It felt heavy too. I flung myself sideways out of bed and landed on the floor with a thud. Pain shot and burned its way through my ankle and up into my shinbone. My entire body felt bruised and stiff. I crawled to the top of the stairs, and peered through the banisters, where I could see the answer phone machine flashing like crazy.

Going downstairs was easier than going up. I could either hang onto the banister and hop, or slide all the way down on my bottom with my good leg as a lever and my bad leg in the air. I tried both. Sliding down won in the end, because it was quicker. I crawled frantically to the telephone and pressed the button on the answer machine. There were three messages, two from Phil, the station manager, and one that was just nothing except white noise and what sounded like music and people talking in the background. Phil wanted to know what had happened to me, and why I hadn't turned up for work. He sounded concerned the second time. I deleted the messages and dialled Phil's direct line number. It went to answer phone. I left an apologetic message, then spent the rest of the day sitting on the sofa, watching daytime TV, going over and over everything in my head, and waiting for the phone to ring.

At six, I heard the sound of a key wriggling noisily in the door lock and the front door opening. I leapt up from the settee and hopped across the room. Larsen stood in the doorway, looking drunk and dishevelled. His eyes were cloudy and red-rimmed, his chin was covered in a couple of days' worth of stubble and his long blond hair was lank and matted. He was wrestling with his jacket, trying to yank his arms out, but he was all twisted up. One arm sprang free and caught the doorknob.

"Ouch," he said, shaking his hand and sucking it. "Ouch, ouch, ouch."

Momentary relief that he was back was quickly replaced with the anger and frustration that had been brewing inside me all afternoon.

"Shut up," I hissed. "And shut the door."

"But it hurts," Larsen whined. He closed the door and leaned against it.

I remained standing on one leg in front of him, hanging onto the banister for support. "You're drunk."

Larsen cocked his head to one side. "What are you implying?"

"Look at the state you're in! Where have you been?"

"Erm. The pub?"

"The pub," I repeated, nodding.

"What have you done to your foot?" Larsen said, suddenly stabbing the air repeatedly in the direction of my bandaged ankle, as if it was something I maybe hadn't noticed.

"What do you care?"

"Is it all right?" His eyes widened in sympathy.

"No, it's not all right," I said. "It's not all right at all."

We stared at each other in silence.

"We had this little party, you see…" Larsen began.

"Who's 'we'?" I said. "I thought you were in Manchester?"

"Ah, and now that's where you're wrong." Larsen wagged his finger. "You're normally right, Lizzie, about everything in fact. I'll give you that. But on this occasion…"

"Where were you then?" I demanded.

"The Juggler's to begin with, and then…" He lowered his head. "Back at Jude's. C'mon, Lizzie, don't give me a hard time."

"Jude? Why were you at her house? What happened to the gig last night?"

"Cancelled." Larsen looked up at me again. "So we came home, went down the pub. Everyone was there. Doug and Marion, Brian..."

"And Jude."

"Well... yeah."

"So what about me? Did you not think to tell me you were back? Why didn't you come home?"

Larsen was sobering up pretty quickly. "I tried to phone you, I left a message..." He tailed off. "Didn't I?"

I took a deep breath. "Where did you sleep last night?"

"At Jude's, I told you. All of us. It was late…"

"Where at Jude's?"

"Where did I...?" Larsen paused. "I need a drink." He walked into the kitchen. I hopped after him. He pulled a carton of milk out of the fridge and swigged from it and, at the same time, switched on the kettle, which started to boil loudly.

"So?" I asked, over the noise of the kettle.

"What was the question again?"

"Where did you sleep? I asked you where you slept. At Jude's. On the sofa? On the floor? In her fucking bed?" I screamed at him. The kettle boiled to a crescendo and switched itself off.

"No. No, of course not. I slept on the floor." Larsen leaned towards me and took my hand. I pulled it away.

"Are you lying to me?"

"I swear." Larsen pulled me towards him again. "Come on baby. Give me a break. We were all drunk. We just crashed."

"God, Larsen, I could have really done with you being here last night — and today. You've been back in Cambridge for twenty-four hours and you didn't even think to phone..."

"Fucking hell, I've had enough of this," Larsen announced suddenly. "I'm going to bed." He pushed past me and headed up the stairs.

He re-emerged a few hours later. I was sitting in the living room, watching the news.

"I'm sorry," he said softly, appearing in the doorway.

"Dave phoned. He's dropping your gear off tomorrow. I'm sorry the Manchester leg of the tour got cancelled."

"Yes, well at least we played Bradford and Leeds. So that paid for the petrol. Makes sitting in the back of a van for hours with Dave's sweaty armpits and a drum kit in your back all worthwhile." He paused. "D'you want a cup of tea?"

I shrugged and stared at the telly. The Chancellor of the Exchequer had announced that high street spending was up by fifteen percent.

"You been out shopping again?" Larsen smiled. I didn't laugh. He sat down next to me and took my hand. I let it flop in his, like a fish.

"How's your ankle?" he asked.

"Sprained."

"How did it happen?"

I told him. Larsen looked shocked. "What the hell were you doing, crossing there?"

"I don't need a lecture," I said. "It hurts."

He folded his arms and sat back, staring at the telly. A minute later he turned and smiled at me, leaned forward and promptly started kissing me. I was so surprised, I couldn't react for a second or two. Larsen took that as a green light, and thrust his hand up my jumper. I pulled back.

"What?" He looked hurt.

"This isn't the time…"

"It's never the time," said Larsen. "These days." He stood up.

I looked up at him. "Where are you going?"

"To get a drink," he said, and disappeared into the kitchen.

The noise of the television suddenly became too loud. I picked up the remote and switched it off, lit a cigarette and looked around the room, trying to figure out something to say before he came back; something to make us both feel better. I looked at the walls — white with a shade of green — that Larsen and Doug had painted when we first moved in, and the framed oil on canvas over the gas fire that Jude had given us as a housewarming present. It was supposed to be a man and a woman embracing, but it just looked like streaks of angry colour and meant nothing to me. I suddenly felt the urge to throw something at it. I wondered if I concentrated hard enough I could make it fall off the wall.

Larsen returned from the kitchen with a bottle of whisky and two glasses. He looked from me to the painting and back again, and frowned.

I said, "You don't know how tired I get, doing a different shift every week. And I'm in quite a lot of pain, you know."

Larsen said nothing. He twisted the top off the whisky bottle and poured two generous measures.

"Not everything can be solved by jumping into bed or downing a bottle of Jack Daniels," I added.

Larsen handed me a glass and I took it. "I can't do anything to please you anymore," he said. "I don't have anything you want."

"Oh Larsen, that's not true!" I protested weakly. "It's just… different now, that's all. Things have changed."

"Well, I haven't changed," said Larsen.

I sighed. I realised he thought of this as some kind of plus point.

"No, you haven't," I said. "You never change. You're still exactly the same as you were when I met you, only you drink more, are at home less, and I'm sorry to tell you, Peter Pan, you've got a few more wrinkles on your face."

Larsen's hand flew automatically to his cheek. He stood up and started pacing the room.

"That's so bloody typical," he said, angrily, and stopped to jab his finger at me. "You used to like me the way I was. You thought I was funny, even when I was drunk. I never pretended to be anything I wasn't."

"Well, it stops being funny after a while."

"And what about you?" he continued.

"What about me?"

"Well, if I'm Peter Pan, then you're bloody Wonder Woman. All you care about is reading the bloody one o'clock news and roaming around the countryside, chasing after the story that's going to get you that news editor job that you're after."

I took a large swig of whisky. "What's wrong with roaming around? I like roaming around. I want to go everywhere. You don't want to go anywhere. I want to go to Paris… Rome… I want to go to Africa. Bosnia, maybe."

"*Bosnia*?" Larsen looked up at me as though I were an alien. "You *are* kidding, right?"

"It's important, what's happening to the people there. The Serbs…"

"There is no *way* you are going to Bosnia!"

"My problem," I said, ignoring him, "is that I don't know where to go first. With you it's a choice between the Juggler's Friend or the flipping Dog and Duck."

"Oh, that's great," said Larsen. "So everyone's got to be a high flyer like you. Well, maybe I like being here."

"But you never are here!" I spluttered, and banged down my glass. Larsen stared at me, wide-eyed. I bit my lip and said, more softly, "You're never here when I come back."

Larsen sighed and refilled our glasses. "If you're talking about last night, I'm sorry."

I lit a cigarette. Larsen looked at his feet. "I love you," he muttered, eventually.

I shook my head. "No. No, you *don't*."

"What?"

"You don't love me, not really. That's just something you say to keep me loving you." Larsen opened his mouth to protest, but shut it again. "If you loved me, I'd feel it," I added. "But I don't. I just feel…" I tailed off. "Tired," I said, finally.

"Tired? Tired of what? Tired of me?"

"No. No, I don't mean that." I sighed. "Not tired of you. Just tired. Tired of being the strong one."

"I'm no good for you. You don't need me," said Larsen.

"How do you know what I need?" I sighed, frustrated. "You think you know, but you don't."

"Funny that, isn't it?" said Larsen, his voice loaded with sarcasm. "I've only lived with you for the last six years—"

"Seven," I interrupted.

"What?"

"It's over seven years."

"Is it?" Larsen looked at the blackness outside the window for a minute, then nodded. "Yep, you're right." He turned and grinned at me. I smiled back, the tension between us broken. We both fell silent and sipped our drinks.

"Bosnia," said Larsen, half-smiling and shaking his head, as if I were child. "You don't want to go to *Bosnia*."

"No, *you* don't want to go to Bosnia," I said. "I'm not you!"

Larsen looked hurt. "Have you any idea what it's like reporting from a war zone? It's not just about getting your face on the telly, you know. People go missing, get kidnapped…"

"I know…"

"You know. You know it all, don't you? You won't be told anything!"

"Well, why do you want to *tell* me everything?"

"Because I care about you! That's why!" Larsen got up and lit the gas fire and sat down in front of it with his back to me, staring into it as if it were a real one. After a while I got up and settled onto the floor beside him. He put his arm round me and I leaned my head against his chest. My face was pleasantly warm and the whisky was making me dozy.

The telephone was ringing. Larsen stirred beside me, but neither of us moved. The answer phone clicked on and I could hear Phil's voice telling me he hoped I was all right and that I shouldn't rush back. I wasn't sure if that was a good thing or not.

"Is that a good thing, do you think?" I asked Larsen.

"They're not going to sack you, Lizzie. They love you." Then Larsen added, "And I love you, you know. I really do."

"I know," I said. "I'm sorry."

"But maybe," he said, looking not at me but at the small blue and white flames that were dancing around in the fireplace. "Maybe we should break up."

I looked up at him. He was still beautiful. He smiled down at me and I could see in his eyes that nothing had changed for him. He still loved me in exactly the same way that he always had — too much, but not enough, at exactly the same time. He held me tighter.

"Maybe you're right," I agreed. "Maybe we should."

4

LARSEN MOVED OUT THE FOLLOWING DAY. I sat helplessly on the sofa with my crutches and watched as he hauled three boxes and a suitcase down the narrow stairs into the living room and out of the door to Dave's van.

I hobbled to the doorstep and kissed him goodbye.

"I still love you," he told me, with what sounded like a question mark at the end.

"I still love you too," I told him back, the same question hanging silently in the air between us.

We locked eyes for a moment and both stood waiting in the doorway for the other to say that this was a mistake. Then Larsen grinned, ruffled my hair, and leapt into Dave's van. He reached out and shut the door as he had done so many times in the past. Only this time he wasn't going down the M11 to London, to the Fulham Greyhound or the Mean Fiddler, or up North to Manchester, or round the M25 to Oxford. This time he was going just a few streets away to Brian's house; but he was leaving our home. The familiar heavy metal slam of the van door echoed in my ears like the clunking of a prison cell door, only I was now locked out, instead of in, where I could have been — with him. Right then, at that moment, my newborn freedom felt hollow, cold, and strange.

On Thursday it was Polling Day, but all I could do was lie on the sofa and stare at the telly. I watched old movies: "Calamity Jane" and "The Way We Were", and cried for Robert Redford and Barbara Streisand and for everything they had lost. I desperately needed to talk to someone, but there was no one I could call. Except… Catherine.

Maybe? But she didn't know me, or at least not me with Larsen, and she was getting married, and I was breaking my heart, and none of it was right or ripe for discussion.

Doug rang at around tea-time, when he got home from work, and asked if I wanted to come over; but, again, it didn't feel right somehow, with him being Larsen's friend first, before mine. Besides, I didn't want to talk with Marion there. She had a way of looking like the cat that had got the cream when anyone else appeared to be having a bad time. Deep down, I was wondering if Larsen would come back; pretend he'd forgotten something, say he wanted to talk. I waited up late into the night, while the election results rolled in, with one eye on the telly and the other on the door, and eventually fell asleep on the sofa in the early hours of the morning.

This must be the right thing, us breaking up, I reasoned with myself. All we ever did these days was argue. I wasn't happy, and it was clear that Larsen wasn't happy. But I hadn't expected it to be this sudden, this final, and this soon.

By Friday morning the Conservatives were back in power, despite a severe recession, despite losing 38 seats, and despite all forecasts to the contrary. The phones would be ringing off the hook in the newsroom and I needed a piece of the action. I couldn't bear the empty silence of the house any longer. Finding that I was able to both smile and walk with a degree of dignity and just one crutch, I caught a taxi to the radio station.

It took a long time to get up the stairs. I pushed open the door and caught my breath, inhaling the rubbery scent of hot machinery, of newsprint, and of freshly ground coffee, the smell that defined the newsroom. The printer that gave us the feeds from the General News Service was clunking and whirring noisily in the corner of the room. Simon Goodfellow, the lunchtime reporter, was sitting at my desk. He peered over his shoulder as I entered and stood up, slowly.

"Good lord, that looks painful," he commented, but didn't offer to help.

I sank down into my chair, exhausted. On my desk was a letter from Phil marked "Private and Confidential". I glanced briefly round the newsroom. Everyone was milling around, carrying out their daily routine, except Simon, who was looking curiously at the letter in my hands. I stuffed it into my handbag and pushed it under my desk. I logged onto my computer, and started to type up the news feeds for the lunchtime bulletin, which Simon had left for me.

It was an extraordinary coup for the government, their fourth consecutive victory and one for which the Sun newspaper was taking full credit, following their provocative headline the previous day urging the last person to leave Britain to "turn out the lights" if Labour won the election. It was clever all right; it fed right into the paranoia of the national psyche. That headline was for anyone who worried about trade unions taking over the country, about immigrants stealing their jobs and their women, about reds under the bed. I quickly typed up the rest of the national bulletin and then began to search for a local story. There was nothing from the police today. I glanced again through the feeds that Simon had left me.

"And finally," I typed. "A farmer in Whittlesford is lobbying parliament this week with a petition signed by four hundred Kent and Sussex farmers against the proposed Channel Tunnel link." I stopped writing and spun my chair round.

"Why?" I asked Simon, who was now sitting at the desk behind me, eating a pork pie.

"Why what?" He looked defensive.

"Why," I asked impatiently, "does a farmer in Whittlesford give a flying one about the Chunnel link?"

Simon didn't answer.

"It's going from London to Paris," I elaborated. "There's no detour planned via Whittlesford."

"So?" said Simon. "Maybe he's coming out in solidarity." I knew that this was a dig at Larsen's left-wing politics, with me as the object of torment. I hadn't told anyone at work that we had split up. I certainly wasn't going to tell Simon.

I folded my arms. "Am I going to have to delete this news item?" I asked him.

Simon grinned. "The farmers — united — will never be deleted," he recited, punching the air with his fist. He chuckled and rocked back in his chair.

"It's not funny, Simon. This is supposed to be a story. Either it is or it isn't." I stood up and went over to the desk where all the information came in from the General News Service.

"Listen to the clip…" Simon began.

"I don't have time," I said, edgily, sitting back down at the computer screen. "If it's going in I need it now, finished." I was aware that my voice had risen by at least a couple of octaves.

I could hear Simon getting up and moving around behind me. He leaned over my shoulder and placed a pile of carts onto my desk in front of me, then left the newsroom.

I glanced at my watch, picked up the carts and my crutch, and stepped into the studio.

When I came out Greg Chappell, the programme editor, was waiting for me. He smiled and sat down at the desk behind me.

"That was quick," said Greg, when I came out again. "You had another two minutes to play with there. You'll be giving those lunchtime listeners indigestion."

I slumped down into my chair. Greg put down his pencil.

"Look," he said. "Don't let him get to you."

"That's easy for you to say," I muttered. "I'm fed up of doing Simon's job for him and then feeling like an autocratic old nag for minding. It's like working with my brother."

"I didn't know you had a brother," said Greg, trying to be tactful, trying to change the subject.

I hesitated a moment. I wasn't sure that I wanted to have a discussion about my family. "Yeah. Just the one. His name's Pete."

"And he wound you up, right?" Greg continued. "That's what being a brother is all about. It's in the job description."

"Yes, well, it's not in Simon's, is it?" I said.

Greg looked at me sympathetically. "You need to get out of here. You need a new start somewhere else. You've outgrown this place."

I felt a glimmer of hope inside me, something I hadn't felt in a while. "Do you really think so? I thought I was only just getting somewhere."

Greg wheeled his chair over to mine. "Look, Lizzie. You've got loads of potential. You could easily get a job in town."

"I already am in town." I was confused.

"I'm talking about London," he laughed. "One of the independents, or the BBC stations even. You're hardworking, you've got what it takes. Don't keep selling yourself short."

I eyed him suspiciously. "You're leaving," I said. "Aren't you?"

"Yes," said Greg.

"When?"

"End of the month. It's an attachment, but..." he trailed off.

"So who's going to cover for you?" I asked.

"Well, who do you think?" Greg smiled. "I thought Phil had told you. He said he had."

"What?" I turned and grabbed my bag from under the desk and ripped open the letter. "I thought I'd got a warning..."

"But listen to me, Lizzie, you can do more. Don't let it be forever..."

"It's enough," I grinned. "For now."

I got up, flung my arms around him and kissed him on the cheek. "You've just made my week. Month. Year," I said, hugging him.

"Good," said Greg. "In that case, I forgive you for you for not caring that I'm going."

"Of course I care," I protested. "I'll really miss you, you know I will. But this is great news for both of us."

I swung round and logged back into the computer.

The following Friday, I picked up the phone and dialled Catherine's number. She answered after a couple of rings.

"Lizzie!" she said. "I am so glad you rang! That's so spooky. I was going to call you tonight."

"Really?"

"Yes. I've been thinking about you all week, how nice it was to see you again." Something in her voice didn't sound quite right. "How are you? How's the foot?"

"Much better, thanks. I had to have a few days off work. But I'm back now, and in fact I've just been promoted."

"Congratulations!" Catherine sounded genuinely delighted. "Let's go out," she said. "Tonight. We'll celebrate!"

"Oh, I'm not sure. My ankle's still not great. I mean, it's better than it was, but... I've broken up with Larsen," I blurted out.

"What? Are you serious?"

"Yes. Sorry. I didn't mean to just dump that on you."

"You're not dumping anything, Lizzie, we're friends, remember?"

"Of course. Thanks."

"I'm so sorry. I thought you and he were...? Well, the way you described him, he sounded great."

"He *is* great," I said.

"So why, then?"

"I don't know. Maybe it's me. How long have you got?" I laughed ironically.

"Right. That settles it. We're going out. Tonight. Celebration or commiseration, it's your call."

Your call. I remembered Larsen saying that to me, the night we met, when I was talking about leaving college. I wondered how much of anything that had happened in the last seven years really had been my call. And I realised with sudden clarity that this was no one's fault but my own.

"Come on," Catherine persisted. "You can stay at mine, that way we can get a cab back together. We'll have a great time, don't worry."

"Go on, then. Why not?" I was wondering what it was about Catherine's voice that sounded different. She sounded kind of high. "So, are *you* okay, then?" I asked.

There was a pause. "What have you forgotten?" Catherine asked, and I realised she wasn't talking to me. I could hear a voice in the background, getting louder, shouting. It was clearly Martin. "Well, of course I would have washed it. Calm down. Hang on, and I'll help you look." The phone went dead for a moment and then Catherine was back on the line. "Lizzie, sorry, I've got to go. I'll call you back. No. I'll see you at eight. The Free Press. You know it? Near Parker's Piece. Okay?" And then she was gone.

Catherine was waiting outside the pub when my taxi pulled up. She helped me out onto the pavement and threw her arms around me and held me tight, and I realised that she was the first person who had touched me since Larsen left. I felt suddenly and pathetically grateful for her friendship, but realised that she was equally pleased to see me because she was holding me so tight, for so long, that I nearly lost my balance. When she stepped back I realised that she was trying very hard not to cry.

"Catherine? What is it?"

She waved her hand in the air. "Oh, nothing. Ignore me. I'm just being stupid. Let's get a drink."

The pub was warm and inviting. The familiar pub smells of hot chips and roasted peanuts mingled with cigarette smoke and the sour stench of ale. I sat down at a table while Catherine went up to the bar and ordered the drinks. A small fire flickered in the open grate beside me. I leaned forward briefly and warmed my face in its amber glow before shrugging off my coat and sinking back into the cushioned leather of my armchair. A group of students, deep in conversation at the table next to me, suddenly let out a loud roar of laughter. I glanced over at them and wished for one strange moment that I were back there with them, with a chance to do it all over again, the whole student thing, only properly this time, to integrate myself fully into that other world and with those people. Maybe that was where I had belonged after all; maybe the past seven years had been a mistake. Maybe fear and insecurity at leaving home to study — at starting a new life on my own — had caused me to go the entirely wrong way through the sliding doors of fate, into the club on Mill Road and into Larsen's life.

"So where's Martin tonight?" I asked Catherine, when she returned. It didn't take Einstein to work out that her low mood was something to do with him.

"He's coaching. The team's got a tournament in Manchester," she said. "It starts early tomorrow, so they've got to go tonight."

"Everything okay?"

"Yeah. Just a silly argument."

"Does he mind you going out with me tonight?"

"Of course not. He's fine about it. It's nothing, honest. Anyway, I want to hear about you."

I took a sip of my drink and thought back to Martin's shouting in the background when Catherine was on the phone to me. He had sounded really angry. I also recalled the unpleasant way he had treated Sean, the junior staff member at the swimming pool. And then there was his flirting. But maybe it was all something and nothing, like she said. I didn't know enough about their relationship to pass judgment, let alone interfere.

"So, come on then," she said. "What happened? With Larsen?"

"I don't know where to start," I said. "Except that everything I told you about him is the truth. He's a lovely guy. He's funny. And kind. And I was crazy about him, you know?"

"Was?"

"Am. Was. I don't know."

"Are you sure it's over?"

"He's moved out," I said. "I haven't heard from him since he left. It's well over a week. Ten days to be precise. I haven't gone this long without speaking to him since the day we met."

"So is this not what you really want?"

"I don't know," I admitted. "It feels like a release at times, like I can breathe again. We were just so merged into each other. Or I was merged into him, more to the point. It's like we were the same person. It was suffocating. Even our initials were the same: Larsen Tyler and Lizzie Taylor. He loved that, things like that, our sameness. He thought it was great, how close it made us. And that was what I wanted, too, in the beginning. I let it happen. It was so secure. And he had a ready-made life, friends, everything was there, set up for me. All I had to do in return was love him, and believe me, I did. He loved me back and it was everything I needed. And when he got up on stage... well, being his girlfriend, basking in his reflected glory... it was intoxicating. It was the headiest thing that ever happened to me."

"So what changed?"

"I just don't know. Me, I suppose. Like I say, I felt stifled, suffocated. As if I just wasn't being myself, as though I was living his life, not mine. But now... it's lonely without him. It's strange. I keep thinking he's just gone away on tour and he's going to come home any minute. Except that all of his stuff is gone. Except he just doesn't— come home, that is."

Catherine took my hand across the table and squeezed it. "It must feel awful. Even if breaking up with him *was* what you wanted. It must be really hard."

"It is," I said, looking up at her. "And there's nobody I can talk to who understands. How can you know something's not right but still miss someone so much?"

"*I* understand," said Catherine. "It's like being torn in two."

"That's it. That's exactly what it is. There is the bit of me that is him and me, and the bit of me that is just me. And the bit of me that is just me wants this, this new path, this new start. But the rest of me... is missing that closeness. Missing him. So much."

Catherine gave my hand another squeeze and bit her lip, pausing for a moment before she asked, "So when did you first notice that the bit that was just you was not getting a look in?"

I looked into my empty glass and thought about that for a moment. "The truth?" I asked her.

Catherine nodded.

"Around seven years ago."

"You mean…?"

"Yes. Right in the beginning. I switched degree courses. For him. My second year at college was meant to be my year abroad. I had picked Paris as my study placement. The city. Where better to learn French? I was so excited. It wasn't that far away. I thought: it's only a year. We can visit each other. He can come and stay. I can come home in the holidays. But when I told him, he said that it would be the end of us. He gave me an ultimatum. He said I was either in this relationship or I was out. So I dropped French and switched to Politics, and moved in with him instead."

Catherine didn't say anything for a minute. "I can understand that," she said finally. Which was not what I had expected her to say, at all.

At closing time, Catherine decided that we should go to a nightclub.

"I really want to dance," she said. "Do you mind?"

I wasn't in much shape for dancing, but I didn't want to go home just yet either, and was still feeling so happy to be with her again that I would have gone for a wet weekend in Cleethorpes if she'd asked me.

"I'll watch you," I laughed.

We paid our entry fee and found a seat near the dance floor, where I sat sipping a gin and tonic while Catherine disappeared into the crowd and the dry ice. I watched the flashing purple and yellow lights and the spinning silver baubles that hung from the ceiling and soon spotted Catherine amongst the other dancers, all swaying and jerking to the rhythm of the night. Catherine danced without inhibition and looked happy, lost in the music, as she swung her hips from side to side, her arms in the air and her long dark hair swinging round her face as she moved. I smiled as more than one man watched her, then came towards her and began to gyrate around her, trying to catch her attention. She didn't seem to notice, or simply turned her back and danced away. Eventually she got tired and came back and sat down beside me, but the music was so loud that we soon gave up trying to talk to one another. We sat and stared at the lights and the dancers instead.

I started to wonder what Larsen was doing right now. He would be at a gig, probably; in fact he would be finished by now and packing up, drinking backstage with the other band members. And no doubt some girls, who would have found their way backstage too. Either that or he would be with the others, Brian, Jude and Doug — our crowd. Maybe they were all down the pub still, at one of the many lock-ins, playing cards, laughing, singing along to the Juke Box or an acoustic guitar. One thing was for certain, he wouldn't be on his own.

A wave of insecurity washed over me and I realized that that was where I wanted to be too, right now — at a lock-in in the Jugglers Arms, with Larsen, not here with a bunch of strangers, with this deafening music thudding and vibrating through my body. But I couldn't admit that, not even to Catherine. If this — going out to a nightclub with a friend that wasn't Larsen's friend — was the first on my list of new experiences, a step forward into my new life, I didn't want to fail at the first hurdle. Besides, it would come across as a slight on her company. More than that, I just couldn't say it out loud that I had made a mistake in letting him go. Because that would make it true.

"I can't believe we're doing this," I yelled, downing the remains of my third gin and tonic.

Catherine didn't answer. I looked round and realised she was asleep.

A young guy appeared next to me. He must have been all but twenty. He mouthed something at me and raised his eyebrows.

"What did you say?" I hoped he wasn't asking me to dance.

"Do you want to dance?" he leaned forward and shouted into my ear, nearly bursting my eardrum.

"I can't." I looked up at him, apologetically. He seemed nice enough, in a gangly kind of way, but I suddenly felt panicky. I didn't want to lead him on.

"My name's Michael," he added.

"I can't, Michael," I said firmly. "I've got a bad ankle," I added, nodding at my crutch, although my ankle was actually feeling much better.

"That's a bit of a lame excuse," he shouted, in my ear. "Get it? Boom boom."

I shot him a withering look. He shrugged, and started jigging around. "All right then," he shouted. "What about your mate?"

We both looked at Catherine, whose head was tipped back over the top of the leather seat, her mouth slightly ajar.

"I don't think so," I said.

He didn't appear to be leaving. "What's your name?" he asked, crouching down beside me.

I told him.

"Busy Lizzie," he said, and smiled as if that meant something.

The DJ announced the last dance and the music changed to a slow song. Catherine was making a snuffling noise and her hand was twitching in her lap.

"Come on," said Michael grabbing me by the hand. "I'll hold you up, don't worry."

I hobbled resignedly behind him onto the dance floor. He put his arms round my waist and pulled me to him. I reluctantly draped my hands over his shoulders. It felt too intimate, my breasts pushed up against his chest like that, when I barely knew him. I could feel his breath on my cheek and his hair tickling my forehead.

The song was Madonna's "Crazy for You". You couldn't actually dance to it. So we just went round and round, like you do to slow songs at discos. It had always seemed a bit stupid and pointless to me, not actually going anywhere, especially with a load of strangers dotted around you doing exactly the same thing. It wasn't as if any skill or dexterity were required, either, like when you tangoed or waltzed. It was simulated sex, really, which is fine when you feel like simulating sex, but I didn't. Not there, not with him, in spite of all the gin.

When the song ended, he tried to kiss me. I let him for a moment out of a combination of pity and curiosity, until he started trying to push his tongue into my mouth. It felt hard and dry, and unpleasantly alive, like a small furry animal. I pushed him gently away and limped back to Catherine, who was sitting up and rubbing her eyes. The lights were coming up and the bar staff were collecting glasses. Sinead O'Connor's "Nothing Compares to You" was now blasting out of the speakers, and it was just about all I could bear.

"What time is it?" Catherine asked.

"Time to go home. Very much so, in fact."

We joined a queue at the taxi rank and eventually got into a mini-cab. As we turned into Catherine's street and pulled up outside the house, she stiffened and peered nervously out of the window. Amidst the row of darkened terraced houses, one glowed with light from every window.

"It must be Martin," she said, looking startled. "What's he doing back home?"

I paid the driver and followed Catherine up the path. Just as she was putting her key in the lock the door swung open and in a flash she'd disappeared inside, the door slamming shut behind her. I stopped on the path, stunned, not quite sure what had happened. I turned and looked back at the deserted street behind me. The taxi was just turning round the corner out of sight.

There wasn't a sound from the house. I looked at my watch; it was a quarter to three, and I had no idea where I was. I'd just decided to take my chances on hobbling back down the road when the front door opened and Catherine appeared, looking flushed and apologetic.

"Sorry about that," she whispered. "Come in."

I stepped inside and caught sight of Martin, surveying us both, stony-faced, from the top of the stairs. I followed Catherine into the front room.

"Don't worry, he'll be all right in the morning," she said in a strange voice as if talking to herself. Gathering up an armful of cushions that were scattered on the floor, she patted the sofa and disappeared out of the door. A few minutes later she reappeared with a pillow and a blanket, which she handed to me without a word before she left again, switching off the light and closing the door behind her.

Moonlight was streaming in through a gap in the curtains, casting a shaft of light across the carpet. I lay back on the sofa, pulling the blanket up to my chin. Through the silence and stillness of the room came the heavy sound of footsteps pacing up and down overhead and Martin's voice, booming through the plasterwork in didactic tones. Every now and again I could hear the faint sound of Catherine, responding, wheedling, coaxing, and finally sobbing. I pulled the blanket over my head and stayed that way with the blood rushing in my ears long after the noise had stopped.

Slowly, I became aware of another presence in the room. Opening my eyes tentatively, I blinked in the darkness, seeing nothing but the shadows of the furniture. I lifted my hand slowly from under the blanket and reached for the table lamp beside me, found the switch and pushed. It clicked, but nothing happened. I lay rigid, my heart pounding in my chest. I wanted to get up, get out, but I was too afraid to move. I screwed up my eyes tight and prayed. Sensing something at the foot of the sofa, I slowly opened them again. In an instant, the blanket was whipped away from me. I screamed. Then I felt my body rolling over as the sofa creaked and sank beside me.

"Shhh," said Martin, putting his hand over my mouth.

"What… what are you doing?" I whispered, pulling his hand away.

"You screamed. You were having a bad dream. I came to see if you were all right."

I blinked and moved my head. "What time is it?"

"Early still. Around six." I realised he was right, that it was now morning. A shaft of early morning sunlight now beamed into the room through the gap in the curtains and specks of dust were dancing through the air. I saw that the blanket was still over me, after all. My body was stiff and aching.

"Are you okay?"

"Yes. I think so."

"So what were you dreaming about?"

"Nothing. Like you say, just a bad dream."

Martin reached out and stroked my hair back from off my forehead. "Poor thing."

This didn't feel right, but I didn't know what to say.

"I'm okay, really," I sat up slightly. I was relieved to remember that I was still fully dressed. "I'm sorry if I woke you."

"You didn't. I was up anyway. I was about to go for a jog."

I glanced up at him and saw that he was wearing tracksuit bottoms and a sweat top. "Don't let me keep you."

"It's okay." He made no move to leave.

I shifted away from him slightly and tried to think of something to say, before he could touch me again. "Where do you go? Jogging, I mean?"

"Just round the block. Up to the shops, round the park, back again."

"Sounds good. I would like to say I'd join you, but… I don't think I'm going to be jogging for a while. Or swimming, come to that."

"That's a shame." Martin paused. "I used to compete, too, you know. Nationally. I was on the verge of turning professional, until I injured my back. That put an end to a lot of things."

"Like?"

"My career for a start."

"I'm sorry. That's tough. What happened?"

"I had an accident. On my bike."

"Your bike? You were on a bicycle?"

"Motorbike. I had a Kawasaki. A Five Hundred. I used to import and sell them, bikes. And cars, too. A real good crack, it was, got to drive them all over, delivering them to customers. I had a good little business going. Till I hit a tree. It was wet. I just skidded off the road."

"God. How awful. Were you badly hurt?"

"You could say that." A wry grin. "Both legs broken, and, worse, damage to my spinal cord. 'Incomplete'. That means it wasn't a total loss of function, thank God. But I didn't know that at the time. I was in traction for weeks. It was bloody miserable. It felt as if my life was over, at the time. That was back in eighty-four."

The year I'd met Larsen. There I was, all tied up with the business of falling in love, while Martin was in pain, lying on his back in a hospital bed. I felt a stab of pity for him.

I said, "You must think I'm a real baby, then. All I've got is a sprained ankle, and look at me, moaning about it."

Martin smiled. "The trick is to keep it moving. And put pressure on it. Try standing on it. Stand on one leg."

"What, now?"

Martin laughed. "I'm serious. As often as you can. You need to strengthen it. Physio's what you need — and lots of it. I can help you if you like."

"You're a physiotherapist?"

"Well, no. Not exactly. But I've picked up a few techniques along the way. Believe me, I've come across more than a few serious injuries since I've been coaching." He paused. "That doesn't sound very good, does it?"

I laughed. "I know what you mean."

"Anyway, I got interested after the accident, in rehabilitation, I mean. After I got some movement back in my spine. I kept telling myself, making this bargain with God, you know, that if He would let me walk again I would do something positive... and then I did walk. And, well, every cloud, you know. I figured if I can't train enough to compete myself, I can help other people."

"That's very... well, big-hearted of you."

Martin shrugged. "It took me a while to get there. I kind of gave up for a while, after the accident. Got a bit down. You know. But I got there in the end. And my back's much better now. Good enough for lifesaving, anyway. And I keep in good shape."

"I can see that," I said, then wished I hadn't. "So," I added quickly, "How long have you been working at the complex?"

"A couple of years."

"Ever had to save anyone's life?"

"Once or twice. There was one time when a very overweight woman came in eating a kebab.

"What?" I laughed. "You're kidding."

"Straight up." Martin was smiling now. "I was just about to go over to her, tell her we didn't allow food by the pool side. Next thing, she's screwed up her wrapper, lowered herself into the shallow end, flopped onto her stomach and sunk straight down to the bottom."

"Oh my God, what did you do?"

"Well, jumped in, of course, pulled her out. Resuscitated her."

"You gave her the kiss of life?"

"Of course. Had to. That's my job."

"And she was okay?"

"Yeah, she was fine. I had onion breath, though, for the rest of my shift."

I laughed. Martin looked down at me and smiled. He placed his hand on top of mine. "So. How are you feeling now?"

I glanced down at my ankle and, under the pretext of making myself more comfortable, slid my hand from under his and used it to shift my body weight. "Better. I'm fine. Really."

"Good." Martin leaned forwards and kissed me gently on the cheek. He let his lips pause there for a moment and I could feel his breath, warm against my face.

"Please," I said, quickly, to stop him.

He looked into my eyes. His face was still very close to mine. "What?" he whispered.

I stumbled for words. "Catherine," I said, and added, "Don't hurt her."

I knew I'd said the wrong thing. Martin sat up and shook his head.

"It's none of your business," he said, quietly.

Then he left the room.

It was still early, and there was no sound from upstairs. I found some paper in my handbag and scribbled a note to Catherine. I left it on the kitchen table and slipped out of the front door. The street was empty, apart from a few cats and a paperboy doing his rounds. I limped to the end of the road and stood on the corner, and looked in both directions. I could see a newsagent and a grocer's shop at the bottom of the road that I recognised. I realised that I knew where I was, at the top of Cherry Hinton High Street and Fulbourn Road. I spotted a phone box on the corner and started towards it, pulling my purse out of my bag to check if I had change.

Suddenly, I heard a whistle, looked up, and saw my father walking down the street towards me. I stopped in my tracks and stared at him, but he didn't seem to notice me. He opened a gate further up the street and disappeared up the pathway. I continued to stand there, rooted to the pavement, holding my breath while time stood still. The gate opened and the postman came back out. It was the postman. It wasn't my father. Of course it wasn't my father. How could it be?

"Morning, love," said the postman, cheerfully, as he passed.

"Morning," I replied, in a whisper.

When I got home the house was cold. I switched the heating on but the boiler had gone out in the kitchen. After a couple of indifferent flicks at the pilot light, I gave up on it. I made myself a cup of tea and sat in the living room by the window with my jumper over my knees, watching a couple of pigeons pecking away hungrily at the cracks in the pavement outside. My stomach churned, demanding food, but I couldn't think of anything I wanted to eat. I couldn't think of anything at all, except that I wanted Larsen back. I couldn't remember what could have been so bad, bad enough for me to give him up. I thought of all our arguments and longed for even that. Anything had to be better than this. As Sinead O'Connor had so pertinently reminded me, nothing compared to him. It was that simple. He was Larsen. Nothing — no one — compared to him.

I sat curled up in the chair until my toes and my nose were numb, then climbed wearily up the stairs and into the bedroom. I pulled the curtains to shut out the light, pulled off my jeans, and crawled under the heavy feathery folds of the duvet.

5

LARSEN HAD BEEN GONE for nearly three months when Marion and Doug threw a party at their new flat on Chesterton Road.

"You've got to come," Doug had insisted on the telephone. "We never see you these days."

On the evening of the party I took a taxi to the address he'd given me. I knocked on the door and took a deep breath. Doug answered. He put his arms around me and squeezed me tight.

"How are you?" asked Marion, as I entered the kitchen.

It was hard to judge whether this was an invitation to tell her how I was coping without Larsen, or just the standard British pleasantry, to which the response "Fine. And you?" would prompt another "Fine," and allow her to get her drink and go back into the living room.

"Oh, fine," I said, watching her. Something about Marion's face told me that she had rather hoped I wasn't fine at all. She was the sort of person who would slow right down to look at a car crash.

"Drink?" she said. She tipped a three litre wine box onto its side and squelched the remains out of the silver paper and into two glasses.

"So," she said, finally, "How's things between you and Larsen?"

"Well, we've split up," I said. I knew that she knew that. I was just hoping that if I started from the very beginning, someone might come into the kitchen and interrupt us before I had to say anything very much else.

"I know that." Marion looked confused. "I was just wondering if, you know…" she trailed off.

"No." I shook my head. "If what?"

"You won't mind seeing him?" Marion still looked confused.

"Why should I?" I laughed, rather too loudly. "We're still friends."

"Oh yes," said Marion. "Of course."

I raised my glass and smiled.

"Hello," said Larsen, coming into the kitchen. He was wearing an old baggy blue jumper that I'd never seen before.

"Hello," said Jude, from behind him.

I was sitting on the stairs with a bottle of wine.

"Alright," said Larsen, sitting down beside me.

"Hello," I said.

"How've you been?" he asked, rather woodenly.

"So so," I said. "New jumper?"

"Not really." He glanced awkwardly away towards the living room door. I felt disappointed. I wanted to know how he'd been coping. I wanted him to put his arm around me. I wanted us to talk like we'd meant something to each other.

"What about you?" I asked. "How've you been?"

"Not bad. But Julia's moving in with Brian…"

"Who's Julia?"

"His new girlfriend."

"Oh. I see."

"Yeah… so, I think I'm going to have to move out." He still wasn't looking at me.

I wondered if there was a reason for him telling me this. I wasn't sure how I'd feel if he said he wanted to move back in again, into the spare room. Of course it was still his house too. And I missed him so badly. Seeing him here, now, feeling him next to me, so close, but acting like a stranger, was almost impossible to bear.

"So, what are you going to do?" I asked.

"Well…"

"If you need to… you know, move back…" I trailed off. "Into the spare room, of course," I added, and laughed stupidly. Larsen still wasn't saying anything. I suddenly remembered his words the night we met: "I never go back. Once it's over it's over."

"How's work?" Larsen asked me.

"Good," I said. "I did a seven-day shift last week, so I've got a few days off. I'm programme editor from Thursday."

"You got it." Without exclamation.

The living room door opened and Jude poked her head around and looked at us. I smiled. She went back inside and shut the door.

"Well, I'm only acting up," I said. "You know, just a secondment…" I was aware that I was speaking very quickly. I was also aware that Larsen wasn't really listening properly but I seemed unable to stop myself from telling him and hoping that he cared. "It's for the lunchtime show, in fact. Greg Chappell's got an eight week attachment at IRN. But in realistic terms it means he's unlikely to come back again."

"Well, aren't you on the up and up?" said Larsen. He stood up. "See you later," he added, and went back into the living room.

I poured myself another glass of wine and considered the up and up. I decided there was no such thing. With an up, it seemed, there was always a down. Laws of gravity, I supposed.

I wandered through the darkened living room and stood there for a moment. The Happy Mondays were blaring out of the speakers. Karen and Marion were dancing together in a manner that didn't invite me to join them. Larsen was sitting on the sofa, talking to Jude. I spotted the back of Doug's head on the balcony outside and opened the door.

"Hey. Mind if I join you?"

"Hey." Doug patted the ground beside him and I sat down. We stuck our legs up against the railings and surveyed the car park below

"So how are you?"

"I'm okay. Thanks. You?"

Doug nodded. "Roll up?" he offered. I shook my head. "It's nice to see you," he added. "I'm glad you came. It's a shame when people break up and people disappear off the scene."

I smiled. "By people, do you mean Zara?"

Doug glanced behind him through the window to the living room.

"It's alright," I said. "Marion can't hear. And everyone else knows you and Zara had a thing going on."

Doug didn't try to deny it.

"So… have you seen her lately? Zara, I mean?"

Doug shook his head.

"Nice girl," I said. "I liked her."

"Me too," said Doug, and smiled. "Off her head, though."

I laughed, remembering the first time I had met her in the bathroom at Larsen's house, when she'd told me about the stars talking and then we'd fallen into the bath. "She's a lot nicer than Marion," I said.

Doug sighed. "Yeah. Well, she didn't stick around. After…"

"After what?"

Doug hesitated. "She wasn't very well," he said, and then, "You'll have to ask her."

"So where did she go? Is she still in Cambridge?"

"No. I don't know. I think she moved to London."

"London? Really?"

"She got offered a job there, I think. It was in one of those big hospitals, a teaching hospital she said, in North London. I can't remember which one."

We sat in silence for a while and Doug rolled another cigarette. I felt a glimmer of hope and something that felt like pride, in Zara. She had always remained on the fringe of things, her relationship with Doug never discussed. Her occasional presence had been accepted because of Doug. But I hadn't really noticed, until now, that she had stopped being around, made the break, moved away.

It was possible, then, to get a new life, to start afresh, without the blanket of love, friendship, and familiarity that had shrouded me for such a long time. Zara had done it. Though, unlike me, she had always had a life away from Doug, outside of our crowd. She hadn't invested everything into her relationship with him, the way that I had with Larsen. I recalled her having friendships with fellow nurses at the hospital where she worked. And I also remembered her being interested in art, talking about some paintings she'd done, and once or twice inviting me to a gallery. Once she had put on an exhibition of her own paintings, and she had invited me to that too. But I had made some excuse and never gone.

I realised now how shallow my friendships had been with all of these women, largely of my own volition. I hadn't really tried to get to know them at all, in all these years, because for the most part all we had in common was that our boyfriends were friends. That was the glue that had held the group together. And now that I was no longer Larsen's girlfriend, there was nothing left. Zara was the one person that I had felt a real connection with, but I had never nurtured that. I had been too wrapped up in Larsen. I now regretted my inertia; Zara could have been a good friend.

I glanced back through the window into the living room. Larsen and Jude were still sitting on the sofa talking. I noticed that their legs were close together, touching. Jude then said something, and smiled up at Larsen, who laughed, put his hand on her leg, and then kissed her, full on the lips.

"Oh," I said. "Now I get it."

Doug followed my gaze. "Oh. Larsen and Jude. I thought you knew."

I stood up. "How could I have been so stupid?"

"Lizzie — wait!" Doug jumped up after me and tried to grab my hands from behind me. I yanked them free and tripped over the step into the living room. Karen turned round and nudged Marion, who turned the music down.

Jude looked up. "Lizzie..." she began.

"How long has this been going on?" I demanded.

"A few months," said Jude, looking at Larsen for backup.

"A few months?" I repeated. I looked at Larsen. "You mean... from the moment we split up? Or longer?"

"No," said Larsen, quickly. "No, not longer."

Jude glanced at him and I knew instantly that this wasn't true. And I realised suddenly how naive I had been. I should have known that he would never have ended our relationship unless there was someone else waiting in the wings. All this time that I had been reeling from the blow of losing him — imagining him to be doing the same — and he hadn't felt a thing.

I looked up and Larsen's eyes met mine briefly, then flickered away.

"Don't go breaking your heart," I said.

Larsen said nothing.

Doug followed me as far as the front door, but nobody followed me out.

I woke the next morning with a throbbing headache and as the events of the previous night began to crash in on me, I also realised that I wasn't well. I cast my mind back and remembered that I hadn't eaten since lunchtime the day before. I'd been too nervous before the party about seeing everyone again. I sat up slowly, then walked unsteadily downstairs into the kitchen. I filled the kettle and put two slices of toast into the toaster. I was rummaging through the drawers for coffee filters when the phone rang.

It was Larsen. "We need to talk."

I felt bile suddenly rising in my stomach and my forehead prickled. I said, "I'm really not feeling very well."

Larsen didn't seem to have heard. "Okay, Lizzie, I don't blame you for being upset. But there are things we've got to sort out."

It was as if we were having two different conversations. Which wasn't that surprising, after all, as we were clearly having two entirely different experiences of breaking up. His was soft, cushioned; Jude and his friends had broken his fall. Mine was cold, empty, and bereft. I was freefalling in space and time, with nobody standing by to stop me hurtling headlong into obscurity.

I sank down onto the sofa. "This isn't a good time."

"Let's face it, there's never going to be a good time, is there?" he said gently. "I know you probably don't feel like talking to me right now, but you have a right to know what's going on…"

I laughed ironically. "I kind of figured it out for myself, actually. But thanks for your concern."

Larsen paused for a second, then continued. "And I want you to hear it from me."

"There's more?" I croaked.

"I didn't plan this, Lizzie."

I didn't say anything. My head was pounding and a wave of nausea was sweeping over me.

"I'm not saying I'm not equally responsible," Larsen was saying. "But it just happened, and that's that, and if you can try and understand ..."

My stomach contracted and my jaw tightened. "I have to go," I said.

"Lizzie, wait. Look, I can't stay at Brian's for much longer." He paused. "I'm going to need to move back into the house. I'll buy you out."

"What? You can't afford to buy me out. You can't even afford to pay the mortgage!"

"Maybe not, but… Jude can."

"Jude? You have got to be kidding."

"Okay. Her parents can. That's what I meant. They can buy you out."

"Her parents? Why would her parents do that? You've only been together a few months!"

"We need the house," said Larsen. "Jude's pregnant."

The room was moving. I placed the receiver down, lurched up the stairs to the bathroom, and was horribly, violently sick.

Three hours later, the sickness still hadn't stopped. I couldn't even lie down in bed in between bouts, because whenever I did, the room started spinning. I was desperately thirsty, but every time I tried to drink my stomach muscles contracted so violently that I could almost feel my stomach lining getting ready to rip. I lay in the bathroom for what seemed like hours, my cheek resting against the cold white enamel of the bath, my legs curled up underneath me.

I had lost all track of time and was almost dozing off on the bathmat when I heard a noise downstairs and a voice called through the letterbox.

"Lizzie?! Are you there?"

"Mum?" I lifted my head up, relief flooding through me.

"Lizzie? Are you home?"

"Yes!" I called, as loudly as I could, but my voice was so hoarse that all that came out was a whisper. I levered myself up onto my feet and almost threw myself down the stairs. My stomach immediately started to tighten.

I fiddled with the latch and flung the door open. "Mum!" I screamed.

I could see that my mother had been about to leave, her car keys in her hand. She turned at the sound of my voice "Oh, you are there. Are you all right?"

"I've been better. A lot better, in fact." I sank to the floor and clutched at my stomach.

"What's wrong? Are you ill?"

"Just a bit."

"Oh Lizzie, what's the matter?"

"Don't know." I hiccupped. "Can't stop being sick."

My mother pushed open the front door.

"Come on. Let's get you into the car," she said. "We'll soon get you home."

I shook my head. "I can't move."

My mother stepped over me, fetched a bucket from under the kitchen sink and pulled my jacket off the coat peg by the door.

"Up you get," she said, firmly.

She took hold of me by the shoulders, tugged me up and pulled my arms into my jacket, through the sleeves, from the cuffs, the way she used to do it when I was little and had my mittens on bits of elastic inside. She steered me out of the front door and towards her car. One of my neighbours walked past and stared at me. I realised I wasn't looking my best. My hair was unbrushed, my face unwashed, and I was still in my pyjamas, with my arms now round the bucket. I didn't have the energy to care.

"How long have you been like this?" she asked, hoisting me into the front seat of the car.

"Forever, I think." I slumped back and fastened my seat belt. She started the engine. I watched the windscreen wipers, flicking back and forth. My head was spinning; I felt as if I was in space.

"You should have called me before," she reprimanded.

"I know," I said.

"You never know when to ask for help."

"I know," I said.

"You're too independent for your own good, sometimes. Just like your father."

"I know," I said.

"Silly girl," smiled my mum, and stroked my hair.

6

I WOKE WITH A START. I opened my eyes and waited for the room to come into focus. My body was stiff and hot, my heart beating heavily in my chest, my clothes drenched with sweat and clinging to me. The room was darkened, the curtains drawn, but it was clearly still daylight outside. The remnants of a nightmare faded into the light.

My mum appeared in the doorway with a tray. "How are you? Did you sleep?"

I nodded.

"Here you are." She placed the tray on my lap and lifted me up, plumping up the pillows behind me. My limbs were weak and I moved with difficulty.

"What is it?"

"Chicken soup. It's homemade."

"Thanks. It looks better than that disgusting drink. What was it?"

"Salt and orange juice. You were dehydrated. It did the trick though, didn't it?"

I nodded and looked round the room. I was in my sister Keri's bed. It no longer smelled of plasticine and old apple cores the way it used to. It must have been years since I'd set foot in here. In the meantime, it had undergone a complete transformation. The childish crayoned pictures of houses and flowers that she'd stuck to the walls with blue tac had been replaced, and the room was now a splash of red and white. The Liverpool team photo took pride of place in the centre. Surrounding it were individual pictures: Ian Rush heading the ball, John Barnes striking, Peter Beardsley in mid-air looking over his shoulder at his backside, both legs flung out beside him.

Mug shots of the less prolific goal scorers were dotted around the window opposite. At the end of the bed sat a scruffy, one-eyed teddy bear wearing a red and white bobble hat. With a pang, I found myself wishing for one very long moment that I could come home again, that this was my room.

I finished the last of the soup and was relieved to note that it was staying down. "Where's Keri?" I asked.

"At her dad's."

"Oh. Him. She sees him, does she?"

My mother's face tightened for a moment. "He's her dad," she said.

"He was supposed to be mine, too. Ours; mine and Pete's. And look how that went."

"Let's not do this," pleaded my mum.

"Why not, Mum? It's time we talked about what happened."

"Because I can't. That's why. Because we'll both say things that we regret and then we'll both be hurt. I know how you feel. It doesn't do to keep raking it over."

She sat on the bed with her back to me and began undoing the bandage on my foot.

I sighed and put my soup bowl down on the floor. "So, what were you doing in Cambridge?"

"Shopping. Keri needed some new school things. I thought I would stop by and see if you were home. I did try to phone. I can see now why you didn't answer. It's a good job I came by when I did."

"I know. Thank you. And I *am* grateful."

I watched my mother as she then got up and moved around the room, picking up errant socks and crumpled t-shirts and putting them into Keri's washing basket. She opened the curtains and the late afternoon sunshine lit the room.

"What's wrong with me?" I asked her.

My mum looked up. "You got dehydrated. You have low blood pressure. Hypotension. You know that. Did you eat yesterday?"

"Not much. I had a bad day."

"Oh, love," my mum put my foot up onto a pillow and turned to face me. "What's happened?"

I told her about Larsen, and Jude, and the baby. She sat on the bed next to me and listened, stroking my hand tentatively, and didn't speak until I'd finished.

"It must hurt," was all she said.

"I can't believe he could just replace me like that," I said. "It feels like she's pirated my life. He wants her to move in, sleep in my bed, and bring up their baby in my home. And he wants me to just... go."

"Poor Lizzie," said my mum, unhelpfully. She stroked my hand, back and forth, over and over again. I could feel the calluses on her work-weary fingers rubbing gently against my skin. Then she asked, "Did you want him back?"

I picked at the throw on Keri's bed. "Maybe. A part of me did, at least. I think that's what I had hoped for when we first decided to break up, that we would work through our problems. Be there for each other, perhaps. And maybe after some time apart... I don't know what I expected. But I should have seen this coming. I should have known."

"Don't blame yourself."

I sighed. "So anyway, I'm going to have to move out."

"Do you really have to?"

"Either that or find forty grand. I can't afford to buy him out."

My mum paused. "I wish I could help. But you know I don't have that sort of money."

"I know that. I wasn't expecting you to do that for me."

I collapsed back onto the pillow with a thump. A book slid off the bed and dropped onto the floor beside me. I picked it up.

"'The Water Babies'," I said, wiping my eyes and turning the yellowing pages. "I haven't seen this for years."

"I found it in the attic. We must have brought it with us when we moved," my mum said, a little apologetically.

I flicked through the pages, pausing to marvel at the beautiful fairy-like illustrations of dragonflies and lobsters and little rounded babies, with 'Lucie Mabel Atwell' printed on them at the bottom, and captions underneath which I used to read myself. There was an ink stain on the corner of the back cover.

"This was my favourite book," I said, spellbound. I turned back to the beginning, looking for my name inside to prove it had been mine. On the imprint page was an inscription. It said: 'To my own Water Baby, with love from Daddy,' which took me completely by surprise. I hadn't remembered it being there at all.

"I didn't know my dad wrote this," I said. My voice sounded hollow. It felt strange, sitting there looking at it his handwriting. It was big, slanted, and old-fashioned; it was proof that he'd really existed. "Why did he call me that?"

"He used to take you swimming; he taught you to swim. Don't you remember?"

"No. Not really." I waited for my mother to tell me more, to remind me, but she didn't. I looked again at the cover and tried to remember. "I didn't know he gave this to me."

"Oh yes," said my mum. "For your birthday, that year..." she tailed off, got up off the bed and opened the curtains further, letting the sun beam in onto the bed. "And the doll," added my mother. Her voice sounded tight. She was looking away, out of the window, onto the street. "Don't you remember the doll we gave you? We chose it together. For your sixth birthday."

"No." I shook my head. "I don't. But I should. I should remember being six, right? There's so much that I seem to have forgotten."

My mother turned to face me with an expression that looked almost like relief. She gave me a quick smile, picked up my empty soup bowl, and started to leave the room.

"Only things have started coming back to me," I said. My mother stopped in the doorway, turned, and then came back again. She placed the soup bowl down on the oak chest of drawers next to Keri's bed and sat down again beside me.

"Little things," I continued. "Like the street that we were living on. I close my eyes and I can see it. A quiet avenue, leafy. Lots of trees."

My mother nodded. "That's right."

"And I had a pink dress."

"It had a kitten on the front. You loved that dress."

"Was the kitten white? And furry? When you stroked it?"

"Yes." My mother smiled.

"And I remember, dad was a postman, wasn't he?"

"Yes. But you knew that."

"You told me that. But I didn't have any memories of my own of him dressed like that, in his uniform. Until now, that is. It's just a tiny picture of him in my head, though, just a tiny picture of this big man in a postman's uniform, that's all I've got. I can't remember *him*."

"He was very handsome. He had your lovely red hair."

"It's auburn, mum."

"Auburn, then."

"And I remember the ambulance coming. And there was no one there. Just me and the ambulance."

My mother's face tightened. "I was there. I was there as soon as the ambulance arrived, Lizzie. I know it was awful, you seeing him die like that. But I didn't know until I heard the siren... it was nothing we could have helped..."

"I'm not saying it was, I just—"

"You always went to the end of the garden to wait for him to come home at the end of his round... you waited for him, you sat on the gate and waited for him, every day. And that one time... well, you just stayed there, you didn't come and get anyone. You just stayed there, standing in the street, and that's where we found you. You must have been in shock..."

"The car came too quickly," I said.

My mum looked at me for a moment as if she had seen a ghost. "That's what you said. 'The car came too quickly.' Those are just the words you used. That's all you said. All you *would* say." She reached out her hand and touched my arm. A tear slid down her cheek.

"I remember the street," I said. "I remember his uniform. I remember the ambulance. I even remember the *words*. But I just can't seem to remember *him*."

"It was a long time ago." My mum put her arms around me for a moment and we were still. She leaned her head against my shoulder. Then she stood up and picked up the soup bowl. I noticed her wiping her face with the sleeve of her cardigan as she turned. "Get some rest," she said. "You're tired."

I nodded.

After she had gone, I picked up *The Water Babies* and read it from cover to cover.

The following day I felt much better and decided to go for a drive and a walk. There was a forest nearby that I remembered visiting as a child. I ate a big breakfast and soaked for a long time in a hot steamy bath. I hadn't brought anything with me except the pyjamas that I

had been wearing when I arrived, but my mum offered me free reign
of her wardrobe. I settled for a pair of black tracksuit bottoms and a
black polar neck jumper. I looked like a cat burglar but I didn't care.
I was just glad to be well again. I found a pair of Wellington boots in
a cupboard that my mum had bought in a jumble sale and that were
two sizes too big for both of us. Mum offered me the use of her car.

"Lizzie," she called, as I left. "Here's something you might want
to think about."

"What?"

"You know my old friend, Lynne?"

"The paediatrician? The one who lives in London? Hampstead,
isn't it?"

"Marylebone. Baker Street. Except that she's just been offered a
job in Edinburgh. It's only a two year contract, a locum position. But
I think she wants someone to look after her flat for a bit."

"Me?"

"Well, anyone. But she'd be happy for you to take it, I am sure."

"I don't know. It's a long way to and from work."

"Just a thought."

"Thanks. I'll see you later."

As I drove through the Essex countryside, looking for the forest,
I realised that I was near Dunmow, heading towards Takeley, the
village where we'd once lived. I smiled as I recognised the post office
and the sweet shop. I turned right at the pub on the corner and
drove past my junior school with the climbing frame and the house
where we'd bought lettuces and tomatoes in summer, then halted in
confusion and horror at a roundabout I'd never seen before. The
house was gone, so was the neighbouring caravan site and Lesley
Mead's house, whose barn we used to play in. The barn was also gone.
And Mrs McCormick's garden, and the wall we used to climb over,
and the apples we used to pinch (only it wasn't really stealing; it was
called scrumping).

Instead, spread before me and glimmering like the Emerald City,
was London's third airport. I looked at the road signs that had
sprung up like weeds in my absence, and guessed that I must have
lived somewhere in the region of the departure lounge.

The road ended there. There was nothing left to do but leave. I stood in my mum's wellies on the oily tarmac and watched a plane that was heading down the runway and taking off in the distance. When it was lost beyond the horizon, I got back into the car and drove south towards the river.

It was late afternoon. I parked beside the lock and sat for a while, looking through the windscreen at the water rippling gently in the breeze. The sun was low but the clouds had disappeared, and the tops of the fir trees stretching into infinity beyond the river were tipped with an amber hue. I climbed out of the car and locked the door. I crossed the little wooden bridge to a dirt track on the opposite bank. I reached out to touch the shrubs that flanked the pathway and the edge of the forest where willows and poplars loomed up through the undergrowth, camouflaging the birds that whistled and twittered invisibly around me. I trailed my hand over thistles and catkins and squeezed the tip of a snow-white cornucopia, which dutifully popped out of its bud and landed at my feet. I felt a sudden pang inside me at the sheer beauty of it all, combined with a newfound nostalgia for a feeling I'd loved and long forgotten, the kind of feeling you're left with after all the best flying dreams. My mother's wellies were rubbing at the back of my legs and I could feel my socks had worked their way down and bunched up under the arches of my feet, like they used to do when I was a kid. The ground was dry and the path by the river covered in a springy layer of mossy turf. I squatted down and yanked off one boot and then the other, and pushed them under a bush.

It was only a few months since my life had begun to change forever. But it felt like forever, an eon ago, in my head. I'd floated along for so long, with everything just happening to me, but now I had come to a fork, where several branches led off into uncharted waters. I needed to make some decisions. But I didn't know how, or what to do for the best. What I really needed, I told myself, was a big hand to come out of the sky and point me in the right direction.

I peered into the water and studied my murky reflection, looking back up at me. A twig bobbed backwards and forwards over my nose. I looked confused. Was Greg right? I wondered. Did I really sell myself short? Was I really that good at what I did? And why did

I need Greg to point it out? I had always cared far too much what other people said about me. I'd always seen myself as a reflection of what everyone else saw when they looked at me, or at least what I thought they saw.

I thought, I must be giving away a lot of power.

For a moment I stood on the bank and looked deep into the water. It was unusually clear, so clear that you almost couldn't see where the rushes began and the water ended. I could just make out the silhouette of a lone minnow as it fought its way determinedly through the tangled weeds and up the river.

I turned and followed, padding in my socks over a carpet of springy moss.

7

I MOVED HOUSE ON A SUNDAY in late July. On the Saturday, Catherine came over to help me pack. We stood in my tiny kitchen drinking tea while Catherine went through my cupboards.

"You mean you're not taking any of this?" she asked, opening and shutting the pine cupboard doors and peering inside.

I shook my head. "No. Let them have it. I don't care. And anyway, Lynne's got stuff."

"But you won't be there forever. You'll need plates, and cups and cutlery at some point. And saucepans," she said, clanging two pans together as she pulled them out of the cupboard. "Hey, this is a good frying pan. You can't leave this."

"It's a wok. And I can't cook anyway."

"That's not the point."

"It's nothing. I'll get it all new. Or from a boot sale or something. It's no big deal."

Catherine shrugged. "I'd take the lot."

"No, you wouldn't," I laughed. "You say that, but you're soft really. And anyway, it's his stuff too. How do we decide who gets what? Two knives, two forks and one saucepan each? I don't want to seem petty."

"Petty? You're hardly that. He's throwing you out of your home. You're taking it really well."

"He's not throwing me out. He's buying me out."

"Whatever." Catherine sipped her tea. "I can't believe he got her pregnant that quickly."

"It was an accident, apparently."

"For him, maybe. I bet she did it on purpose. I bet he still loves you."

"Who knows? But one thing's for certain, he's made the decision for us both. There's no going back now; it's too late. They've got a connection, now, forever — whatever happens in the future, they will always have their child. It's over for me and him. It's time to move on."

Catherine nodded. She levered herself up so that she was sitting on the work surface and poured more tea from the pot next to her. "What about the teapot?" She grinned.

"No."

"Go on. Take the teapot."

"No!" I laughed.

Catherine pulled a face and stuck her bottom lip out. "I can't believe you're leaving. I've only just found you again, and now you're going. What am I going to do without you?"

"I know," I said. "But I'll be back. I'm still going to be working here. I'll be coming back here almost every day. And you can come and stay."

Catherine looked doubtful.

"Can't you?" I persisted.

"Sure." Catherine picked up a piece of bubble wrap and with her thumb and forefinger started to burst the bubbles, one by one. I jumped up onto the work surface opposite.

"That's if he'll let you, you mean," I added.

Catherine looked up, crossly. "Of course he'll let me. He's okay, you know. I know he can be a bit moody sometimes, but he's been through a lot. He had dreams. They got smashed when he had that accident."

"I know. But..."

"He's never quite got over that, not being able to compete any more. And sometimes it frustrates him, that's all. But he's a good person. He helps other people. You should see how he is with the kids on the junior swimming team. Really caring. And he loves me. I'm sure of that."

I didn't answer.

"What, you don't believe me?" Catherine pushed her hair out of her eye and frowned. "You don't think he loves me?"

I sighed. "I'm sure he does love you. Why wouldn't he? You're gorgeous."

"But?"

"Well..."

"Go on." Catherine spoke gently as she always did, but I could tell she was getting angry. "Say it, Lizzie. Say what's on your mind."

When people say that they never actually mean it. The last thing Catherine really wanted was to hear what was on my mind. "Nothing," I said. "It's nothing. I'm just going to miss you, that's all."

"When I first met him I had nothing," Catherine continued, ignoring me. "I was living like a student, in a shared house, in a rough part of London. And I was on the dole…"

"You had just finished drama school. You were looking for acting work."

"But I wasn't getting any! At least, I wasn't getting paid for anything I did. I was just bumming around. Martin sorted my life out, showed me that I needed to work, helped me get a job…"

"You hate your work, Catherine. You're a trained actress and you've settled for being a secretary."

"I'm a PA, not a secretary. And I don't hate it. Anyway, there's nothing wrong with being a secretary, Lizzie. Not everyone has to be a high flier like you."

I sighed. Here we go again, I thought. Where have I heard this before? "No, they don't," I said. "And no, of course there's nothing wrong with being a secretary if you want to be a secretary. Or a PA. It's a good job. If that's what your goal is. But it's not yours."

"It's not what I want to do forever, no, but…"

"When was the last time you performed?"

"I'm looking into that. I am applying for parts. But it's tricky, because you can't tour when you're working and there's a lot of competition for the local theatre parts. Anyway, we're getting off the point. The point is that Martin has done a lot for me. I had nothing when I met him, now I've got a man who loves me, a home, a job…"

"Okay, okay," I said, putting my hands up.

Catherine looked up at me. "When you are in a relationship there have to be some compromises, you know."

"What are you saying?" I asked her. "That I'm uncompromising? That I should have tried harder with Larsen, given up more for him?"

"No. I'm not saying that. That's you and Larsen. That's different. You wanted different things. But this is what I want. Martin. Me. A life together." She paused and neither of us spoke for a moment or two. "Look, I know you didn't get a very good welcome when you came over that time, but he was just worried, that's all. He came back late at night and I wasn't there. He didn't know where I was. And that was my fault for not leaving a note…"

"You weren't expecting him back till the following day! Why would you leave a note?"

"Well, that doesn't alter the fact that he was worried. Anything could have happened to me."

"He knew you were going out with me," I argued. "That's what you told me."

"Not 'til that late, though!"

I sighed.

"Look Lizzie, I don't know what you've got against him. It wasn't personal, him shutting the door on you like that. He likes you. When I told him I was coming over today to help you pack he offered to come and help too, straight away."

I sighed again, lost for words.

"I said we could manage — and he had to go to work, so he couldn't come, not really, but he offered all the same, and was even willing to get his shift covered. To help you. I told him he didn't need to, but he wanted to, that's the point."

The doorbell rang. I jumped down, grateful for the interruption, and went to answer it, moving a box of books to one side with my toe as I walked through the living room. Catherine followed me, padding softly across the carpet behind me. I felt upset and uncomfortable. I didn't want my mistrust of Martin to drive a wedge between us, but I knew that Catherine sensed it and it was hard not to speak my mind. Until it was spoken about, the wedge was there in any event; it was hard to be close to a person when there was something you couldn't talk about, especially something as important as the man she was going to marry.

I opened the door. Martin stood on the doorstep, smiling.

"Oh, hello," I said. "Are you looking for Catherine? She's here."

"I've brought some more boxes," said Martin, nodding towards the car. "They're flat packed but I can soon put a few together."

"Thank you," I stood aside to let him in. "I don't think I need any more, though. I haven't got much more packing to do."

"She's hardly taking anything," said Catherine.

"Don't blame her," said Martin, standing in my living room and looking around him. "Clean slate. Best thing."

I followed Martin's gaze round the room at the apple-white walls and the half empty bookshelves, down to the magnolia and fawn flecked carpet and across to the red corduroy Habitat sofa that Larsen's mother had given us when we first moved in. At the black leather wingback armchair Larsen had found in an antiques shop on Mill Road one afternoon and had dragged all the way home, with Doug. And at the oak coffee table that we had splashed out on at Clement Jocelyn when I had first got my job at GCFM. I had removed Jude's painting that had hung over the gas fire and had slid it down behind the sofa. That was one thing that was definitely not coming with me. "I don't have that much that's just mine," I muttered.

Martin slid an arm round Catherine's waist, pulled her to him and kissed her full on the lips. "Hello baby," he said. "Pleased to see me?"

Catherine looked up at him adoringly. "Yes," she said. "But what happened to your shift? I thought you were working 'til four?"

"They didn't need me today, after all. Closed the pool. Some kind of problem with the heaters. Had to get the engineers in." Martin kissed her again. Catherine put her arms round his neck and kissed him back.

I averted my eyes, picked up a roll of sellotape that was sitting on the coffee table, and began picking away at it to find the end. I hated sellotape. It didn't matter how many times you found the end, all it took was one snip of the scissors and it was lost again, your fingernails ruined. I lowered myself to the ground in front of the box of books and kneeled on the carpet.

"So, I thought I could help," Martin said. "Where do you girls want me? Kitchen? Bathroom? Bedroom?"

"All of those," said Catherine in a sexy, but loud, whisper.

Out of the corner of my eye I saw Martin slap Catherine on the bottom. She let out a squeal. I located the end of the roll, and pulled a strip of tape with a loud screech. Both Catherine and Martin stopped grabbing at each other and watched as I taped up the box of books.

"It's all done. Really. Like I said, I don't have much." I wrote "BOOKS" on the box with a marker pen, which was a bit pointless really since I didn't have any other box to mistake it for.

"When are you leaving?" asked Martin. "You want me to start loading up?"

"Tomorrow. First thing. I suppose you could put these in the boot if you don't mind. The rest can wait till the morning."

"No problem. Here." Martin bent down beside me and picked up the box. He followed me out to the car. I opened the boot and took out my map and my swimming bag to make room for the books. As I turned, my goggles fell out of my bag onto the pavement. Martin and I both bent down at the same time to pick them up. Our heads collided and we both crouched on the pavement for a brief moment, looking at each other awkwardly. I rubbed my head.

Martin grinned. "You okay ?"

"Fine." I reached out and retrieved my goggles.

"Look…" said Martin. I waited. Behind him, Catherine appeared in the doorway of my house, a few feet away. She leaned against the door frame, watching us. I stood up and Martin, glancing over his shoulder, did the same.

"I never meant…" said Martin. "I hope we can..."

"Catherine's waiting," I said.

Martin gave me a look that I couldn't decipher and slammed down the door to the boot.

After they had gone, I picked up the phone and dialled the number for the pools complex.

"When are you going to be open again?" I asked.

"When are you looking to come?" asked the receptionist.

"Well, as soon as I can. As soon as the pool reopens."

"Re-opens? What do you mean? We're open now," she said.

"Oh, great. I heard the pool had been closed today. Power failure. Heaters or something?"

"No, love," said the receptionist. "You heard wrong. We're open all day. 'Til ten tonight. Lane Swim only from seven though."

"Thank you."

I put down the phone and wandered round the house, collecting up items of clothing and bed linen from the upstairs rooms and throwing them into a big black bin liner. What was his game? I wondered. Was he making excuses to see me? Was that it? Or was he jealous of my friendship with Catherine? Afraid I'd pack her up in one of my boxes and whisk her off to London?

In the living room, I picked up a woollen purple throw with black and white crocheted flowers that my mother had given me from the back of a chair and put it in the washing basket, which was sitting on the floor near the door. I paced the room, briefly switching on the telly and switching it off again. Whatever he was up to, Catherine was completely taken in. There was no point in trying to tell her something she didn't want to hear. And maybe he was right; maybe it was none of my business. Maybe I was just jealous, after all. Maybe he had just wanted to spend the day with Catherine, whatever she was doing, whoever she was seeing. Maybe he really loved her. Maybe I was wrong.

I paused and looked up. In a corner of a book shelf above the telly was an old photograph of Larsen which I had taken soon after I met him. I wasn't sure if that made it his or mine. I picked it up. He was on stage, smiling, his head bent over his guitar, wisps of his shoulder-length blond hair falling into his face. His beautiful face. My heart leaped; he still took my breath away. But he was gone. And now our home together was gone — packed up and laid bare, all ready for his new life with Jude. All bar the cot that would soon be in the spare bedroom, the Moses basket that would soon be sitting beside the bed. Our bed. The bed that we had rolled around in naked together. The bed that we had curled up in together, laughing and talking dreamily until sleep overcame us. The bed that would soon have Larsen back in it again — Larsen and his new family, lying tangled up sleepily together.

I put the photo back on the shelf where I had found it, laid down on the sofa, and turned out the light.

8

THERE ARE GOOD DAYS and there are bad days and then there are those days from hell that leap up out of nowhere and smack you right between the eyes. These are the days when you wish you'd stayed in bed, or in the womb. "Nobody told me there'd be days like these," sang John Lennon once. Nobody told me either.

Not that any of it had been particularly easy of late. Even moving was scary at first. Apart from my first term at college, and the few months since Larsen had left, I'd never really lived on my own. Now, aside from the practical details like worrying alone (which is different from worrying with someone else) about the rent and the bills and the poll tax and TV licence, there were more fundamental and complicated problems to be faced — like what to do with moths, beetles, and spiders in the bath, what to do when the water pipes froze and burst and flooded the kitchen, what to do when things went bump in the night, and, with no one to direct me or to be my excuse for inactivity, how to decide what to do with the rest of my life.

I'd been lucky with the flat, I knew that. My mother's friend Lynne was more than happy to let it to me. It was a modest but distinctly up-market two-bed upper floor flat conversion in a cobbled mews in Central London, just off Marylebone High Street. The house itself was pretty — white brick with timber sash windows, a cast iron downpipe, and a Juliet balcony leading off my living room at the front. A pair of authentic looking stable doors opened onto the neighbour's garage downstairs. At the rear, a black iron staircase provided a fire escape which led up past the living room window to the kitchen.

The living room had the original floorboards, cornices, and picture rail, and was decorated simply in white and lemon. Two small sofas with cream and tartan throws sat in front of a gas fire, and a large vase of dried flowers stood by the door that led onto the two small bedrooms. Two large Gaugin prints filled the walls in the hallway. The overall effect was light and bright, chic and feminine, and it would ordinarily have been completely out of my price bracket. But, to my immense surprise, Lynne had only wanted to recoup the cost of her considerably cheaper rented flat in Edinburgh, on the basis that I was semi-house-sitting and therefore doing her a favour.

I moved in with two suitcases full of clothes, the cardboard box full of books, a bag of cassette tapes, Jeffrey, my beige woolly teddy bear, and an Ikea bedside lamp that had seen better days. I couldn't believe that this sparse collection of chattels, small enough to load into my car and out at the other end all by myself, was the product of my seven years with Larsen — of my twenty-seven years of life. It occurred to me with some sadness how many people I'd also left behind over the years along with my belongings.

The flat seemed very empty, and it was cold for July. It had been overcast and wet for days and didn't really feel like summer. I should be having a housewarming, I mused regretfully, but there was no one to invite. After a quick spring clean, I lit the gas fire, hung my clothes up in the wardrobe, and went off to Europa for bread, cheese, olives, and a bottle of red wine. Soon I was sitting on the living room carpet in front of the fire, drinking an ambivalent toast to my new home.

Being alone, I discovered, is a state of mind. At its best it brings serenity. It could recreate for me the sunshine days of my solitary youth, when all I needed as friends were my books and the fields at the back of the house where we lived.

On my days off, I'd go swimming, then lie on my bed wrapped up in my duvet and read for hours. Or I'd catch a bus up to Finchley Road and take long brisk walks over Hampstead Heath. Sometimes, as I plodded past the ponds and up to Kenwood through bracken and stretches of reedy grass, I'd pause to smoke a cigarette and watch the sun go down over the city below. Whether my mood was blissfully happy, or reflective and melancholy, I'd achieve the state of inner harmony that I now realised I'd been missing for so long. My senses reawakened, I'd feel so completely and utterly at peace that it would almost bring tears to my eyes. At those moments, I'd feel I'd achieved the perfect equilibrium between the security I needed so desperately on the one hand, and the freedom I craved on the other. I'd see my future as bright and hopeful, with an infinite number of choices open to me.

Other times, being alone was just plain lonely, and hard work to boot. The effort of travelling well over a hundred miles to work and back each day, combined with shopping, cooking, cleaning, and paying the bills, then climbing into bed at night with no one to touch or to talk to about the way I was feeling, often made me wonder what I was doing in London and whether I'd made some huge mistake.

I'd plough on for days, even weeks, barely acknowledging to myself that anything was wrong, until I'd wake one morning, early and off balance, after a dream about Larsen in which he'd been holding me and stroking my hair and whispering that everything was going to be all right. I'd stretch out my hand and feel the emptiness of the bed beside me and my heart would sink. I'd lie there apathetically for hours, staring into the dim and dusky bedroom, seeing nothing but one more empty day ahead and then more and more days exactly the same, stretching on and on into infinity. I'd see the crossroads of my future looming up ahead, but instead of enthusing over the various paths I could take, I'd feel lost and confused and long to run back the way I'd come, knowing deep down that I never could, and this would frighten me more.

Sometimes loneliness would creep up and catch me unawares. I'd spend an entire weekend holed up in my living room, content and happy. I'd read and cook and listen to music, watch a film on TV, or sit with a cup of coffee and stare out of the window at the pretty cobbled streets and houses. Then suddenly, the silence would become oppressive; I'd hear a humming noise in my head and start to feel a bit weird. I'd start to worry that I was going slightly mad, and I'd realize by Sunday afternoon that maybe it was because I hadn't spoken to a solitary person in forty-eight hours. So I'd put on my coat and walk down to Oxford Street, just to be near people. Now I began to see why old people spent so much time talking to shopkeepers, or to me on buses.

There was the telephone, of course. I phoned Catherine in Cambridge and, less often, she phoned me back, but I could always sense Martin hanging around in the background and our conversations were stilted and distracted.

"We must get together, really soon," Catherine would say every time we spoke.

"Whenever you like," I'd answer, flicking through the blank pages in my diary.

"I'll call you then." Catherine would sound panicky, as if she didn't know quite how she was going to manage this.

"Fine. Whatever." I didn't want her having any guilt trips on my account.

Occasionally I'd take the train into Cambridge and go out for a drink after my shift with people from work, but mostly they were either driving, or married and couldn't stay for long. Those who did seemed bored, or fed up with being stuck where they were and the conversation would become negative and ultimately depressing. I knew it wasn't really where I wanted to be either, out there in no man's land.

By mid-August, I was getting frustrated. Everyone knew that there was no chance of Greg coming back to the station, but there had been no mention of his long-term replacement. All kinds of speculation had been made about his future but nothing official had filtered down.

On the Friday before the Bank Holiday, I woke up with a toothache. I realised I must have been grinding my teeth in the night. I swallowed a codeine tablet and stood by the kitchen sink in my pyjamas, drinking coffee and emptying the last few slices of bread out of the packet onto the work surface. I realised that it was time to confront Phil about the job. While I buttered and peanut-buttered sandwiches for my lunch I started to compose my opening dialogue. As I dressed for work I practised in front of the mirror.

At ten o'clock that morning, I tapped on Phil's door.

"Ah, Lizzie," he smiled vaguely, looking up from a pile of rosters. He was a short, stocky man in his early forties, although he looked older, and his receding sandy hairline revealed a complicated configuration of lines that looked as though they had been etched in with a stencil. He looked like someone does when they're irritated but trying hard to be polite. I stood in the doorway until he put down his pencil.

"What can I do for you?"

"I need to talk to you," I said.

"Sounds serious," Phil laughed, a little condescendingly. "I'm incredibly busy. Can it wait?"

I paused for a moment, then decided it couldn't. I'd lose my nerve by this time tomorrow and he'd still be just as busy.

I took a deep breath. "I'm sorry, it can't."

Phil waved me good-naturedly into a chair in front of him and gave me his full attention, levelling his eyes at my chest.

"Fire away," he smiled at my breasts. I crossed my arms and his eyes flickered upwards and met mine. I abandoned my pre-meditated preamble and decided to be direct.

"I've been acting up for Greg for three months this week," I began.

"You're doing very well, Lizzie," Phil interrupted. "Very well indeed."

"I like to think so," I agreed. "What I want to know is, is Greg coming back and, if not, what's going to happen about replacing him?"

Phil's surprise at my forwardness was stoically masked, almost to perfection. He shifted and leaned forward towards me, placing his elbows on top of his rosters and pressing his stubby fingers together. He spoke slowly, as if he were talking to a child. "Greg's attachment at IRN was for eight weeks initially—"

"I know that," I interrupted, impatiently. "But it's been three months now. That's my point."

"—and we expected him back before now. However," Phil continued, just as slowly, "it appears that they've decided to extend the contract."

"How long for?" It was beyond me how someone who was allegedly so busy could spend such an inordinate amount of time playing with his words.

"Initially a further ten weeks." Phillip was losing interest in the conversation. He began shifting the papers about on his desk. He held a letter up to the glare of his desk lamp, scrutinized it closely, tore it into strips and dropped it in the bin.

"And then?" I persisted.

"There's every chance that his position there will be given long-term consideration."

"Long-term consideration," I echoed, frustrated anger welling up inside me. I knew my voice was wobbling. "It's at least four weeks into the extension of his contract. You must know what's going to happen. When were you going to tell me?"

Phil sat back defensively, picked up his pencil and wagged it at me.

"Now just calm down a minute, Lizzie."

"I *am* calm."

Phil sat and stared at me, tapping his pencil. Under the pretence of waiting for me to recover from my loss of control, I could tell that he was playing for time; he was barely managing to conceal his own annoyance at my refusal to play out the role of demure child to his kindly parent. He'd hardly passed the time of day with me since he'd sent me the letter offering me the opportunity to cover for a senior member of staff on half the pay and a quarter of the respect, for which I was supposed to remain eternally in his debt.

"An announcement will be made once the vacancy becomes official." Phil's tone had become detached and professional.

"An announcement?" I shook my head in disbelief. "You mean you were going to stick up a notice on the staff board?"

"The job has to be advertised," Phil said. "You will be welcome to apply, naturally."

I stood up. "I'll do that," I said. "Naturally."

I spent the rest of the morning preparing the twelve and one o'clock bulletins for someone else to read and news wraps for the programme that someone else would present and cues for interviews that someone else would conduct. By the time the programme finished at two o'clock, I'd had enough. I had been up since five and had been too worked up to eat all day. Now I was tired and starving and awaiting the moment when I could sit down with a coffee, eat my sandwiches, and read a chapter of my book before I faced the long drive back to London.

I pushed open the door to the staff room. There sat Phil, smoking a cigarette and reading a magazine. I couldn't believe it. He almost never mingled with the minions, and there he was, feet up, occupying two and a half seats and leafing through a copy of Cosmopolitan, chortling affectedly, in the nearest thing to a retreat that could be found in the building and in my first free ten minutes all day. I stormed into the toilets and poured my coffee down the sink. I glared at my reflection in the mirror. Pink spots of anger were forming on my cheeks. Time to get out of here.

One advantage of the lunchtime shift was missing the evening rush hour. I cruised down the M11 at a steady seventy, pushed Ella Fitzgerald into the cassette deck, and fished around in my handbag for my sandwiches. However, as I passed the Bishops Stortford turnoff, I noticed the traffic had slowed down considerably. Within a mile of the M25, the dual carriageway was down to one lane, the road was strewn with police warning beacons and I became another reluctant statistic in a tailback a mile long.

I sighed and leaned back in my seat. I ripped open the packet on the passenger seat beside me; my stomach growled in anticipation. Inside, I discovered that my peanut butter sandwiches now exhibited small rings of blue and white mould.

It was gone five by the time I pulled up outside the flat. The street was jam-packed with cars and I had to drive round the block three times before I could find a space. Finally, as I rounded the corner onto the road parallel to mine, a Volvo pulled out sharply in front of me and I edged nervously into the gap behind a gleaming bottle-green Mercedes.

As I crossed the street to my flat, I felt my jaw aching with tension. I closed the front door behind me, dropped my bag onto the floor and poured myself a large glass of red wine. I checked the answer phone: no messages. I lit a cigarette and sank to the floor, leaning my head against the telephone table.

The wine went straight to my head. I knew I should eat something really, although by this point, the idea of drinking myself into a stupor was infinitely more appealing. Eventually, after half an hour of staring inanely into space, I managed to motivate myself into taking a final journey round the corner for a Chinese takeaway and another bottle of wine. Dragging myself wearily up with the aid of the table legs, I went to fetch my purse. After an agitated rummage through my bag, I realised that it must have fallen out of my bag in the car. I found my car keys, grabbed my jacket and stepped out into the warm night air.

As I rounded the corner I stopped suddenly and stood rooted to the pavement. My car was gone; a black cab sat purring in its place. At first I wondered if I'd got the wrong street, but with a sick lurch of the stomach I saw, beyond the taxi, the shiny silver bumper of the bottle-green Merc, still gleaming under the streetlight.

The cab driver drew back the glass and popped his head out.

"Need a cab, love?"

"My car's gone," I said, bewildered.

"Gone?"

"Stolen." The word seemed to echo around me. "It's only an Astra," I added, pointing at the Merc. "Why didn't they take that instead?"

"Doubt it's been nicked, love, not round 'ere," said the cabbie. "How much did you put in the meter?"

"What? No, no... I've got a permit," I explained.

"Not along here you haven't," said the cabbie. He pointed at the pavement. "Meters only."

I turned round; a few yards away stood a parking meter.

"You've been towed," said the cabbie, smugly.

"Thank you," I said. "You've been very helpful."

"Need a cab?" he repeated.

"No thank you." I sighed, my vision of a night by the fire with a Chinese take-away and a bottle of wine flickering before me and fading out of sight. "I've got no money. And anyway, I don't know where I have to go to get it back."

"West Kensington police pound," said the man from the Met.

"Thank you." Thank you for towing my car away and then telling me how to get it back again.

"Make sure you're there by seven," he added. "Otherwise you'll have to pay for an extra day."

My neighbour, when I knocked, was having a better evening. She was evidently somewhere in the middle of a working out session, as Larsen used to call it. She just managed to deposit a couple of pound coins into my hand before her other half appeared behind her and dragged her off squealing by the belt of her dressing gown, kicking the door shut in my face in the process.

I sighed and headed up the road to Baker Street. As I walked into the tube station my bad ankle gave way. I lost my footing, stumbled forward, and tumbled down the steps.

"Tell me, is it Friday the thirteenth today?" I asked the sister in charge. I was sitting in the A & E department at St Bartholomew's Hospital, my left ankle once again elevated in front of me and wrapped in a bandage.

"No," she replied confidently, after a moment's consideration. "That's next week".

I looked up at the ceiling. "Oh Christ."

A bony finger tapped my arm. "You watch your language, young lady," croaked its owner, a spindly geriatric patient, who had stopped beside me in her wheelchair. I stared at her, dully, until she clicked her tongue and wheeled herself off again, glaring back at me as she went.

"There. You'll live," said the Sister. She patted my shoulder reassuringly. "Nothing broken, just a sprain. Keep it up for a few days, and you'll be right as rain."

I smiled; it sounded like a song.

It was all quite funny really, I reflected, a little hysterically. I'd gone out for a Chinese takeaway in Marylebone, I was supposed to be at the police compound in West Kensington, and now here I was in hospital in Islington. I glanced at my watch. It was too late to pick up the car, in any case. I might as well worry about that tomorrow.

I'd been lucky to get offered a lift to the nearest hospital by a kind couple who had been parked up on Marylebone Road. It was *their* nearest hospital in fact; they lived in Clerkenwell. The sister had also very kindly given me a cup of tea and a biscuit, which was strictly beyond the call of duty, I was well aware, and probably beyond the budget of the National Health Service. You normally at least had to give them a pint of blood first. I wasn't complaining, not really. It was just that I was tired, hungry, and in pain and now I wasn't at all sure how I was going to get home again.

"Good lord!" said a loud voice, very close to my ear. I jumped in my seat and turned to see the starched corner of a nurse's cap and a familiar elfin face, its bright blue eyes peering amusedly at me from behind a stray lock of honey blonde hair.

"Zara? My God, what are you doing here?" I asked, redundantly, as she stood back to reveal her light blue uniform.

"What have you done?" she indicated my bandaged ankle.

"I fell. Down some steps."

"Well I never," said Zara, shaking her head and twisting back and forth on her heel, her hands behind her. "Fancy seeing you here." Suddenly, she leapt forward, bent down towards me, and grabbed both my wrists. "Hey, where are you going now?" she asked.

I looked beyond her at my extended leg. "Well, I don't exactly have any plans."

"Stay right where you are. I'm off duty in fifteen minutes." Zara leapt to her feet and hurried off down the corridor.

"Don't go away!" she yelled back over her shoulder.

"Right," I muttered, staring at my bandaged ankle.

A quarter of an hour later, Zara reappeared with the same old black raincoat on that I'd seen her in all those years ago. She had a woolly beret on her head that looked like a tea cosy. She was pushing a wheelchair.

"Hop in," she ordered.

I shook my head. "You can't be serious."

Zara regarded me for a moment, puzzled, and then, before I could protest any further, came round behind me, grabbed me under both arms and hoisted me up in one swift movement and deposited me into the canvas seat. I was amazed at her strength; her tiny and frail-looking appearance was belied by the muscularity of a brawny six-footer.

"Christ, I'm not going to argue with you," I laughed as Zara wheeled me down the corridor, through the double doors of A & E and out into the car park. "You're like Rambo. Or the Incredible Hulk."

"Six years of lifting old codgers onto bedpans," said Zara, pushing faster and skidding along behind me. "And old ladies into baths."

A balmy breeze whipped my hair round my face. I screamed with laughter and Zara giggled from behind me as she got faster and faster, negotiating her way deftly through the parked cars and ambulances and out through the gates onto the road.

"I hope you don't do this to your patients," I yelled.

"'Course I do — they love it," Zara shouted back.

"Where are we going, anyway?" I lifted my head towards her.

"King's Arms," said Zara, slowing down as we headed out of the gates and across the square outside.

"The where? I haven't got any money..." I protested. "I've lost my car. And my purse."

"You are *so* accident prone, Lizzie," said Zara. "Anyway, don't worry about that. I've got money." She levered me up onto the kerb and parked me outside a small, noisy pub. "Boy, do I need a drink," she said. "I've had the shittiest day you would not believe."

From my wheelchair, I twisted my head back again, and surveyed her caustically.

"Really?" I said. "No kidding."

9

THE KING'S ARMS IN SMITHFIELD was a classic seventeenth century back-street pub with a beautiful half-beamed exterior, hanging baskets and wooden beer casks lined up along the outside. Inside the public bar was an expanse of wood panelling, oak beams and a polished wood floor. The seating was provided by antique settles and benches and there was a beautiful inglenook fireplace in the corner. That evening the pub was jam-packed with hospital staff who had just come off duty. They stood or swayed around the bar area in an imposing mass, the hum of excited chatter filling the air along with loud screeches of laughter and clouds of cigarette smoke, the nearby tables overflowing with drinks. One girl had removed her stockings and used them to blindfold one of her male colleagues, who was now the delighted recipient of a lengthy embrace from an unknown female on tiptoes. She was being egged on by the crowd behind her.

"Friday night," said Zara, as she edged her way into a gap at the bar. "Everyone goes a bit mad. What are you having?"

"A pint of lager please. And I'd better have some crisps."

"Two pints of lager," she said to the barman. "A bag of cheese and onion, and," - looking at me for approval and finding no argument - "a couple of whisky chasers?"

We found a table at the back of the pub. Zara hopped me into my seat, placed my leg on the chair in front of me and went back to fetch the drinks. I looked around me at the old black and white photos of Smithfield market that were pinned to the oak beams nearby. In one, a slim man in a white apron who looked like Charlie Chaplin was grinning broadly in the sunshine and holding up a very

large fish. He looked so ridiculously happy that it made me wonder
if that was all it took for some people: a sunny day and a big fish.

I lit a cigarette and exhaled deeply. Zara reappeared with the
drinks. "So, how have you been?" she asked, slipping in beside me.
"Tell me everything."

So I did.

"I never liked that Jude," said Zara, loyally, when I'd finished.

"I never liked that Marion," I smiled back.

A cheer exploded from the crowd next to us.

"Hooray!" said Zara. "Hooray for us!" We clinked glasses.

"Just look at that lot," Zara smiled. She nodded in the direction
of the bar. "They're going for it tonight."

"Wild," I agreed.

"Are you shocked?" she asked.

"Not really," I said truthfully. I'd seen worse.

"I suppose we have a bit of a reputation, nurses ... you know. It's
being surrounded by sickness all day that does it. You become more
impulsive, like there's a desperate need to enjoy life to the full. I
suppose it's because you're constantly reminded how quickly it can
be taken away from you."

"Live fast, die young," I smiled.

"No," said Zara sharply. "I don't hold with all that rock 'n' roll
rubbish. Maybe this," - she raised her glass - "is a bit self-destructive.
But I value life; I really do. I wouldn't spend all day trying to save it
if I didn't. But it's hard, sometimes. Last night I was on the Neuro
ward. The staff nurse had to tell two young girls that their mother
was dead. An aneurysm, it was. Which caused a haemorrhage. One
minute she was there, the next ... well, she wasn't. The oldest must
have been my age, about twenty-five or six. I tried to persuade them
not to, but they still went in to see her. In the end we had to drag them
screaming off her body.

"When I got home I rang my mum." She stopped abruptly and
glanced away from me up at the ceiling. I jerked my head upward to
see what she was looking at but there was only an oak beam. "I only
wanted to talk, hear her voice. It was late," she muttered. "She was
tired, I think, just wanted to go to bed."

She hiccupped and I started to laugh, then realised stupidly that she was crying. I squeezed her fingers, tentatively.

"It's nothing really." Zara mumbled and wiped her eyes with the back of her hand. "It's just…like I said, not a very good day."

Zara shifted in her seat and leaned forward. She looked like she'd spotted someone at the bar. She glanced back at me, her watery eyes suddenly alert, and lifted her glass. "Another?"

I nodded, and leaned back into my seat. I watched as Zara weaved her way quickly through the crowds towards the bar area. Just before she reached the bar she stopped and tapped the arm of an attractive black man. Her back was to me but I could clearly see his expression as he swung round to face her. It was one of extreme annoyance. He looked back at the man with whom he'd been talking, who smiled and backed away towards another group. He shoved his hands into his pockets and turned back to Zara. They spoke for a few minutes before he lifted both hands up abruptly as if he was a policeman stopping traffic, then he turned round and walked off in the direction of the door. Zara disappeared after him.

I lit another cigarette and waited patiently. After ten or fifteen minutes she returned to the table with two large whiskies and slipped in beside me again. We drank in silence for a minute. The whisky was starting to have a pleasantly anaesthetic effect on my ankle.

Zara sat beside me and sniffed and wiped at her eyes with her sleeve while I tried to think of something to say.

"I can't take the exams, you see," she said eventually. "If I was qualified ... things would be different. Bloody exams." She took a huge sip of her whisky and turned to me. "You know I only became a nurse because I failed my art degree. Or dropped out, I should say. Three months before my finals."

"What?" I was horrified. "After all that work?"

"I know, I know." A wry smile flickered on Zara's lips and was replaced by an anxious frown. "But I'm serious, Lizzie. I just can't handle the pressure. I worked hard at school and somehow got through, but I only sat one A-level. I've studied and trained for every module of the first two years of the RGN, but without sitting the exams. Until I do," she shrugged, "I remain Nurse Bedpan. There's this other staff nurse on the Neuro Ward, she finds fault with everything I do. It's getting so I can't bear working with her. I'm losing my confidence around her. Today she started making snide comments about Joel. He's my - one of the doctors I'm seeing." She glanced at me sideways. "Kind of. We're supposed to be a secret," she added. "Also he's black. She's found out and she doesn't approve."

"Jesus, Zara, you want to report her, you know. That's harassment," I said.

"It's not that easy though," she sighed. "She's a good nurse; she has a lot of respect from senior staff. And it's so covert that no-one else is ever witness to it. I'm sure she would just deny it, and make me out to be paranoid or over-sensitive or something. That's the sort of person she is. And then it would be ten times worse. I'd end up believing whatever was said about me. At least at the moment I'm hanging on by a shoestring to my self-respect."

I nodded and sipped my drink in silence. It was easy to give advice when you were on the outside of things looking in.

"And then there's Joel. That's the other problem," Zara confessed finally. "He was here tonight, actually, but he left."

"I know," I said. "I saw him."

"Ah." She sipped carefully at her drink. "It's not going very well," she admitted. "It really isn't going anywhere. He's very..." she tailed off.

"Very what?" I asked her.

"Uncommitted. Ambivalent."

"Your usual type, then," I smiled.

Zara pursed her lips. "I don't know what you mean."

The bell rang for last orders. Zara went to the bar and came back a few minutes later with another large whisky for each of us. I lit another cigarette. It had been a long day and I had eaten practically nothing; I was already decidedly far from sober, but I was feeling ridiculously happy to be with Zara again, and wasn't looking forward to going home again to my empty flat. As if reading my thoughts Zara took my arm and said, "Come back and stay at my place. I share a house with three other nurses. It's only round the corner. You can't walk, and besides it's ages since I've seen you."

"When *was* the last time we saw each other?" I asked her.

Zara shook her head and shrugged her shoulders. "I don't know. I left Cambridge after Doug and I parted. It was nearly two years ago."

"So, what happened?"

"Nothing. He chose to stay with her." She paused. "And he didn't want the baby."

"The *baby*? What baby?"

"Our baby."

"You were pregnant?"

"For a while, yes."

"So… what happened?" I asked again.

"I had a termination," she said. I leaned forward in my seat. Zara was speaking so quietly I could barely hear her. "There were reasons."

"Well, I'm sure there were. It's not easy bringing up a baby by yourself."

"No, but I would have done. That wasn't it. I would have loved it. More than anything in the world."

"So why, then?"

"I don't know. I was crazy. I've regretted it ever since. If I could turn back the clock, I would."

"There's no point regretting things, Zara," I said. "You can't live in the past."

"Wanna bet?" she said.

When we got outside, the wheelchair, inevitably, had gone. The cool air and the final whisky were having the same effect on Zara as they were having on me, and when it came to walking, she wasn't faring much better than I was.

"Just hold on to me round my neck," she said, grabbing me round the waist. I put my arms round her. Her head only came up to my shoulder and, despite her strength, the inequality in our size and build and the whole situation struck me as suddenly very funny. I began to giggle, and was soon shaking with laughter.

"Stop it," pleaded Zara, laughing herself. "I can't carry you when you're wobbling like that!"

I laughed even harder. Immobilised by the stitch that had developed in my stomach and the giddiness in my head, I doubled up and with Zara laughing as loudly as I was and loosening her grip on me, we both sank to the pavement. People were walking past on the way home from the pub. They watched us as they passed but, typically, didn't stop. Eventually, Zara sat up and shook me.

"This is serious," she said. "I've got to get up. I need to go to the loo."

"Oh no," I moaned. "You can't leave me here."

"Of course not," said Zara. "I can carry you. As long as you stop laughing. Now come on."

Getting me up again took a long time. Every effort on Zara's part to lift me was thwarted by my renewed fits of giggles, which were caused by her putting her hands under my armpits, where I was incredibly ticklish. In the end, she swung my legs across the kerb and stood in the road over me, yanking me forward by the wrists. She caught me as I reeled towards her.

"Now hold tight." She hoisted me over her shoulder and we set off again in the direction of the hospital.

Zara was deep in concentration, bent on her mission. I was feeling less hysterical and slightly sick. We stumbled wordlessly through the grounds and out onto the opposite side.

"We're nearly there," said Zara, stopping for a moment and crossing her legs. "Not far now."

Finally, we turned into an ill-lit street and stopped at a dark and crumbling three-storey town house. Zara pushed open the gate and propped me up against the porch while she fiddled around trying to get her key in the lock. As soon as it opened she shot inside and bolted up the stairs. I hobbled in after her and hauled myself slowly up in the direction she had gone.

A door opened on the first landing and a head popped out.

"That you, Clare?" asked a male voice.

"No." I paused, and leaned weakly against the banisters. "I'm Lizzie." I suddenly felt overwhelmingly tired.

The door widened, casting a shaft of light across the dingy landing, and the speaker stepped out of the room. He was tall, dark, and completely naked.

"Oh, hello," he smiled, apologetically and cupped one hand between his legs. "I thought you were…" He shrugged, grinned and then held out his spare hand. "I'm Tim."

"Hello, Tim," I said, and passed out.

10

I WOKE WITH A BLINDING HEADACHE. Zara was sitting up in bed beside me reading a magazine. Little by little, the rest of the room came into focus. It looked as if we were in a squat. We were lying on a thick and lumpy mattress on the floor in the corner next to a window, which was hung with one drab-looking curtain and a sheet of clear plastic, nailed down at the edges to keep out the wind. The walls were cracked and the paint was yellow and chipped. Along one wall was a shelf of books, and below it an old table stacked high with files and folders, some wooden frames, pieces of canvas, and several murky jam jars full of painted water and brushes. On every spare surface — on the table, on the mantelpiece above the gas fire, on the floor — were paintings of flowers. Large, bright, multi-coloured sunflowers, snow-white water-lilies floating on a leaf-green pond, and intricate weaves of buttercups and daisies set against a pink and purple backdrop.

"You're awake," said Zara. "How d'you feel?"

"I've definitely felt better," I murmured, resting my arm over my forehead. My mouth was so dry that I could barely speak. Zara handed me a glass of water.

"Do you remember what happened?" Zara paused while I cast my mind back to the night before. The pain in my ankle was beginning to make itself felt.

I shook my head. "No. At least not after we got back here."

"You passed out," said Zara.

"Ah," I said, a little embarrassed. "Sorry. Where did I land?"

"It's a good job Tim was there," she continued. "You were standing at the top of the stairs. You'd have gone right down them, backwards, if he hadn't been there to catch you."

"God." I shivered at the thought. "Who's Tim?" I added. A vague recollection was hovering at the back of my mind. On cue, there was a knock at the door. It opened, and a dark curly head appeared.

"Hello?"

"Tim, come and meet Lizzie," said Zara.

"I believe we've already met," he said, stepping into the room and smiling broadly at me.

Tim had one of those faces that made you want to laugh before he'd even said anything. He was grinning widely, the corners of his mouth seeming almost to touch his ears, and his eyes were big and round and so dark that you couldn't see his pupils; they looked like cartoon eyes. His thick eyebrows were arched quizzically and there was a dimple on his chin. He was very tall, and thin. My memory came flooding back. I was relieved to see he had clothes on.

"And how's the patient this morning?" he asked me.

"Alive," I croaked. "Thanks to you."

"All part of the service," said Tim. "You should probably stay where you are today. Get some rest."

"That would be nice," I said. But something was nagging at me. I cast my mind back to the events of the previous day, and sat up in bed. "Oh my God," I said. "What time is it? I forgot about the car." I scanned the room for my clothes.

"What car?" asked Tim. I explained briefly, about the police pound, about my ankle, and about how I'd ended up at Bart's.

Zara pushed me gently back down again. "You're staying right here, and I'm staying with you. Tim will get the car, won't you, Tim?"

I looked at him, uncertainly. "Sure," he said. "Where are the keys?"

"In my pocket, I think," I replied, confused, unsure where my pocket was. I was unable to believe that I could really lie back and that everything would be taken care of. Tim went over to Zara's desk and wrote down my registration number.

"My purse," I said, sitting up again. "It's in the car — or at least, I hope it is. You'll have to give them my credit card. If it's there. Oh, God."

"Stop worrying. I'll sort it out," said Tim. "Now relax. Everything's under control." He picked my jacket up from a chair that was tucked under the table, fished the keys out of my pocket, and left.

I lifted the bedclothes, and glanced down at myself. I was wearing a very tight pink nightdress.

"That's one of mine," said Zara.

"Oh," I said, worried. "Who undressed me last night?"

"Me and Tim," said Zara, dismissively. "Do you want a cup of tea?"

She caught my expression, and smiled as she got up. "Don't worry, he's a nurse," she said. "He's seen it all before."

I lay my head back on the pillow. I supposed that made us about even.

We stayed in bed and talked all day, Zara and I, about the past, the present and the future. I watched her eyes twinkling as she spoke and recalled the first time I'd met her, up in the bathroom at Larsen's house, when she had told me about the stars talking and we had fallen into the bath. It seemed such a long time ago. And yet up until now, I'd known so little about her deep down, the things that really mattered. As she moved, I noticed for the first time a scar protruding from the sleeve of her nightdress.

"What's that?" I asked her.

Zara pulled up her sleeve to reveal the shiny traces of a number of incisions, running horizontally across her left forearm. "I had a difficult time, she said. When I was six."

"You did that when you were *six*?"

"My mum couldn't cope. I got taken into care. I hated it there. It was awful. The matron was just like the nurse on the Neuro ward. A bully. It was more a kind of release than an attempt at anything else. Some way I could let go of what I was feeling."

I thought back to me at six, and it felt like there was a connection between me and Zara. That was the age I had been when my father had died in the road in front of me; it was a misty, scary age, when everything and nothing made sense.

"I didn't really know what was going on," said Zara, reading my thoughts. "Except that I thought I was going to be left there forever, and I thought it was all my fault because my mum didn't want me home again."

She paused. "That's when I started drawing. I've got a picture somewhere, of me in bed in the dorm. Just lying there. No one else around. It's from a funny angle, too. Looking down, as if looking from the ceiling."

Zara turned and looked at me for a moment as if I were someone else, and then the same anxious frown of the night before shadowed her forehead. "My mum had me too young," she said after a pause. "She just wasn't ready to have a baby."

"How awful. What about your dad? Did they visit you?"

"Yes. At first they did. And I begged them to take me home. But my mum just got upset, and then she stopped coming. I knew by her reaction that it was my fault," Zara continued. "I thought I was evil, and I thought I'd made my mum crack up. There was nothing to say, but be strong for her, so that hopefully she'd get better and come and visit me."

"And did she?"

"Well, no. Not really. She had another two babies, my brother and sister. But things got a bit better for me. I drew a lot, everything I was feeling. And one of the staff would bring me flowers, that was really nice, so I drew them too. That was the happy bit." She waved at the walls. "Flowers make me feel happy. Then, when I was nine, I came home."

"What happened then? Was everything okay?"

"I guess," said Zara. "But the bond was gone. Me and my mum. We just never bonded. And that's why I want that... *dream* of that. That's why I just so *need* a baby of my own."

At around midday, Zara put her coat on over her nightdress and went out to get some lunch. Tim returned in the meantime, and dropped my keys and my purse onto the bed in front of me.

"How much?" I asked.

"I'll tell you later," he said. "Right now you're still in shock. We don't want any relapses."

"That bad?"

"Put it this way," he grinned. "Don't go planning any holidays abroad for a while."

"Tim," I called, as he left. He turned at the door. "Thanks. And thanks for last night as well."

"You're most welcome," he said, and then hung his head in mock-modesty. "I like to think I was kind of responsible, in a way."

I smiled. "Do you always wander around in the middle of the night with no clothes on?"

"I thought you were Clare," he said. "My girlfriend."

"Oh. I see."

"Don't worry," said Tim. "You're not the only one. Clare nearly passed out too, the first time she saw me naked."

Zara came in with a large wooden tray, which she settled on my lap before she climbed back into bed beside me. On it was a pot of tea with a woolly cosy on top that looked a bit like the hat she had been wearing the night before. Also, there was a piece of cold smoked mackerel wrapped in tin foil, a jar of pickled herrings, two hard-boiled eggs, and a packet of oatcakes.

"And I've got these." She produced a tin from under the bed and handed it to me.

I pulled the lid off and smiled. "Fairy cakes. Did you make these?"

"No..."

I took a bite of cake and began to choke. Zara put down her cup, and walloped me on the back. A piece of cake flew out of my mouth.

I stared at the bed. "Zara, this cake is green inside."

"Ah. Don't eat it." She snatched the remaining piece out of my hand, put it back in the tin and put the lid on. "Uncle Silbert made them," she said, looking at me apologetically. "I'm sorry. I forgot to check."

"Uncle Silbert?" I laughed. "Who's Uncle Silbert?"

"He's not really my uncle, I just call him that. He's one of my old patients from when I was on the district." Zara smiled at the cake tin. "He's seventy-six, and he's got really bad arthritis, but he still lives on his own. He can't get out, or do much for himself, and I don't know what's happened to his family. He says he has a nephew in Hackney Downs, but I've never seen him."

"Where did he get his name from?" I asked.

"Oh that," said Zara. "That was a mistake. He was supposed to be called Gilbert, but they wrote it down wrong on his birth certificate. One of those funny G's, you know," she explained. "He's been Silbert ever since. I still go and visit him, every Sunday," she added, grinning and grabbing the teapot from me as it wobbled and hot tea splashed over my leg. "And fetch him things from the shops."

"Where does he live?" I asked, dabbing at my leg with a tissue.

"In a council block, just off Essex road. Would you like to go and see him?" She looked up at me, hopefully.

"Sure," I smiled. "Why not?"

"Oh, that's great," said Zara, looking pleased. "We could go tomorrow… if you're feeling okay, that is, and if your ankle's a bit better."

I smiled. "Tomorrow will be absolutely fine."

Uncle Silbert lived on the twelfth floor of a fourteen storey tower block. I got out of the lift, which smelt of urine, and clung with vertigo to the metal railings outside while Zara banged on the door and called through the letter box.

"Uncle Silbert!"

The wind whistled round my ears. When I looked over the edge at the street below, I felt sick. After several minutes, the door opened. An old man stood stooped behind a walking frame. He was painfully thin. I could see he had once been tall, but his back was hunched and his frail bones were knotted with disease. He shuffled backwards in the narrow hallway and waved us in.

"Zara. My little angel of mercy." He spoke softly, his bright blue eyes shifting keenly between the two of us and finally resting on me. "And who've you brought with you?"

"Hello," I said. "I'm Lizzie."

"Uncle Silbert," said Zara. "This is an old friend of mine."

He looked deeply into my eyes. It was an odd sensation, a bit like deja vu. He reminded me of someone, but I couldn't think who.

"Hello, my dear," he said. "Do come in."

We followed him slowly down the cold hallway to the kitchen, where one ring on the old gas stove was burning. The flat smelled of dust and pastry. As we passed by open doors, I noticed that two of the rooms were completely empty, apart from some plastic bin-liners and boxes full of books, which were pushed up against the walls. In the room next to the kitchen, I could see a single bed against the wall behind the stove. The rest of the room was also empty, apart from more bin bags and a cardboard box stuffed full of what looked like old newspapers.

"I sit in here," said Uncle Silbert, pointing at a stool by the stove. "It's warmer."

He lowered himself into a brown leather armchair with stuffing coming out of the sides, and proceeded to cough convulsively into his fist for several minutes. Zara stood beside him, rubbing his back, then folded a blanket over his lap and put the kettle on.

I sat down and studied his face. It was angular but gentle, and delicately featured with skin the colour of old icing, stretched tautly over his high cheekbones and aquiline nose. He had narrow pink lips and a full head of white hair.

"There's some cake there." He pointed to a tin on the table. Zara grinned at me and poured the tea. She passed me a plate and a cup and saucer, then sat down on a stool next to Uncle Silbert. She picked up his hand and held it in hers. I watched them affectionately and played with my cake, pushing it around on my plate.

"So, are you a nurse too?" Uncle Silbert asked me.

"She's a journalist," said Zara.

"A journalist," he repeated. "Very interesting. Well, it's nice of you to come," he said, patting the hand that held his, but looking at me. "I don't get many visitors."

"What about your family?" I asked.

"All gone away." He didn't elaborate. He sat and nodded silently for a few minutes, smiling.

"The nurse visits you every day, though, doesn't she?" asked Zara.

He nodded.

"And she helps you with your bath, and brings your medication."

He nodded again, and looked a little embarrassed. I smiled at him sympathetically.

"Can't bath on my own," he said to me. His voice was soft, and throaty. I had to strain my ears to hear him. "Dignity," he said, "is a luxury afforded to the fit and well."

"I'm sorry," I said.

He shrugged his shoulders, and smiled at me. "Oh, it hardly matters anymore. You get used to it, like everything else. But I'm a proud man," he added, turning to me again and fixing his blue eyes once more on mine.

I know you, I thought suddenly. He continued to stare at me. I felt confused, light headed.

"You shouldn't be living like this," Zara was saying. "You should be somewhere you can be taken care of properly."

"I can manage," Uncle Silbert protested. "I won't be a burden to anyone..."

"A burden." Zara sniffed, and looked at me. "This man fought in the war, you know, risked his neck flying across Europe for four years, and parachuted into France with the Normandy landings. Ended up in the military hospital with shrapnel wounds in his back, arms, and chest, and took home the George Cross..."

Uncle Silbert was still looking into my eyes. I could have sworn he was saying something.

"...a pride that must never die," finished Zara theatrically, and gazed ironically around the kitchen, and through the doorway into the bare hallway. She started as if she'd said something wrong, stood up, and left the room.

"Why is everything all packed up in bags?" I asked.

"Oh, to make things easier," said Uncle Silbert.

I stared at him, lost for words. I thought about the shrapnel wounds. He looked so noble, so distinguished — and yet so vulnerable. I couldn't bear for him to say anymore. He continued to look into my eyes, then leaned forward and passed me his handkerchief.

"Are you in a lot of pain?" I wiped my eyes, embarrassed.

"Pain? Of course. But then so are you," he added. I looked down at my ankle, and started to protest.

"Not that." He stopped me, and tapped his chest. "I'm talking about in here."

I began to wonder if we were really having this conversation out loud.

"Maybe I am," I said slowly. "But yours is different. Worse."

"Possibly. Possibly not." He lifted his hands. "Who's to say whose pain is greater, or lesser than anyone else's? We are all unique beings and pain... we must try to empathise; but never measure."

Zara had come back from the loo and was standing in the doorway.

"So how do you bear it, then?" My voice sounded strangled.

"You get by," he said, looking from me to Zara. "With a little help from your friends."

It seemed very bright outside. We took the lift down to the street below in silence. Zara took my arm and we hobbled down the road to the car. I was feeling very tired. Everything felt strange, as if we were in a dream together.

"Isn't he lovely?" said Zara eventually.

"The best," I agreed. "I'd like to see him again."

"Oh, you can. You will. He liked you very much."

"His eyes," I said. "What was it about his eyes? They reminded me of someone, but I can't think who."

"Did you ever go to Sunday School?" asked Zara.

"Yes..."

"Remember those pictures of Jesus?"

"Yes, that's it! The same solemn, gentle face, and the deep blue eyes..."

"Although of course Jesus would have been dark," she added. "With black curly hair and brown eyes."

"Like Tim," I suggested, and we both cracked up laughing at the image.

I drove Zara home and we sat in the car outside talking for a bit. I really didn't want to say goodbye to her. Eventually, I put my arms round her and kissed her cheek. She hugged me and stroked my back.

"Call me," she said. "And make it soon."

11

MY INTERVIEW TOOK PLACE a week later and was merely a formality. Hurricane Andrew had just hit the North-Western tip of the Caribbean and Southern USA, leaving devastation in its wake. I looked at the floor and tried to imagine what it would like to be buried underneath a collapsed building, whilst Phil sat opposite me in his office and asked me a series of pointless questions to which he already knew the answers. The appointment of the new programme editor was announced the following day. Two weeks later, I found myself once more driving round the countryside, talking to farmers about government subsidies and mechanisation, and frantically scanning the *Guardian*'s media pages for jobs in London.

"Don't take it personally. He just happened to be the right man for the job, that's all," Phil told me. "You're next in line."

The following week, a family was murdered in an arson attack in Cherry Hinton, creating a temporary diversion to the issue. I attended the inquest with anticipation, did a two-way from the Radio Car with the Drive Time presenter and the Cambridgeshire Chief of Police, and was congratulated over the talkback by Phil, who assured me that the interview would be channelled through to the national network. By some strange quirk of fate, Simon Goodfellow managed to tape over it before it could be sent off and my supposed moment of glory passed unceremoniously.

"Well I heard you, and I thought you sounded great," said Catherine that evening. It was the third time she'd rung that week. Last night we'd broken both our individual records for the longest telephone conversation ever. It had lasted two hours and fifteen minutes.

"Thanks, sweetie," I said, balancing the telephone receiver between my ear and my shoulder and lighting a cigarette. "But I don't suppose anyone else did."

"Maybe it'll be on the air tomorrow at breakfast time," she said hopefully.

"I don't think so somehow."

"Lizzie," Catherine sounded edgy, suddenly. "Could I, maybe, come and stay with you for a day or two?"

"Of course you can!" I was delighted. "You know you're always welcome."

"Maybe you could pick me up on your way home tomorrow?"

"Not a problem." I paused. "Is anything wrong?"

"No, no," she said, quickly. "Just need a break that's all. And I miss you," she added.

"I miss you too," I agreed. "It'll be great to see you in person. I'm getting Telephone Ear, at this rate."

"What's that?"

"You know, when your ear goes flat and develops a numb, tingling sensation from too many hours spent on the telephone. I'll see you tomorrow. I can't wait."

Catherine was waiting for me at the Newmarket Road Park and Ride. I knew there was something wrong the minute I saw her. Her face was pale and drawn, and her left cheek red and slightly puffy. Her hair hung loose and lank around her shoulders. She was wearing a grey flannel skirt and a navy blue jumper. It looked as if she was wearing our old school uniform. I opened the car door and hugged her as she got in. She clung to me and buried her face in my shoulder. We stayed like that for a few minutes, then I started the engine.

"Do you want to tell me what happened?" I asked her, as we drove round the ring road and onto the motorway.

"I guess I've got Telephone Ear," she joked. "I spent too long on the telephone to you and got a thick ear for it."

I gasped. "Are you serious?"

She nodded.

"Oh Catherine... I'm so sorry."

"It's not your fault."

"I know." I squeezed her hand. "I'm just sorry, that's all."

I glanced at her sideways as she sighed and stared ahead through the windscreen at the road ahead. It was starting to rain. I flipped on the wipers. Catherine sat mesmerized, watching them flick backwards and forwards. I remembered doing that when I was a kid, trying to coincide each flick to the left with a telegraph pole by the roadside. I slipped into reverie, relaxed in her company, remembering past car journeys, driving in the rain. When I glanced over at her, Catherine was fast asleep, curled up in her seat like a baby.

She woke as we pulled up outside the flat, and put her hand to her mouth.

"God, I was dreaming," she said. "I dreamed my teeth were falling out."

"That means you're worried about money," I said.

"Am I?"

I laughed. "Well, maybe not yet," I said. "But after tomorrow you will be."

The next day, the rain had cleared and it was warm and sunny. We walked down to Bond Street and then, with several detours, along Oxford Street to Tottenham Court Road. Catherine bought a pair of strappy sandals with chunky heels from Shelly's, a pair of earrings, and a beautiful pink, white, and blue floral dress. I bought a pair of jeans and a very expensive brown suede jacket that I couldn't afford from a shop on Carnaby Street.

"I feel wonderful," said Catherine as we sat outside a café in Soho drinking cappuccinos. "I feel ten years younger. I'm not going to be able to eat for the next month, of course, but who cares?"

"Retail Therapy," I smiled. "Nothing like it."

We took a bus up to Finchley Road. I told Catherine we were going to The Heath. On the way, however, I stopped at a hairdresser's and dragged her inside.

"What are we doing?" she asked.

"Ha ha," I smiled as the hairdresser came towards us. "Appointment for Donoghue? Three o'clock." The hairdresser nodded and ticked Catherine's name off in her book.

"Aah, help! I'm about to be scalped!" Catherine screamed, hanging out of the door with her hands over her head. People were turning in the street to look at her.

"Come back here, you coward," I said, pulling her back inside. The hairdresser led her to a washbasin. "Just sit back and close your eyes. You won't feel a thing."

"I can't afford this!" she protested, as a towel was put round her shoulders.

"My treat." I smiled wickedly. "You're not getting out of it that easily."

After Catherine's hair had been washed, I sat behind her to direct, and to make faces at her in the mirror until she allowed the hairdresser to chop off more than a couple of inches. Eventually, as it struck her how much better it looked, she started to get excited, and her hair got shorter and shorter. When we emerged out onto Finchley Road an hour later, Catherine had a bob.

We walked up through Hampstead village to the Heath and across to Parliament Hill where we sat on the bench looking out over the city, spread beneath us.

"What the fuck am I doing?" said Catherine. "You were right. I should be here, getting involved in productions, student stuff even, just getting my foot in the door, making contacts in the theatres, not rotting away in a dead end, with..." She paused. "I've done nothing, since I've been with him, you know. Nothing. No wonder I'm depressed."

She twisted the engagement ring on her finger, nervously. "God knows what he's going to say about my hair," she continued. She looked at me. "You know I haven't had a haircut or bought an item of clothing in four years without consulting him, or at least thinking first, 'Would Martin like this?' I'm lost," she announced miserably. "I don't know who I am anymore."

I took a deep breath. "Then leave him, Catherine."

"Leave him?" She stared out Eastwards towards Canary Wharf. "I can't leave him. I'm supposed to be marrying him."

"Do you really want to marry a man who pushes you around, who controls your life — who hits you?" I asked her.

Catherine flinched at the former implication now put into words. "Where would I go?" she asked.

"You can come and stay with me," I said.

She looked doubtful.

"Catherine, it's not that difficult. You're not married yet; you don't have any kids."

"I don't know," she said. "I'm frightened. What if it doesn't work out?"

"If what doesn't work out?" I asked her.

"Me," she said. "Without him."

That evening, we were sitting up at the bar in the King's Arms. Catherine was wearing her new dress and sandals. Her hair was tucked behind her ears, and her fake diamante earrings were sparkling. She looked like a million dollars and I told her so. She beamed happily. The door opened and Zara flew in and hopped up onto the bar stool beside me. I introduced the two of them and ordered a drink for Zara.

"So." Zara was grinning like the Cheshire Cat.

"So what?"

"I've done it," she announced, proudly.

"Done what?" I asked.

"Entered for the RGN. The exams," she said. "They're letting me start on the fourth module, so I'll sit the finals next year."

"Well… wow," I said. "That's great. So you feel okay about this?"

She took a large gulp of her drink. "I don't want to sit the exams, if that's what you mean. But I don't want to remain stuck where I am either. You were right," she added. "It may be an uphill struggle, but if I stay where I am, I'm stuck. Either way, it's bloody difficult. So what have I got to lose?"

"Nothing," I said. "Nothing at all."

"You're an inspiration," said Catherine.

"Really?" Zara was pleased.

"Really." Catherine tucked a stray lock of hair behind her ear. "I think you're very brave."

"You want to know what I think?" I said. "I think you are too. We all are. We are three brave women."

"The three musketeers," smiled Catherine.

"What were their names, now?" Zara scratched her chin.

"Athos, Porthos, and Aramis," said Catherine.

"Blimey, that's impressive," I said. "Hold up, what about D'Artagnan?"

"I think he's over there," said Zara, suddenly blushing and smiling at someone over my shoulder.

"All for one and one for all," announced Catherine, raising her glass.

I raised my glass to meet hers. Zara was still looking over my shoulder and smiling coyly. I glanced back to see a stocky, handsome man in a green rugby shirt. He was sitting at a table behind us, looking straight back at us and smiling.

Zara raised her glass slowly. "Yep. All for one, and all that. Unless, of course, that handsome guy over there walks across to the bar and offers to buy us a drink. In which case it's every man for himself."

"Woman," said Catherine.

"Whatever," said Zara, fluttering her eyelids and cocking her head to one side.

It was nearly eleven. Catherine was asleep with her head on my shoulder while Zara was busy being chatted up by the stocky, handsome man whose name was James. He had a strong Irish accent. Catherine and I sat across the table from them; Catherine snored softly while I played with my beermat and tried not to listen to everything they were saying, which was somewhat difficult.

"So come on James, what's your last name?" asked Zara.

"Bond."

"No, it's not!" Zara collapsed in a fit of loud giggles. "You're so funny."

Catherine stirred beside me, and sat up.

"Get your clothes off," said James. "And I'll buy you an ice cream."

"Don't give in to that!" I said, indignantly.

"No, no… it's 'For your Eyes Only,'" laughed Zara. "The film. James Bond says, 'Get your clothes back on and I'll buy you an ice cream.'"

"Oh. I see."

"Only she hasn't got them off yet," added James.

Catherine leaned over and whispered in my ear, "Can we go now?"

"Sure." I turned to Zara and raised my eyebrows. "Coming?"

"So, you're a builder, you say?" Zara was leaning on one hand, gazing intently up at James. I raised my eyes heavenwards and looked at Catherine. She shrugged and yawned.

"Ay," said James.

"What do you build?"

"Houses."

"Can you build me one?" said Zara.

"Tell you what, love, I've got one I could show you right now, if you're interested?"

"Great. I'm just going to the loo, and then we can go," said Zara, laying her hand on his shoulder.

"Fair play," said James, downing his pint.

Catherine caught my eye and jerked her head over her shoulder. I stood up.

"So, what's about you, love?" said James, turning to Catherine.

"Huh?" Catherine rubbed her eyes.

"Tell me about yourself, why don't ya."

"She's a Thespian," I told him.

"Oh, right, right." He smiled at her, then frowned.

"So does she speak English?" he asked me.

"Of course I do," said Catherine.

"Excuse me," I said, squeezing past him, and heading towards the toilets.

"So, where's Thespia, then?" I heard him say from behind me.

Zara was, putting on her lipstick.

"You cannot be serious," I said at the mirror.

"Why? I think he's cute," said Zara. Her face was all pink and twinkly.

"Well, he's good-looking alright..." I admitted. "But what are you going to talk about?"

"He's quite clever really," said Zara. "You're just prejudiced because he's a builder."

"Zara, he says 'love'," I pointed out.

"'Love'? What's wrong with that?"

"Well, it's like 'Birds', isn't it? It's derogatory."

"'Birds'? Did he say, 'Birds'? Oh well, I'll have to talk to him about that."

I shook my head, despairingly. "So, you're going to go back to his house and sleep with him?"

"He told me," said Zara, glossy-eyed, "what he'd like to do to me. He's been talking dirty to me."

"He told you..." I stared at her in the mirror. "What?"

"I'll tell you tomorrow," she grinned, pulling on her raincoat. She winked at me and kissed me on the cheek. "Gotta go."

"Zara, be careful," I said. "Please."

"I'll be fine," she said. "Stop worrying."

Catherine and I caught the tube to Baker Street and walked down Marylebone Road. As we neared the flat and I fished in my bag for my keys, a car door opened and a man got out.

"Oh, God," said Catherine, stopping dead in her tracks and grabbing my arm.

Martin leaned up against his car door with his arms folded, staring at us, or more specifically at Catherine.

"So, where the fuck do you think you've been?" he asked in a cool voice, loaded with angry sarcasm. Catherine didn't answer. "Look at you," he sneered, contemptuously. "Dressed up like a tart. And what the fuck have you done to your hair?"

He unfolded his arms and took a step forward. Catherine flinched, a knee-jerk response, and stepped back. "What are you doing here, Martin?" she asked, her voice wavering.

"What am I doing here?" he retorted, his voice rising. "I've been looking all over for you, you selfish bitch. Sneaking off like that. What the fuck do you think you're playing at?"

"I needed some space, Martin," Catherine pleaded.

"Space?" Martin snorted. "You and your fucking dyke friend over there."

"Now just a minute," I began.

"Get in the car," he ordered. Catherine didn't move.

"I said, get in the car!" He reached out, grabbed a handful of her hair and yanked her over towards the car. Catherine screamed.

"Let her go!" I shouted. I rushed at him and started tugging at his arms. He turned around and brushed me off like a fly that was bothering him. I fell backwards and sat down on the pavement.

"My things are inside," I heard Catherine cry as she was elbowed into the car.

Martin turned to me. "Get her things."

"Don't bloody-well order me around!" I yelled at him, but stood up anyway, and shakily let myself into the flat.

I went into the bedroom and picked up Catherine's overnight bag. I peeped out of the window; there was no movement in the car. I glanced around the room at the relics of our day: the unmade bed, the empty chocolate wrappers and the make-up scattered all over the sheets, the tape recorder and cassettes spread over the dressing table, the wine bottle on the floor. I bent down shakily and picked up Catherine's clothes and stuffed them in the bag. I sat down on the bed and picked out her eye shadow and lipstick, then went into the bathroom for her toothbrush. All the while I was boiling with anger, knowing there was nothing, absolutely nothing I could do. Except call the police. But I knew Catherine wouldn't want that. And somehow, neither did I.

I went back downstairs and out onto the street. Martin opened the car door and held his hand out for her bag. Catherine was slumped down in the passenger seat. It was dark, and I couldn't see her very well.

"Are you all right?" I asked her. She gave a barely perceptible nod. Martin snatched the bag from my hand and closed the door.

He started the engine, and the car roared off up the street.

12

ON A SATURDAY IN LATE OCTOBER, Catherine returned. It was early in the morning when the telephone rang, making me jump.

"It's me," said Catherine in a strange voice, that didn't quite sound like hers. "I've left him, Lizzie."

"Where are you?" I asked. "I'll come and get you."

"Liverpool Street," she said. "I got the first train. And don't worry, I'll get a cab. It will be quicker. I just wanted to make sure you were home."

When I opened the door, Catherine looked as though she had shrunk. She was wearing sunglasses, and her dark hair was lank against her head. She stood on the step with two bags. I leaned forward to help her with them but then I noticed that there was something wrong with her face. I reached up and lifted up her sunglasses instead. Catherine flinched. Underneath she had a black eye and a badly swollen cheek.

I breathed in sharply. "Oh Catherine," was all I could say.

She smiled, tight-lipped, the whites of her eyes glistening. "It's not as bad as it looks," she said, but when she spoke her voice was all lispy and I saw that one of her front teeth was missing.

Tears sprang to my eyes. "Oh Catherine," I said again. "You've lost your tooth."

"No I haven't," she said. "It's in my pocket." And then she started to cry as well.

I took her into the kitchen and made coffee. Catherine sat down at the table and I placed a mug in front of her and sat down opposite.

"What happened?" I asked her.

"I don't know… I just don't know. Things were all right. For a while, you know. After I came to stay, before." There was a slight whistle between her teeth as she spoke. "He apologised for what happened when he came here to find me. Said he had just been worried about me. He didn't know where I was. He got back from a tournament in Manchester to find me gone, he said, and he just flipped out. I mean, I left him a note — it wasn't like before. I told him in the note that it was just for a few days. But he said that not knowing where I was frightened him. He was scared. I'd never done that before. I said I understood. I forgave him." She paused. "And that was the end of it. Things were perfect for a while. So perfect." She sighed and looked out of the window at the fire escape where a blackbird was pecking at some crumbs I'd put out there earlier.

"So, what happened this time?" I prompted her.

"You know, I don't really know what started it. I quizzed him over something. He was being cagey about some girl he knows. She had phoned him, and I asked him who she was and he got angry. He stormed out. And when he came back I asked him if he had been to see her. He just went mad. I told him it didn't matter, after all, that I didn't mind. And then he saw my head shots... publicity shots, you know? Lying on the kitchen table. I'd just had them done at a studio in town. I was thinking I could just start making a few applications, see how it went."

"Well, that's great!" I said.

"Well it wasn't, not really. Because he started insulting me. Picked up my head shots and threw them across the room." She started to cry, softly again. "He called me names, said I was an ugly, useless whore, that I couldn't act. Would never make it as an actress. Then the phone rang and I went to answer it. He ran after me to get there first and that's when it happened. I don't think he meant to, but he just... punched out... punched me out of the way."

I took her hand across the table and squeezed it.

"I fell. I hit my cheek on the corner of the table. And that's when I looked down and there was blood coming out of my mouth. Then I felt something else in my mouth, besides the blood, I mean, and I spat it out and it was my tooth. When he saw what had happened I think he was more shocked than me. And, you know, it was almost funny, ironic, really. Me on my hands and knees, blood dripping from my mouth while I picked up all these smiling photos of me that were lying all over the floor. It was like that wasn't the real me, smiling away, make up, hair all perfect. It made me feel what he said. I *am* useless," Catherine sobbed. "Completely useless."

"Catherine, you are not!" I shouted. "You're a brilliant, talented, wonderful person. And I am so angry that he has done this to you."

Catherine wiped her eyes. "I'm going to have to get a false one, aren't I?" she said, placing the tooth on the table.

"Catherine… that's your front tooth. They are really deep rooted. And he's knocked it out. This is serious," I said. "You should let me call the police."

"No. I don't want that. He knows he's gone too far. He won't come after me."

"He shouldn't be allowed to get away with this," I persisted.

"No." Catherine looked up at me. "Please. I don't want that. He didn't mean for this to happen..."

"But it did."

"...and, besides, it was loose, anyway. I think I have that thing… you know, what's it called? When your teeth are loose…"

I sighed and fastened my hands round my coffee cup. I stared silently at the tooth sitting on the table between us. I hoped that she wasn't going to try and mitigate this. If she did, there was no hope.

Catherine was wiggling another tooth with her forefinger. "This one feels a bit loose too," she said.

"Let me see." She opened her mouth and waggled it back and forwards. "Okay, leave it alone," I said. "I'll ring my dentist, get an emergency appointment."

"You know all those dreams I had about my teeth falling out?" said Catherine, trying to make a joke. "Well, I don't think I was worried about money. My teeth are falling out."

I said, "Yes, well, they didn't fall out by themselves."

We sat in silence for a minute or two.

"He hasn't always been like this," she said. "Deep down he hates himself for it, you know."

"Good," I said. "I hate him for it too."

Catherine sighed and peered into her coffee cup.

I reached out and took her wrist. "Stop feeling sorry for him," I said. "And start feeling sorry for you."

"I know," she said. "I know you're right. But, you know what hurts the most? When I remember what it was like in the beginning. I've still got this image in my head of the guy I fell in love with. He would never have done this." She shook her head, her voice wavering. "It's like he's possessed, or something. I know deep down there's a good, decent person inside him. And that's the person I miss... that's the person I want back." She looked up at me, as if it were in my power to do something, to change it all.

I stroked her arm. "Sometimes people change," I said. "But you have to face it; maybe he's not coming back. Maybe this is how he is. Maybe this is how he always was, but you brought out the best in him just for a little while."

We drove round Regents Park to Sainsbury's in Camden. It was a crisp cold morning, and the tree-lined pathways along the outer circle were strewn with fallen leaves.

"I suppose it's a good job I've got some decent head shots," said Catherine. "That's one thing. I'm not going to look so great now with a false front tooth. When I smile, it's going to show. Oh God. What am I going to look like?" She pulled down the passenger sun visor and flicked open the mirror.

"It won't notice," I said. "Not when you're on stage."

"At auditions it will. Men will notice," she said. "It will age me."

"You could get any bloke you want," I said. "Teeth or no teeth."

Catherine laughed out loud.

"I'm serious," I said. "You're lovely. A false tooth is not going to change that."

"You know I used to fancy your brother."

"Pete? Really?"

"Are you kidding? He was gorgeous. All the girls in our year did."

I laughed. "I didn't know that."

"So, do you hear from him? Ever?"

I paused, and looked across at her. All the years with Larsen and I'd never really talked about Pete. Or my dad, come to that. Not to Larsen, not to Marion, Doug, Karen… any of them. Because he was gone and I didn't want to remember, not then. But now it was all creeping back, everything. And Catherine was back too, a timely witness to the truth of what had happened. She remembered me in the days before I had had a chance to shut it all out. I was grateful that I didn't have to explain things, to start from the beginning.

"Occasionally. But not often. Not since he left home, the year after he left school. Maybe that's why I let you go too. I was trying to forget my past, put it all behind me. But I don't think it works like that."

"I wondered why you never called. I thought it was because of your new boyfriend, David whatshisname, that you had just got really involved with him and that you just didn't need me as a friend anymore."

"I think it was that too, I'm ashamed to say. David was like a… a transitional object. A teddy bear."

"He looked a bit like a teddy bear," agreed Catherine.

I smiled. "He came along at the right time in my life. He allowed me to move away, like Pete did, without being too scared. He gave me strength, strength enough to leave him too, in the end, and to go away to university — and that was what I really wanted to do. Study, learn French. And then go abroad. Travel. Only, my first year at college… well, I didn't expect to feel so lonely. But then along came Larsen. He helped keep it all at bay. But I knew something was missing. It was like a part of myself had been buried. Along with my dad."

"Your dad was horrible to you," Catherine said.

"I meant my real dad," I said. "Not him."

Catherine nodded. "Of course."

"Although he was supposed to be a dad too. To me and Pete. That was the deal. But he only ever really wanted my mother. And so he tore my family apart. Destroyed me and Pete. Or tried to."

Catherine placed her hand over mine. I changed gear, with her still holding on, and we both smiled.

After a couple of minutes, Catherine spoke. "I know what you're thinking. Martin's not like him, you know."

"How do you know that?"

"Because he loves me. Whatever he's done, I know that's true because I feel it. Felt it," she corrected herself. "Your dad just enjoyed hurting you. He did it for pleasure. That's different. And I'm sorry."

I turned off Albany Street and stopped at the traffic lights. As I looked ahead down Parkway I noticed a kid with a guy propped up in a cart and realised that it was the last day of October, Halloween.

"I still have bad dreams," I confessed. "Nightmares. Really frightening ones. About ghosts. I know they're to do with what's happened. The bits that I can't remember. The bits that I've blocked out. It's like I know that intellectually. But I can't seem to make the connection emotionally. It feels like the nightmares won't go away until I do."

"Maybe that's what people go to counselling for."

"Maybe. Maybe that's what I need to do. But then I think to myself, maybe it wasn't that bad. Sometimes, I don't know what's real and what isn't," I admitted.

"Everything's real," said Catherine. "If it's real to you. Your nightmares, the way you feel now, all these years later. They're proof that it *was* that bad."

I looked up at her gratefully and nodded. "I guess that must be true."

I turned into the supermarket car park. We got out and Catherine pulled on her black furry coat and her sunglasses.

"You know fate is guiding you," Catherine reassured me, as we entered the store. She grabbed a trolley and I followed her to the fruit section. "It's all happened the way it was meant to. Everything. There's a reason why you're only remembering things now. And there is a reason why I am here right now."

"So you're saying everything's pre-destined, written in the stars?" I asked her.

"Yes. That's exactly what I'm saying. We're all on one long spiritual journey. Maybe this is my fate... being with Martin, I mean. The Universe is trying to teach me something about how to deal with it."

"Deal with it?" I frowned. "You're not going back to him?"

"No," said Catherine, uncertainly. She picked up a pack of bananas. "Of course not."

I stopped dead in my tracks. "I'm sorry, Catherine, I just don't believe that you can see anything positive in what Martin's done to you. I think you make your own fate."

Catherine shrugged. "Maybe."

"What do you mean? Are you trying to tell me that this was all meant to be? You getting your face smashed in?"

"No, that's not what I'm saying." Catherine moved off with the trolley ahead of me and I worried that she was hurt by what I'd said.

I ran and caught her up. Neither of us spoke for a minute as we turned a corner and entered the canned goods aisle. Then Catherine stopped the trolley and put her arms around me. "I love you, Lizzie," she said. "I am so glad you came back into my life again."

"Ditto," I said. I buried my face in her shoulder. "I really need a friend like you, right now."

"Me too."

"And I'm so sorry if I sounded harsh. It's just because I care."

"Don't ever stop speaking the truth. It's what's so great about you. You always tell the truth about things. I know you're on my side. And that's what matters. And I'll always be on your side, too, Lizzie. Even when you're wrong."

"I'm never wrong," I smiled. "I thought you knew that by now. So," I said. "What are you going to do?"

"I'm not going back," she said. "You don't have to worry about that. I'll get a job, or maybe even study. And you?"

"I think I need a new job. And maybe a bit of therapy," I smiled.

"We can help each other," Catherine said.

"Sure we can."

"Deal?"

"Deal. So, who's cooking tonight?" I asked her. "Or will the Universe provide?"

"Skeptic!" said Catherine pushing the trolley at me.

"Hippy!" I laughed over my shoulder, as I sped off down the aisle with Catherine and the trolley in hot pursuit behind me.

13

THE WIND WHIPPED AT MY SCARF and I hugged my anorak tightly round my shoulders as I skipped through Smithfield, past the blue wrought iron gates to the meat market and out into the square. The sky seemed very bright. It looked as if it was going to snow. When I reached the King's Arms and pushed open the door, Catherine and Zara were already there, sitting up at the bar.

Zara swung around. She was wearing her tea cosy hat. "Well?" she said, expectantly.

I grinned and raised my eyebrows.

"You got it!" Zara jumped off her stool and picked me up, wrapping her arms round my waist and lifting me off the ground.

"When do you start?" asked Catherine.

"End of January. I'll have to work out my notice." I sat down next to her. The barman wandered over and I ordered three tequilas. I handed out the shots and the lime.

"That's so great," said Catherine, licking salt off her wrist and grimacing as we slammed. I couldn't help noticing her new false tooth every time I looked at her, and it made me feel like hugging her every time.

The door opened and Tim came in with Shelley, one of the nurses who lived with Zara and Tim.

"What are we celebrating?" he asked.

"Lizzie's new job, at City FM. Come on," said Zara. "Sit down."

I ordered another five tequilas.

"I'll get these. Congratulations," said Tim, kissing me on the cheek. "So what is it?"

"I am a planner-stroke-researcher, working across two programmes again, but it'll be prime-time — Breakfast and Mid-morning and it's, well, 'It's City FM'," I said, mimicking the catchphrase in my best Broadcasting voice. Tim and Zara both sang the City FM jingle. I laughed. "So, I'll be doing a bit of everything, writing material for scripts, bulletins and links, interviewing, some reporting but also presenting and production. It's an amazing opportunity."

Tim put his arm round me and raised his glass. "Three cheers for Lizzie. Down the hatch," he said in a BBC voice. We all tipped our heads back and cheered when we'd finished.

"And guess what?" said Catherine. "I've found a really experienced drama tutor in Highbury and she's going to give me some coaching and help with auditions in exchange for helping her out at home."

"Another drink," said Tim, waving at the barman. Five more tequilas appeared on the bar beside us. "To Lizzie and Catherine," said Shelley. We all slammed in unison.

The tequila worked its way up into my face. I felt warm and a little breathless, and glowing inside; I felt happy. After a while I extracted myself from the mass of arms and beer glasses and stools and went to the toilets. A log fire was crackling and popping in the inglenook fireplace and Christmas decorations adorned the walls and the top of the bar. Thick sparkling snakes of silver and green tinsel were wound around the china plates and horseshoes, and huge puffy scarlet crepe paper bells and smaller golden globes were hanging from the ceiling, interlaced with shiny cut-out paper-chains. And by the bar were my friends. I hung back for a moment in the doorway to take a mental snapshot, something I could bring out again to remind me, when I was down, that I was not alone, after all.

Zara followed me into the toilets and jumped up onto the ledge by the sink.

"I've finished with Joel," she said. "It's over. For good this time."

"Joel?" I said. "You mean that's still on? I thought you were seeing James?"

"Yeah. James. Good idea," said Zara. "I should stick with him."

"I'm confused."

"Well, Joel came back. Sort of. After I started seeing James. And I really like him, you know."

"Who?"

"Joel. But there's no point," she said. "He doesn't want me." Her eyes started welling up and she rubbed at them with her fists.

"Oh Zara, what's happened?" I asked her.

She sighed. "I went round to his place last Friday. He wouldn't even let me over the doorstep. Just said 'Not now, Zara', and waved his hand like I was some kind of annoying fly buzzing round his head that he couldn't get rid of. Said he was entertaining."

"Well, maybe he was," I said. "Maybe it was work people. You're supposed to be a secret, after all."

Zara looked me straight in the eye. "Lizzie, he was wearing a walkman."

"A walkman?" I said.

"He had a walkman on, and earphones round his neck." She shrugged. "He didn't have anyone there. He's just decided it's all too easy again. He just gets off on me liking him. He's having an ego trip at my expense. Every time I walk away and get on with my life, he tries to pull me back again."

"That's not very nice," I said.

"No, it's not," she agreed. "Anyway, I don't care. Really. It won't work. Not anymore."

I could see how hard she was trying to convince herself.

"Never mind," I said, and hugged her. "Maybe you should swear off men for a while."

Zara looked at me as though I were mad. "You've got to be joking," she said. "I need to call James. That's what I need to do."

Later, back at the house, we decided to have a meal together on Christmas Eve before we all went off to our parents' the following morning.

"I've had it with standing around in overcrowded pubs, waiting half an hour to get served and getting chatted up by dodgy guys," said Shelley.

"Yeah," Zara agreed. "Been there, seen it, done that."

"Come on, Zara," said Tim. "You like dodgy guys."

Zara thumped him on the arm.

We arranged to invite Uncle Silbert. "He's never going to agree," said Tim. "How will we get him here?"

"In Lizzie's car," said Zara.

"I think we should borrow a wheelchair," said Tim.

"Unless we have it at his place," Shelley said.

"There's nothing there," I said. "We'd have to take a table and chairs."

"And I don't even know if the cooker works properly," said Zara.

The front door opened and Clare, Tim's girlfriend, came in. "What's all this?" she said, looking at me.

"We're organising Christmas Eve," I said. "'Round here."

She shrugged. "I won't be here." She went off upstairs. Tim jumped up and ran after her.

"I need to go home," I said. "I've got to go to work tomorrow. And there's a resignation letter I need to write."

I shook Catherine, who was asleep on the settee. She waved her arm and rolled onto her stomach.

"Let her stay there," said Shelley. "I'll wake her in the morning." She kissed me and went upstairs.

"It's been a great day," I said to Zara. I put my arms around her. She hugged me back. "I wish you didn't have to go."

"I know," I said. "I'm going to feel rubbish tomorrow. But it'll all be worth it to see Phil's face when I tell him I'm leaving, that I've found something better than anything he could possibly offer."

"Enjoy," she said. "I'll be thinking of you."

I walked a little unsteadily down the street. White flakes appeared under the glare of a streetlight. I looked up and saw that it was beginning to snow.

As I passed a small playground, I heard the rusty creaking of a swing and stopped to peer over the hedge, wondering who could be in there at this time of night. The playground was empty, and everything was still except for one swing, which was moving slowly backwards and forwards, its metal ropes clinking like chain-mail. There was no one on it and no one in sight. Entranced, I pushed open the gate and entered the playground. I felt a rush of adrenaline as I slowly crossed the grass to the tarmaced play area, a combination of excitement and fear. As I passed the climbing frame and neared the swing, it stopped moving, slowing down gradually as if someone had jumped off. I breathed in sharply and stopped in my tracks. Then, tentatively, shaking a little, but with resolve, I walked over to the swing next to it and sat down.

The swing next to me remained unmoving, its seat parallel to the ground. I stared out onto the playing field where the snow was trying to settle over the grass, brightly lit round the edges by the nearby streetlights, but dark and shadowy in the middle. As my eyes adjusted to the darkness I saw, slowly emerging from the grass several feet in front of me, the figure of a man in a dark grey duffle coat and a bright green scarf, his wavy auburn hair tumbling over his forehead and his shoulders hunched against the cold as he made his way across the park and towards the open gate. Then, halfway across the field, he stopped and crouched down to gather up a handful of snow, which he rounded into a snowball. When he stood up and lifted his arm to throw it, I saw who it was. For an instant, he remained standing with his arm in the air, his grin impish and his eyebrows raised enquiringly.

"Throw it," I whispered. "I'm not scared."

He threw his head back and laughed. He dropped the snowball and carried on towards the gate.

"Stop. Wait," I yelled after him, leaping off the swing and running across the field towards him. He didn't seem to hear me. He reached the gate and stepped out onto the pavement.

"Don't go!" I shouted after him, my heart thumping against my chest. "Please, come back!" My voice seemed to echo around the empty playground. I ran out through the gateway and looked up and down the snow-covered street. A car drove past. There was no one in sight. I sighed, dug my hands into my pockets, and headed for the tube station.

Uncle Silbert was all ready to go, sitting in the wheelchair that Zara had borrowed from the hospital. He was wearing a red jumper. The sleeves were a little too short, and quite a lot of his bony arm was sticking out at the bottom. He looked tired. I kissed him on the cheek and helped Zara with his bag, while she wheeled him out to the lift.

"Is he okay?" I mouthed at Zara from behind the wheelchair. She raised her hand and waved it to indicate "so-so".

When we reached the house, the aroma of turkey was wafting out from the kitchen, where Shelley and Tim were busy rushing back and forth with plates and saucepans full of vegetables. They had already decorated the table with a white sheet for a tablecloth and there were sprigs of holly and multicoloured crackers beside each placemat.

"It all looks lovely," I said. I put the wine I'd brought in the fridge.

Tim turned to me and smiled, his cheeks glowing from the wine and the heat from the stove. "There's already a bottle open," he said. "Dive in."

Zara helped Uncle Silbert into a chair behind the table and I poured everyone drinks. Zara pulled a cracker with Uncle Silbert and put his paper hat on. He looked a bit disorientated.

"Are you all right?" I asked him, patting his hand across the table.

"It's good to be here, Elizabeth," he said.

I smiled. Nobody called me that, but I didn't correct him. I thought it lent me a certain gravitas, made me sound like someone important, like the queen. "It's good to see you too."

"I think I need my medication, though," he said. "And a stiff brandy, maybe."

"Coming right up." I went and fetched him his bag and a drink.

"You shouldn't really be drinking, you know, not with your medication," Zara reprimanded him.

"Oh come on, it's Christmas. Let him enjoy himself," said Tim, coming over with a bowl of Brussels sprouts. "What harm's it going to do?"

"Well, actually…" Zara and Tim began a debate about Uncle Silbert's medication and its potential side effects.

"Here." I gave Uncle Silbert his drink and sat down beside him. "Cheers," I raised my glass to his.

"À votre santé, Elizabeth. I'm very pleased to hear about your new job."

"You speak French?"

"Indeed. You?"

"Yes. I mean, I used to. I studied for a year after my A-levels, but I haven't really used it since. I was meant to study in Paris, spend a year there."

"Why didn't you go?"

"That's a good question. I fell in love, I suppose."

"Ah, love," said Uncle Silbert, pensively. "Well, that's a different kind of journey."

"I guess."

"They say it broadens the mind."

I was confused. "You mean travel?"

Uncle Silbert smiled and said nothing.

"Or do you mean love?" I persisted.

"What do you think?"

I stopped and looked at him with a smile on my face. His body was old and tired. But his eyes were bright, penetrating. They were truly windows into his soul. "I think," I said slowly, "that I've wasted a lot of time."

"Ah," said Uncle Silbert. "But have you? What do you hope to gain by travelling that you couldn't gain through love?"

I thought about that for a moment. "Freedom?" I said, realising that I had framed that as a question.

There was a knock at the door. I went to open it. It was Catherine.

"What happened to you?" I asked her, as she squeezed in through the doorway with a carrier bag full of parcels.

"Martin phoned," she said.

I sighed, pointedly. "What did he want?"

"To wish me a merry Christmas," she said.

"And?"

She paused and looked down at her feet. She put the carrier bag down on the floor. "To meet me for a drink."

"A drink?" I echoed. "You went for a drink with him?"

"Well, it *is* Christmas," she said, defensively. "He was in town anyway. It was just a drink."

I shrugged. "It's up to you," I said. "It's your life." I turned and headed back up the hallway towards the kitchen.

Shelley was carving the turkey with an electric knife. Bits of meat were flying off in all directions, and Tim and Zara were yelling at her. She stopped and let Zara take over. Catherine and I sat down and passed the plates and vegetables around. There were mashed and roast potatoes, Brussels sprouts and roast parsnips, and Tim had made bread sauce and sage and onion stuffing all mixed up together because there weren't enough roasting tins.

Throughout the meal, we sang Christmas carols in four part harmonies. Tim sang the baritone and Zara sang soprano, then they swapped around, which had us all in fits of laughter. Uncle Silbert sat there glassy eyed, watching us, like a proud father.

When we finished, we opened our presents. Zara had painted me a miniature watercolour of the sea and the sky with different shades of blue, and silver stars.

"I know blue is your favourite colour," she said.

"It's beautiful," I said. "And those stars look as if they can really talk." I winked at Zara and she grinned back at me.

Catherine had bought me a wok.

"Wok's new," said Tim.

"Catherine," I protested, holding it up and laughing. "You know I can't cook anything but pasta."

"I know," she said. "It's for reheating your Chinese takeaways."

Tim left the room. As he went I caught his eye and he beckoned to me to go after him. Intrigued, I got up and followed him up to his room. I felt happily flushed; the wine and the turkey were combining soporifically. I leaned dreamily against the banister. Tim disappeared inside and came back to the doorway, where he handed me a small package wrapped in tissue paper.

"I didn't want to give you this in front of everyone." He grinned at me shyly, went into the bathroom, and shut the door. I opened up the package. Inside was a beautiful silver necklace with a tiny Saint Christopher pendant.

"The patron saint of travellers," I said to myself, shaking my head. I was touched. It was an almost identical replica of one I'd had and lost many years ago.

"Tim." I knocked on the bathroom door, and he opened it.

"It's beautiful," I said.

He looked pleased, and took it from me and put it round my neck, doing up the clasp behind me.

"Thank you," I said, and stood up on tiptoes to kiss his cheek. He stood woodenly, un-responding, in front of me for a moment. But as I moved away, he suddenly put both arms around me, pulled me back to him behind the bathroom door, and kissed me on the mouth. His lips were soft and warm, and I found myself responding. He kicked the door shut behind us and then he pushed my mouth open with his. I sank weakly against him; I couldn't move. I hadn't been kissed like this in a very long time. Tim moved his hand up my back and pressed against me, sending shivers down my spine. I pulled away.

"We mustn't," I said breathlessly.

"Don't stop," said Tim, pulling me back. "Don't stop now."

"What about Clare?" I said.

Tim didn't answer. He leaned into me and put his lips on mine.

At that moment the door was pushed open, and we both lost our balance and fell backwards into the bath.

"Hello," said Zara, who was holding a glass of wine. "Am I interrupting something?"

"No," I said.

"Yes," said Tim.

"Good," she said, to both of us, and tipped herself over into the bath on top of us.

"Zara," I wailed, laughing. "You're spilling red wine all over us."

"Oops," said Zara. "If we don't get that off quickly it'll stain." And, amid screams of protest from me and Tim, she leaned over and switched on the shower.

Downstairs, all was quiet. Both Catherine and Uncle Silbert had fallen asleep. Shelley was stacking dishes and glasses up by the sink.

"What happened to you?" she said, as we all walked in with wet hair. I was wearing one of Tim's t-shirts.

Zara picked up a tea towel. "Lizzie and Tim were—"

I shot her a warning glance.

"—spilling red wine," she finished, cryptically.

Shelley looked confused. "Red wine?" she repeated.

"We've all had a bath," said Tim.

Shelley leaned back against the sink and gave a vague, uncomprehending smile.

"It was wet," I added, for something to say.

"I think Uncle Silbert needs to go to bed," said Zara.

Zara and Shelley put Uncle Silbert to bed in Tim's room, while Tim made up a bed for himself on the sofa.

"Where am I sleeping?" said Catherine sleepily from the doorway.

"In Zara's bed with me and Zara," I said.

"Okay. I'm going up," she said. "I'm bushed."

Tim came in with a glass of whisky in each hand. He gave one to me.

"I'm worried about her," I said, sitting down on the floor and leaning against the sofa. "She sleeps such a lot."

"She's drunk," said Tim. "And maybe a bit depressed," he added. He sat down on the floor next to me.

"Depressed? She's not depressed," I protested. "She's happier than she's ever been. She's got her acting classes, her work at the theatre, and she's free of that…"

"*That*," said Tim. "Is the problem. She's not very good at being on her own. Not everyone is as strong as you, Lizzie."

"I'm not that strong," I said. "Everyone just thinks I am."

"That's because that's what you show them."

"I have my moments of weakness."

Tim paused. "Is that all it was?" he asked quietly. "A moment of weakness?"

I drained my glass and made a move to get up. Tim put his hand on my arm.

"Don't go," he said.

"I can't do this," I said. "I'm confused. And besides, you're with Clare."

"Yeah, like we're always together," said Tim, sarcastically.

"Well, you have to sort that out," I said. "I'm not going to be her stand-in."

"You're not," he said, almost angrily. "You know that's not how it is."

I turned to face him. I knew that he was right. That wasn't how it was at all. I was being disingenuous, using Clare as an excuse. It was glaringly obvious that Tim had feelings for me, and that it would matter very little to Clare if I did begin to take her place in Tim's life. She already had one foot out of the door; it was only a matter of time before she left completely.

But while it would be so easy just to give in to being loved, held, made to feel alive again, I couldn't tell for how long I would need this, or, more to the point, how long I would need this from Tim. It didn't matter to Tim that I wasn't Clare. That much was clear. But no matter how hard I wanted it, or wished for it to be true, I knew I couldn't love him. Because he wasn't Larsen.

I bent down and kissed him on the cheek. "Good night, Tim," I said.

As I moved away I saw the look in his eyes, the way he was gazing at me, and it took all the strength I had in my aching body to drag myself out of the door and up the stairs to where the girls were sleeping.

14

THE BEGINNING OF 1993 was marked by the inauguration of William Jefferson Blythe III, now President Clinton, and we both began our new jobs on the same day. I sat in the newsroom and watched the ceremony on Sky with my new producer, Kim; Clive Cullen, the breakfast show presenter, who had just finished his shift; and the programme editor, Sandy, who was also my new boss. I looked around happily at my new environment and my new colleagues, and listened to the President while he announced the arrival of spring "in the depth of winter" and pledged a time of dramatic change, hope, and renewal. I was inspired, and gave myself a little message of hope about the year ahead. It had to be better than the last one, I thought.

Martin crept back slowly into our lives. I couldn't understand how this could have happened, but he seemed to be on his best behaviour; slowly I came to accept that this was what Catherine wanted, and it wasn't my decision to make. The balance of power had shifted noticeably between them, though; Catherine was living with me, she was happy, and she had no intention of moving back in with him, or of giving up her new life.

"It's like the beginning all over again," she told me happily one morning as she got ready to go out She was leaving for rehearsals for a fringe theatre adaptation of an Ibsen play that she was staging with a group of drama students she had met at a theatre workshop. "And I want to keep it that way. This is the real Martin. I don't know what happened to us, before, you know. But he's back to who he was again."

I chopped up lettuce and tomatoes and fetched cheese from the fridge. I was going for a walk and a picnic with Zara. "You really think people change just like that?" I said, trying to mask the irritation in my voice.

"Yes. Sometimes they do," she told me authoritatively. "It doesn't always have to be an unhappy ending, you know."

"What, domestic violence?"

A cloud crossed Catherine's face, and she cringed, visibly. "It was only once or twice that actually happened. I know he could be moody and stuff, but that never happened before..."

"He was controlling you, Catherine. In some ways, that was worse."

"He didn't mean to. There's stuff from his past that he hasn't yet resolved. And it makes him unhappy, sometimes. And insecure about us. The problem was that I didn't know how to deal with that before, or how to handle his moods."

"Catherine, you said it yourself, that day — remember, up on the heath? That you didn't know who you were anymore. That you were lost."

"Well, now I'm found." She grinned at me. To her credit, she wasn't defensive; just highly persuasive, like a saleswoman selling me some useless item that I didn't need or want, and trying to convince me that I did. "Look Lizzie, he loves me, he really does. He's so sorry about what happened, you wouldn't believe. He's promised to make it up to me. You've seen what he's like now. He nearly lost me for good, and he knows it."

"Oh, he's trying really hard, I'll give him that." I turned and elbowed a cup off the kitchen counter. It bounced on the floor and cracked in half. I swore loudly and bent down to pick it up.

"Look," she said. "Just give him a chance. Please Lizzie. For me. If things go wrong again you can say 'I told you so'. But he isn't the only one who's changed. I've changed too. I'm stronger, and he knows that. If he gets in a mood, I don't have to react the way I used to. I'll tell him straight, any more of this and I'm out the door. I was part of the reason he behaved the way he did. I was too weak, too much of a victim."

"Oh please," I sighed. "You'll be telling me you walked into doors next."

"It's true!" Catherine stopped loading the dishwasher and grabbed my arm. "It takes two to tango, Lizzie. If I had been less of a doormat, less of a pushover, it may have all happened differently. Next time he gets into a mood, I will stand up to him, fight back."

"Yeah, good luck with that," I muttered and went off to my room.

A moment later, Catherine appeared in the doorway. "Can you honestly say, with your hand on your heart, that you don't like him at all?"

I sat on my bed and thought about how happy the last couple of months had been, Catherine and I both busy all day pursuing our careers, Martin turning up in the evenings with Chinese takeaways for all three of us, bringing flowers for us both, tenderly re-potting an orchid that I had knocked off the windowsill one evening. I remembered him on his hands and knees, carefully clearing up all the scattered soil from Lynne's cream carpet, scooping it up in his hands so that it wouldn't get ground in. Martin popping round after work with a bottle of wine, asking both me and Catherine about our day, showing real interest in the people I worked with, laughing at our jokes. Martin fixing the plumbing in the bathroom when the toilet stopped flushing, without having to be asked.

It was true that he was making an effort. And not just with Catherine. He included me in everything, asked if I wanted to come too when they went out for a drink or a meal. Things had definitely changed, and not just for Catherine, but for me also. I was no longer the enemy, the one that might take Catherine away from him, or help her see the light. He acted as if I was his friend now, and it was hard, very hard to hate him.

"A man hits you once, he'll hit you again," I warned her.

"That's just a cliché," Catherine said.

"Well, clichés are clichés for a reason."

"That's a cliché too," said Catherine. "It's like 'All men are potential rapists'."

"No, it's not. And what was said was actually 'All men are rapists'. That's a feminist doctrine. What I am saying is statistics. I'm not trying to be Germaine Greer here, I just don't want to see you hurt."

"I won't be," pleaded Catherine. "Things are different now. I can see now where I've been going wrong. It's almost as if I was..." she tailed off.

"Asking for it?" I suggested.

"Well, sort of."

"Are you serious? You're saying you wanted him to hit you?"

"Not consciously, no. But maybe on some level, yes, I did. There was a part of me that thought that it proved how much he loved me, that he would get that passionate, that jealous."

"But that's absurd!"

"And maybe there is another part of me that thought that was all I deserved." Without warning, Catherine's face started to crumple. I patted the bed beside me. Catherine came and sat down and I put my arms around her.

"Why on earth would you think that?"

Catherine shrugged and wiped at her eyes. "I don't know. I suppose my dad was quite moody too. Not like yours, not violent or anything. But I grew up watching the way my mum tiptoed around him and deferred to him..." She paused. "Then I meet Martin and… it's like that's how I expect it to be. It's like a dance, and we both know the steps. When he gets moody, I cower and shrink inside myself, instead of standing up for myself. And he disrespects me for that. And so it goes on."

"So how do you change that?"

"You both have to learn new ways of being, of dealing with things."

"But what if he doesn't want to? What if he doesn't know any other way to be? What if he's just one of these men who like to be in control? Like the sort of blokes that whistle and leer at you in the street; they do it to unbalance you, to show they've got all the power."

"Martin's not like that."

"I hope you're right."

Neither of us spoke for a while. There was something else. I was thinking about the time that Martin had kissed me, but I couldn't tell Catherine about that. Seven years of friendship with Marion and Jude had taught me that that kind of honesty never comes out well for the woman. And what if I'd got it wrong? I ran over it again in my mind. All he'd done was kiss me on the cheek. Maybe it was genuine compassion; he was just feeling sorry for me, because I'd woken up screaming. Maybe he was just trying to be a friend. Maybe that's all he was ever trying to be. It was a long time ago. Maybe I'd read it all wrong.

"I love him, Lizzie," Catherine said, eventually. "I've never loved anyone else. It's always been him, for me. Just like it was always Larsen for you."

"Yeah, well, look how that ended up," I reminded her.

"Oh Lizzie, that was your doing. It was always you he wanted, you know that. But he knew he was going to lose you and he feathered his nest. Blokes like Larsen, they'll make sure they're never on their own for long. But you... you've gone to the opposite extreme. Because you're looking for perfection. And you're not going to find it, Lizzie. It doesn't exist. We're humans; we're all flawed. Maybe you just need to accept that, and get on with letting someone love you too."

I sighed. "I haven't gone through all the pain of breaking up with Larsen just to go out and make the same mistakes all over again," I told her. "I want to get it right this time."

"I know. And I understand that. But if you don't get your nose out of the map soon and start driving, you're never going to know if you're getting it right or not."

I smiled. "I will. When I find what I'm looking for."

"Plenty of fish in the sea," she added, smiling too.

"Yes. But most of them are either mackerel or herring."

Catherine looked confused.

"D.H. Lawrence," I admitted. "If you're not a mackerel or a herring, then there are not that many good fish in the sea. Look... I'm not looking for perfection, but I just know what I want. I need someone who is going to love me in the right way, someone who knows who he is and is happy with that, and doesn't need a mirror-image to know he exists. Someone who can respect who *I* am, and is happy with that too; a man who would do anything for me, but who wouldn't suffocate me either; someone who would wait for me if I needed to go away, and not have to replace me with someone else because he couldn't be alone; he'd laugh when I broke things, and hold me when I cried, and he would always be there if I needed him."

"Honey," said Catherine. "You want your *dad*."

It was my turn to cry. Catherine put her arms around me and held me tight.

A few minutes later there was a knock at the door.

"Okay," I conceded. I wiped my eyes and stood up. "I give in. Maybe you're right about Martin. What do I know? But I swear, Catherine, if he lays a finger on you again..."

"I know. Absolutely. Believe me, he'll be gone."

I opened the front door. Zara was on the doorstep, wearing a new cashmere coat, a pair of Jimmy Choos and a new tea-cosy hat.

"Blimey Zara, where did you get all the gear?"

"Harvey Nicks," said Zara, beaming. She lifted up one foot and twirled her gold strappy ankle. "You like?"

"Wow. Yes. I do. But how much did they set you back?"

Zara sniggered into her hand and whispered in my ear.

"What! £400? Where did you get that kind of money?"

"Oh, relax," said Zara. "I put it on my card."

"And the coat?"

"Come on, Lizzie, a girl's got to look good," said Zara. "James absolutely loves them."

"I bet he does," I said. "You look stunning. But I thought we were going for a walk?"

"I know," said Zara. "But I didn't go home last night. I was with James."

"Do you want to borrow some trainers?"

"Hey," said Zara. "Shall we go shopping instead? I saw this really gorgeous Prada handbag in Beauty and Accessories that would really go with my new dress." She opened her coat. She was wearing a beautiful red and black mini dress. "Let's go back there," she chattered excitedly. "They've got jewellery to die for. And we can get our makeup done!"

I eyed Zara suspiciously. "How can you afford a Prada handbag? You don't earn that sort of money. I mean, how much did that dress cost?"

"Oh come on, Lizzie, stop being such a killjoy," laughed Zara. "You only live once."

"That's right," said Catherine from behind me.

"The Universe will provide," said Zara. "Isn't that right, Catherine?"

"It's true," I heard Catherine say again from behind me.

"Oh, all right, then," I agreed, feeling like a bit of a spoilsport. "I guess we could."

We took the tube to Knightsbridge. I would normally have enjoyed the walk, across Hyde Park, but it was clear that Zara wasn't going to be able to do that in six inch heels, and that she wasn't going to swap them for my old trainers.

The tube was packed and we had to stand. Zara chattered incessantly about James, as the train bumped and twisted, and threw us around. I clung onto the hand strap rail and tried to keep up.

"It's amazing," said Zara, who looked like she was suspended from the ceiling. "The sex is just amazing!"

A woman in the seat opposite looked up abruptly from her magazine.

"You seem really happy," I observed.

"Oh, God, Lizzie, he just does it for me," she whispered loudly, whilst dangling seductively from the handrail. "I feel like, well... invincible!"

"You're not..."

"What?"

"Taking drugs or anything?"

"What?" Zara threw back her head and started laughing. "Of course not!"

"It's just... you seem different. Really... well, confident." I sounded jealous. I didn't want to be.

"I know," said Zara. "I feel like I can do anything. And it's all because of James. I've got so much energy. We barely slept last night."

"Shhh," I laughed, looking around the busy carriage. "Enough about the sex, Zara. So, come on then, tell me about him. Where does he live?"

"Kilburn. In a house."

"In a house," I repeated. "What kind of house? Who does he live with?"

"I don't know. It's just sort of an address he uses. There are several people there. He's from Ireland."

"Well, that's the bit I knew already," I said. "So what else have you found out about him? Which part of Ireland is he from?"

"The North," said Zara. "Belfast, I think."

"And what's he doing here?" I asked.

"He's learning to fly, he's going to be a pilot. How sexy is that?"

"I thought he said he was a builder?"

"He is," said Zara. "As well."

"So where's he studying?"

"Oh. Yeah. The London School of... something. I forget."

"Well, where's he working?"

"On a building site. He's building a house. He's very good with his hands, you know." Zara grinned and lifted her eyebrows.

"It all seems a bit sketchy," I said. "What do you actually talk about?"

"Not much," giggled Zara. "He's a man of action rather than words."

We came out of the tube station and waited to cross the road. On the corner, a black man selling flags wolf-whistled as we passed.

"Get lost," I hissed.

"Hello, darling," said Zara at the same time.

"Zara!" I grabbed her arm. "What are you doing?"

Zara was still smiling back at the man, who was calling after her, trying to say something to her. I dragged her away.

"Don't encourage him," I admonished her.

"He liked me," she pouted. "And he was sexy."

"Zara, don't take it personally; you're probably the hundredth woman he's whistled at today."

I felt a bit mean, trying to bring her down like that. But Zara merely smiled a Mona Lisa type smile, tossed her head and her cashmere coat, and swaggered off down Knightsbridge, wiggling her hips as she went, looking for all the world just like a movie star.

Later, back at the flat, we ate dinner and sat watching the news on TV. Martin was there, on the sofa with Catherine. Zara was curled up in the armchair. She was much quieter now and seemed withdrawn. I guessed she was tired now after her night of passion.

"Look at that," said Catherine. "Isn't it awful?"

A bomb had exploded in Warrington, Cheshire, killing a 3-year-old boy and injuring fifty people.

"That's got to be a revenge attack," said Martin.

"Revenge? For what?" said Catherine.

"That's the second IRA bomb attack in Warrington," said Martin. "They bombed a gasworks there last month, don't you remember?"

"Why are they taking revenge?"

"Because of the arrests," I said. "The police arrested three people. IRA."

"God, that's awful," said Catherine, again. "Right in the middle of a busy shopping centre. Poor little boy. Poor parents."

"It's so sad," I agreed.

"I thought there were peace talks," said Catherine. "I thought this was all going to stop?"

"It's not going to happen unless there's a ceasefire," said Martin. "This isn't going to help."

"Did they ever catch the people who bombed the Baltic Exchange?"

"No. This is the IRA you're talking about."

"What do you mean?" asked Zara, suddenly entering the conversation.

"Well, they're a paramilitary organisation. They're highly organised. You've got Jerry Adams and Martin McGuinness and people like that, the political wing, legitimising it, doing all the talking, the public face. But the men behind the scenes, well… you'd never meet them. You'd never know if you were talking to one. Even here in London."

"It could even be James, Zara," I joked. "He might be IRA."

"What? Why?"

"Well, think about it," I said. "You don't know anything about him, other than that he's James and he's from Kilburn…"

"James of Kilburn," interrupted Martin. "Hmmm. It's definitely a smokescreen."

"…and that he is taking flying lessons."

"There you are," said Martin. "Trainee suicide bomber."

"The IRA don't have suicide bombers, do they?" asked Catherine.

"So, why do you think he's a terrorist?" Zara persisted.

I studied her face. She looked alarmed. "We don't, Zara. We were just teasing."

Zara was silent.

"Ah, but think about it," said Martin, "He wouldn't tell you his surname. And we've never met him."

"Lizzie and Catherine have."

"Yeah, we did. Once," said Catherine.

"Is he Catholic or Proddy?" Martin asked.

"I don't know." Zara looked really worried. Her confidence of earlier that day had evaporated, and the anxious frown and shadowy eyes had returned.

"Does he talk like this?" said Martin in an impressive Belfast drawl. "Or like this?" he said in a softer, Southern accent.

"The first one."

"There you are, then."

"What?" said Zara. "What do you mean? How do you know?"

"You can't tell if someone is IRA by their accent," I said. "He's just teasing. Shh, Martin," I said. "She's getting really worried."

Martin laughed, then checked himself, gave Zara a strange look, and sank back into his seat.

In late April, we were all invited over to Zara's for dinner. It was a warm evening, unusually so for the time of year. Somebody had been working on Zara's front garden. It smelled pleasantly of warm earth and cut grass. The habitually tangled mass of overgrown privet bushes had been chopped back to reveal a square patch of lawn, and a pile of dead weeds lay under the fence.

Shelley opened the front door and let us in on her way out to work. "Night shift," she said, wrinkling up her nose.

"Oh well," I said. "At least mostly everyone will be sleeping."

"Or dying," she said, opening the gate.

Tim was in the kitchen, seated at the old wooden table. He was chopping onions. He looked up as we came in, put down his knife and disappeared wordlessly into the old walk-in pantry behind the antique gas stove. He re-emerged a moment later with three chipped wine glasses, which he placed on the table in front of us.

"Where's Zara?" I asked.

"Up there," he said. "Working. As usual."

"Oh," I said. "Well, I'll just go and get her."

"Bet she doesn't come down," said Tim.

I ran up the stairs and poked my head round Zara's door. She was sitting at her desk, scribbling away furiously, a book open on her knee.

"What are you doing?" I asked.

"Oh, hi. I'm just trying to get this finished."

"Tim's cooking dinner," I pointed out. "Catherine and Martin are here."

"I know, I know, I know..." said Zara irritably, flapping her hands in the air. She dropped her biro on the floor.

"Come on, Zara. You have to eat."

"Okay." She dropped to the floor and began feeling around for her pen.

"Have you seen James?" I asked, hoping that her favourite topic of conversation might entice her downstairs to dinner.

"Why, has he phoned?" asked Zara, from under the table.

"No," I said. "I don't think so."

"Oh," said Zara, rummaging around on her hands and knees. "Where did the bloody thing go?"

"Leave it," I said. "You can find it later. "

"Look, I'm not even that hungry," said Zara. "Why don't you lot go ahead and start without me?"

"You invited us over," I reminded her.

"It was Tim's idea—" Zara began, then stopped short and sat up, hitting her head on the table.

"Suit yourself," I said, and shut the door.

Back downstairs, Tim was stirring a saucepan, which was heating on the stove. Catherine and Martin were in the garden, sitting on a bench and drinking wine. I stood by the open back door to the garden and lit a cigarette.

"You want to pack that in, Lizzie," called Martin.

"Yeah, yeah. I know."

Tim came and stood beside me in the doorway. He looked out at the garden and sighed.

"What's up, Tim?" I asked.

"Clare's dumped me," he said. "She's met someone else. She's moved out."

"Oh Tim, I'm sorry." I stubbed out my cigarette, put my arms up around his shoulders, and pulled him against me. He put his arms back around me and held me tight, his chin resting on the top of my head. His t-shirt smelled of patchouli oil.

"Breaking up is..." I searched for something comforting to say which didn't sound like a cliché.

"It's like that feeling that you get in the pit of your stomach when you're about to jump out of an aeroplane," Tim said into my hair. I nodded, stood on tiptoes and kissed his cheek.

Martin looked up from the bench where he was sitting. I could see him watching me and Tim hugging for a moment and then, as he caught my eye, he smiled and got up.

"This looks cosy," he said, walking towards us.

"Can I play?" asked Zara, who was standing in the kitchen looking upset. "I'm sorry," she added, to me.

"Group hug," I announced, and stretched out my arm to her. Martin joined in, putting his arms around me and Zara and squeezing us tight. I looked over at Catherine, who was still sitting on the bench. "Come on Catherine," I called, feeling Martin's arm around me and worrying that she might feel left out. "Group hug."

"It's okay," she smiled.

We ate Spaghetti Napolitana with bread, parmesan cheese and salad on blankets in the back garden. This one had not been tended, and was home to all the neighbours' cats as well as various different species of wildlife which came in through the hedge backing onto the park behind.

"I feel as if I'm in the countryside," I said, looking around at the patchy grass and brambles and at the charred logs that lay in a dirt hollow under the trees where someone had recently had a bonfire.

"We should do something too," said Zara. "Shelley did the front."

Tim topped up our wine glasses. "Only because she's got a new boyfriend she wants to impress."

"Oh," I said. "What's he like?"

"He's a banker," said Tim.

Zara looked up. "I thought he was a sales rep?"

"I wish I could just stay home tomorrow and weed the garden," Tim sighed.

I rolled over onto my stomach. "I thought you enjoyed your job?"

"Oh yeah. Another day of cancelled ops and running around, getting nowhere." He shrugged. "They've closed half the wards — two hundred beds have gone. All so we can balance our books next year." He picked up the wine bottle and shook it. "We've got two new managers instead, paid fifty grand a year each to sit in an office and work out ways to cut costs. Isn't that right, Zara?"

Zara looked confused. "What did you say?" she asked.

Tim pulled his tobacco pouch out of his pocket and began rolling a cigarette. "Britain's oldest hospital," he continued. "Founded in the eleven hundreds, it was, by an Augustinian monk. It escaped destruction by the fire of London and the bombing in the second world war, and now here we are in the nineteen nineties and they're taking it to bits. One thousand years of history..." He clicked his fingers. "Up for sale."

No one spoke. Zara looked depressed, even in the darkness.

"It should be protected," said Catherine. "Like a listed building, part of our national heritage. Under customs law or something. There must be something you can do."

"It's called rationalisation," said Martin. "The existing beds need to be used more efficiently. That's the idea."

"How can you use a bed more efficiently?" asked Catherine.

"Put two people in it?" I suggested.

Martin looked at me and laughed.

"It's all about money," said Tim. "They don't care about people, just money."

"It's got to come from somewhere," Martin said.

"There's plenty of other places it could come from," said Tim. "But that might involve taking a bit of money away from the fat cats."

"It's their money," said Martin.

"No it's not. It's ours."

"I mean 'the fat cats', as you call them. They've made their money."

"Yeah, by paying peanuts. Off the backs of people like me and Zara."

"It's getting dark," I said, sensing an argument brewing. Martin was one of those people that would argue that black was white. I'd heard him saying just the opposite a week earlier. I sensed he was trying to antagonise Tim.

"Do you want to go inside?" asked Tim.

I shook my head. "Just point me to my wine glass." I lay back on the blanket and squinted up at the night sky. "I can only see three stars."

"No, there's more," said Tim, lying down beside me. "You just have to let your eyes focus."

"I wonder," I said, "If they have some sort of test for astronauts, you know, like the number plate test. Okay, Mr Armstrong, how many stars can you see?"

"A lot," said Zara, quietly.

I gave her a sideways glance. "Yeah. You pass. Get in your rocket, Miss Lewis." Zara wasn't smiling.

"I wonder what they look like up close?" asked Catherine.

"Big," said Martin, looking down at me and Tim, lying on the rug. I felt self-conscious, all of a sudden, lying there with my head so close to Tim's. I sat up again, slowly, and shifted slightly away.

Catherine said, "It's comforting to know they're always there, even if you can't see them. Puts things in perspective."

"Souls," said Zara. "Of dead people."

We waited a moment, expecting some kind of amplification.

"Well, the scientific view is that they're big exploding balls of gas," said Tim. "But that's a nice idea."

Zara sat up abruptly and knocked over her glass of wine. I realised with alarm that she was crying.

"When I try to look into the future," she blurted out, "I can't see anything there!"

Nobody wanted to drive home, so we all stayed the night. Catherine and Martin went to sleep in Clare's old room, and I crawled into bed beside Zara, but I couldn't sleep. After tossing and turning for a while, I entered into a strange half-dream about an Augustinian monk in his hooded cloak, wandering around, in and out of the old brick walls of the hospital, and the courtyard, and by the fountain in the middle, then up and down the empty and hollow wards. Shelley appeared briefly with a lamp, wearing an old Victorian nurse's uniform and said, "They're all dying," but then the Augustinian monk was back in the courtyard and nothing much else really happened.

I began to get bored of the same scene with the walls and the fountain and the courtyard playing over and over, and all the time the Augustinian monk kept repeating, "Half the wards, two hundred beds," until I realized that it was still just my brain ticking away and that I wasn't really asleep at all. I opened my eyes and stared dully into the darkness. Zara lay silently beside me in the same position she'd fallen asleep, curled up on her side with her back to me. I always found it remarkable how little she moved, and how deeply but noiselessly she slept.

After an hour or so of lying in the darkness, I got up and went downstairs for a drink of water. When I passed Tim's bedroom, I saw that the door was open and peeped inside. He was lying facing me, his tousled dark hair curling over his forehead. The covers were pushed away from his lean torso and his arms were wrapped protectively around a pillow. As I stood watching him, he shifted slightly on the bed and opened his eyes.

"Lizzie?" he said. "What are you doing?"

"I couldn't sleep," I whispered.

He blinked sleepily and glanced at the clock. He reached out an arm. "Come here."

I went into the room and sat down on the edge of the bed. Tim put his arm around me and pulled me down beside him. He stroked my hair. "Stay with me," he said, putting his arm around me again, and then he fell straight back to sleep.

I must have drifted off because when I woke it was light and I'd just heard the door slam. I looked at the clock. It was eight o'clock. Then I noticed that the door to the bedroom was open and Martin was standing there, looking at me and Tim.

"Sorry," he said. "Wrong door. I wanted the bathroom."

"Next door," I pointed. He paused for a moment, looking at us both, and then he disappeared.

Tim was still sleeping deeply; I could feel his breath against my neck. I lifted his arm, which was still wrapped around me, and slid out from underneath him.

Shelley was in the kitchen making tea. She looked exhausted.

"Do you want a cup?" she offered.

"Go on then." I sat down. "I'll have to go straight to work from here."

Shelley sat down beside me. "God, I need my bed," she said. "A quick soak in the bath. And then I'm going to sleep for England."

"Maybe you'd better wake Zara on your way up," I suggested. "Hasn't she got college today?"

"I doubt she's going in," said Shelley. "She hasn't been in for about three weeks now."

I looked up at her. "She didn't tell me that."

"She's trying to catch up with her coursework," said Shelley. "She's got her first exams in two weeks time and she's getting stressed out."

"I didn't realise," I said.

"I found her crying the other morning when I came home. Tim was on nights and I was at Gavin's."

"Gavin?" I echoed. "Is that his name?"

She nodded.

"Really, Shelley," I said. "A banker called Gavin?"

"He's not a banker," she said, confused. "He's a sales rep."

"Morning," said Martin, appearing in the doorway.

"Oh. Morning." Shelley got up to leave. "Need sleep," she added.

"But Shelley..." I tailed off, as Martin sat down next to me. "Hi," I said to Martin.

Shelley stopped as she got to the door. "I'll talk to you later," she said.

"Okay."

"So," said Martin. "How are you this morning?"

"Yeah, good. Tea?" I got up and fetched him a cup from the sink and added milk.

"Thanks." Martin took the cup from me and spooned sugar into it from a cracked jar next to the teapot. Slivers of sunshine glanced in through the window onto the table in front of us, though the kitchen was largely dark and the air slightly damp.

"So, what's going on, then? With you and him?" Martin nodded up at the ceiling.

"Tim? Oh, nothing. Really. We're just friends."

"That's not what it looked like. You were in bed with him."

"It's not like that. I couldn't sleep. It was just a… a cuddle."

Martin smiled and stirred his tea. "Whatever you say."

"It's true," I protested, then stopped. I couldn't work out if Martin was just teasing me, or whether he actually minded, about me and Tim. But why would he?

"He likes you," commented Martin. "That's bloody obvious."

I looked up, surprised at his tone. "Well, I like him too. But it's not like that."

"So what is it like, then?"

I paused. "Rationalisation," I smiled. "Efficient use of beds."

"You don't want to lead him on." Martin wasn't smiling now.

"I'm not," I protested. "He knows how things stand."

"He's a bloke, Lizzie," Martin said. "Blokes have needs."

"Well, so do women," I said, crossly. "You're not the only ones. But me and Tim are just fine with how things are."

"I doubt that very much."

"Look, Martin," I said. "I'm sorry, but I can't see how this is any of your business."

Martin looked down at his cup in silence.

"More tea?" I suggested, after a minute, trying to lighten the tone.

"Go on, then."

I poured him a second cup. "So. Catherine still asleep?" I asked.

"Yeah. She's always asleep." Martin said. "I was thinking of going for a jog. Want to come?"

I shook my head. "I've got work. I've got a meeting. I have to go soon."

"Okay," he said. "It doesn't matter."

I picked up my tea and pulled my cigarettes out of my handbag. I stood up and opened the back door. The air outside was cool, in contrast to the night before. The neighbour's cat shot into the hedgerow.

"You really want to pack that in." Martin looked up. "Seriously. You're an athlete. It doesn't make sense."

"I'm hardly an athlete," I said. "I like swimming, that's all."

"Well, imagine. Imagine how much faster you could swim if you did."

I shrugged, flicked my lighter and lit my cigarette. "Maybe. You're right, I know. I will. Soon. When I'm ready."

"So. No time like the present." He smiled. "Tell you what. I'll give you... erm. Five hundred quid. If you give up."

I laughed. "Five hundred quid? You're kidding, right?"

Martin smiled. "No. I'm serious. You give up and keep it up for six months, I'll give you five hundred quid."

I blew out a cloud of smoke. "But why? Why would you want to do that?"

Martin shrugged. "Why not? It's only money. It's an incentive, isn't it?"

I nodded. "You could say that. It's certainly a lot of money."

"So? Are you up for it?"

I stubbed my cigarette out on the wall and dropped the butt into the dustbin outside. "I don't know. I don't believe you're serious. And anyway, what would Catherine say? You two could go on a nice holiday for that."

Martin shrugged. "You can't do it. You haven't got the willpower."

"Yes, I have," I objected. I thought about it for a moment. We looked each other in the eye and neither of us gave in until we both started laughing. "Alright," I said, finally. "Game on."

"You're serious?"

"Yeah. That was my last cigarette."

"Okay," said Martin. "Put it there." He held out his hand and I gave him a high five. He grabbed my hand and held it for a moment. "No cheating?"

"I'm not going to cheat," I said. I tried to pull my hand away but Martin held onto it tightly and said again, "You sure?"

"I'm sure." I tried again to withdraw my hand from his grip. The door opened and Catherine's head appeared. Her face fell slightly, unmistakeably, when she saw us. Martin let go of my hand.

"Oh, hi, Catherine," I said. "We were just..."

"I thought you were coming back to bed?" said Catherine, to Martin. "I was waiting."

"Just coming, sweetheart," said Martin. "I was just making tea."

Catherine came into the kitchen and sat down at the table. She was wearing Martin's jumper and she pulled it down over her bare knees.

"Go on back up," insisted Martin. "I'm coming now."

"I'll wait," said Catherine. "I'm here now."

"I've got to go," I said. "I'm going to be late."

Nobody spoke.

"So. I'll see you later, then?" I looked at Catherine.

"Yeah." Catherine nodded.

Martin leaned over and gave her a kiss.

"Bye then," I said and closed the door behind me.

I ran upstairs to the bathroom. The door was open, the walls damp and steamy. A wet towel was draped over the banister. I ran up the next flight of stairs to Shelley's room.

"Shelley?" I called softly outside her door, but there was no answer from her room. I poked my head round Zara's door but she was fast asleep still, curled up in a tight little ball. I picked up my boots and jacket from the floor next to her bed where I'd left them and kissed her on the cheek. Then I closed the door behind me and hurried down the stairs.

I worried about Zara all the way from Clerkenwell to Euston. But when I got into work, there was a war going on in Bosnia and I had that to think about instead.

15

A FEW DAYS LATER, Catherine and I caught the tube down to the Barbican where Catherine was meeting her friends for rehearsals. I had tried ringing Zara but got no answer. As it was a Saturday, I decided to travel down with Catherine and surprise her instead. I knocked on the door and Shelley answered.

"She's up in her room," she said. "She's been up there since yesterday. I can't get her to come down."

When I got upstairs, Zara was curled up in bed, crying. She looked exhausted, as if she hadn't slept.

"Zara? What's wrong?"

"It's James," she said. "He didn't want to see me last night. We had a bit of a row."

"Why?" I sat down on her bed.

"He said he had important things to do today, a flying exam or something, and he had to get ready. And he made me go."

"Well, you should understand that, Zara. You've got your own exams coming up soon."

"I don't believe him. I think he was just giving me the brush-off. He's had enough of me."

"Why would you think that?"

"Because I've changed. I need him now, and he can sense that. And now he's rejecting me. I can't bear the rejection. It hurts so much."

"Zara, listen, darling," I said, bending down and stroking her back. She had always been thin, but I hadn't realised quite how bony she had got lately. "You're reading too much into it. Maybe it's just as he says, it's an important day for him."

"No." She shook her head. "I know what it is. I told him I loved him. And now he doesn't want me."

"I'm sure that's not true."

"Why? Have you spoken to him?"

"Well, of course not. I just meant…"

"He gave me a look, Lizzie. As if to say 'I know'. And that's why."

"That's why what? What are you talking about, Zara?"

Zara said nothing.

"Look, lying in bed's not going to do you any good," I said. "Get yourself dressed. I'll go and make you a cup of tea."

There were three cups of tea in the room already, all cold, sitting on the mantelpiece. I gathered them up and poured them down the bathroom sink. I went downstairs and put the kettle onto the stove. When it had whistled, I poured water into the teapot.

Suddenly there was a rumbling like thunder outside, which went on continuously for several seconds, getting louder and louder, as if it was getting closer to us. Then the windows rattled hard and the kettle wobbled on the gas ring.

"What the bloody hell was that?" yelled Shelley, running into the kitchen. Zara appeared in the doorway in her nightdress.

"I don't know. Can I use the phone?" I asked.

"Of course."

I picked up the phone and called Sandy, my boss.

"Can you get in?" he said.

"What is it?"

"A bomb. Bishopsgate. Outside the Hong Kong and Shanghai Bank. Apparently it's massive."

"I'm in the city, not far away from there."

"Perfect. Can you get yourself straight down there? Tom will meet you there in the radio car as soon as possible."

"I'm on my way."

I glanced over at Zara, who looked petrified.

"Zara? Are you okay?" said Shelley, putting her arm around her.

"I've got to go," I said. "Sorry."

I grabbed my jacket and ran out into the street. A black cab passed and pulled up to my frantic waving. As I opened the door, another loud explosion hit the air like a giant gunshot and the cab rocked visibly in front of me.

I leapt in and shut the door. "Bishopsgate," I said. "As fast as you can, please."

"Bloody hell," said the driver.

We drove quickly through the quiet streets of Clerkenwell and onto London Wall. It was easy to find where we were going. A huge cloud of smoke sat above the City skyline, like a beacon, or some sick parody of Hiroshima.

There were at least nine or ten ambulances on the scene when I arrived, and two double-decker buses which had been commandeered to take the injured to hospital. Teams of fire-fighters were standing by, and the police had already begun cordoning off the area. Nobody stopped me, however, as I picked my way through the street-long devastation of injured bodies and sheets of broken glass.

Nothing could have prepared me for what I was about to witness, and certainly not three years at a small radio station in Cambridge. They didn't teach you on journalism courses what a hundred people shouting or crying out in pain sounded like, or about the sight of people lying bleeding, possibly dying, right before your very eyes.

There were people everywhere trying to help, lifting panels of glass, fallen scaffolding and metal from on top of the injured bodies. One man was holding another man's head with his coat wrapped around it, despite the blood that was matted into his own hair and splashed over the back of his shirt. A woman was sitting on the kerb and holding the hand of a younger girl who was lying in the road, her skirt pulled up above her bloodied knees. She looked about fifteen; she could have been her daughter. Her ankle looked as if it was on back to front.

Windows had exploded in every building within a five-hundred metre radius of the Bank, blowing debris from the bigger buildings and offices through basement windows into the local cafés and restaurants. A middle-aged man in a suit was stumbling towards me. His eyes were wide and terrified, and there was blood running out of both of his ears.

"I can't hear!" he called out, turning his head from side to side, scanning the streets frantically for help. "I can't hear anything!"

I stopped him and took his arm, and pointed in the direction of one of the ambulances that was edging its way through the barricades of fallen bricks. He gripped onto my arm tightly and I walked with him, tripping through the dirt and broken glass.

A few yards from the ambulance I stopped in horror. A man was lying in a crumpled heap, blood seeping from cuts all over his body. He was jerking and twitching, his limbs moving rhythmically, involuntarily. His eyes looked frightened, but unfocused. My stomach tightened and I caught my breath. Memories flooded back, making me sick to the stomach. It was my father lying there. I could see it all perfectly clearly. The road. The car. The man who had hit him, standing beside me, saying, "Oh my God. I didn't see him. I'm so sorry." My father was lying there, dying before my very eyes while I stood there beside him, paralysed with fear.

And then he was gone and it was a man I didn't know, a young man with dark hair and a dark coat, laying there on the pavement. I could feel myself trembling, but it was nothing in comparison to the relentless shaking of the man before me. I bent down beside him and my legs gave way, so that I fell onto my knees on the pavement. I steadied myself with one hand on the ground and tentatively reached out an arm to touch his coat. I noticed one of his shoes was missing.

"It's okay," I told him. My voice came out all high-pitched and squeaky. I cleared my throat. "It's going to be okay," I said again.

I looked around, desperately. A paramedic arrived and took his arm. "Do you know his name?" he asked me. I shook my head. The paramedic bent down to face him. He took his arm and felt for his pulse, speaking reassuringly all the while. A few minutes later a second paramedic arrived and placed an oxygen mask over his mouth. I tried to stand and move away, but my head was spinning, so I sat down again on the pavement.

"Okay, my love?" asked the first paramedic.

I nodded.

"Alright," said the second, as between them they lifted the man and strapped him onto a stretcher. "Off we go."

"Will he be okay?" I asked, weakly, from where I was sitting.

I didn't hear the answer.

A policeman had stopped behind me. "If you're not injured, I'm going to have to ask you to move back away from here," he said. I nodded and stumbled towards the cordon and wobbled down the street.

I met the radio car in Leadenhall Street, not far from the Baltic Exchange.

"Thought to be a ton of explosives," said Tom, poking his head out of the driver's side window. "A truck bomb, they reckon." I went round and got into the passenger seat next to him. "Jesus Christ," he added. "You're looking a bit green."

I leaned my head back against the seat. "What time is it?"

"Twenty-five past."

"Time to call the studio. They'll want a two-way."

"Are you sure you're okay?"

"Let's get it over with," I said.

After the news was over, Tom sat beside me in sympathetic silence while I leaned out of the car and was sick on the pavement.

"Are you okay?" he asked again, finally.

I nodded. "Let's get out of here."

"Do you want me to take you home?" asked Tom.

I shook my head. "Next stop, Scotland Yard and then... St Bartholomew's A & E."

I got home at eleven that night. Catherine was up waiting for me. I sank down onto the settee. Catherine got up and poured me a large brandy.

"I've been listening in," she said. "And watching the news. I can't believe it. It's just... unbelievable."

"I've just seen Shelley and Tim," I said.

"Where?"

"At the hospital. They're working flat out. There just aren't enough staff; so they've both been called in. But it's still not enough. There are no beds. There were people just lying on stretchers in the corridors, some of them had been there for hours."

"I just can't believe it's happened again," said Catherine. "Although I guess there must be a reason," she continued.

"A reason? Are you trying to tell me this is the Universe unfolding as it should, or something?"

Catherine turned away defensively. "Well," she said, after a few moments. "Maybe. Maybe there are things we just can't control. Maybe this was meant to happen for some reason we don't yet understand. Maybe it is just destiny, I don't know."

"Nice destiny," I said.

"Look, I know how you're feeling," she said gently. "I understand — I feel the same as you do. But I can't give up believing that there's some higher power at work. Otherwise it makes a mockery of our existence; then, there'd be no point to anything."

"Maybe there is no point," I said. "Maybe it's all meaningless. Maybe this is all just some sick joke."

"This isn't like you," mumbled Catherine. "You've got bitter," she said. "You used to be a bottle-half-full person."

"Well, sometimes it's just not looking that full," I said.

We sat in silence for a while.

"So have you seen Zara?" said Catherine. "Did she go in to the hospital?"

"No. She wasn't there," I said. "I hope she's okay. She seemed a bit fragile this morning."

At that moment there was an urgent tapping on the window next to the fire escape and Zara's head appeared. I opened the window and she climbed in and fell into my arms.

"What the hell are you doing out there?" I asked, hugging her. She had no coat on and she was freezing cold. "Why didn't you come round the front?"

"It was James," she said, shivering. "Or, should I say his real name, Mickey Finn."

I stifled a laugh. "That's not his real name, Zara."

"Yes, it is!" she protested. "He told me."

"It's a joke," I said.

"Oh, this is no joke," said Zara, shaking her head violently. "You have no idea."

"What was James?" Catherine wanted to know.

"The bomb," said Zara.

"What are you talking about?" I asked her.

"It was him!" Zara screeched impatiently, then checked herself. She ran over to the window and pulled back the curtain. She spun round and faced us, solemnly. "He's IRA," she said.

"What?" Catherine and I both said, in unison.

"Shhh," hissed Zara. "They'll hear you."

"Who?" I turned round and glanced at the window. "Who are you talking about? Who are 'they'?"

"I told you," said Zara, sighing and rolling her eyes. "They're IRA."

I said, "I don't think so, Zara."

"It's true. I have evidence. I saw them yesterday. I saw James. Mickey. Talking to his house mate, this guy, whose name I've never even been told — it's like you said, it's all hush-hush." Zara was speaking so quickly, I could barely follow what she was saying.

"And?"

"And he said 'all set then', and James scratched his head — which was of course the signal — and that was it, James says 'yes' and that's when he told me to go."

"Because he had an exam today," I reminded her.

"But that's just it, it wasn't! It was just a smokescreen, like Martin said."

"Martin didn't mean it," said Catherine, who was sitting on the sofa looking baffled.

"He rang me," said Zara, her eyes wide. "He told me it all went well, that it was a success."

"His exam," I insisted.

"No!" yelled Zara. "He wanted to see me, to celebrate. But I know he knows."

"Knows what?"

"That I know," said Zara, going to the front window, pulling back the curtain again and peering out. "He gave me a look. And I looked back. And he knows." She paused. "That car shouldn't be out there," she said.

"What car? Why?" I said, going to the window. I looked out, but all I could see was my neighbour's Volvo.

Catherine stood up and went into the kitchen. She came back a minute later with a glass of brandy.

"Here," she said to Zara. "Drink this."

"What is it?" said Zara.

"Just brandy," said Catherine. "Come on, sweetheart. Sit down and drink it. And then you can tell us everything, from the start."

Zara looked at Catherine for a moment with something that almost looked like hostility. But then she seemed to change her mind, took the glass, and sat down on the sofa. She kicked her shoes off, and folded her legs underneath her, and took little sips at her drink.

Catherine and I sat and watched her.

"Strong," she said, smiling.

"I think we all need a strong one," I said. "I'll go and get the bottle."

Zara smiled and laid her head back against the cushion. I got up and went into the kitchen. When I came back in again with the brandy bottle, Catherine had her finger to her lips and Zara was asleep.

"What did you give her?" I whispered.

"Liquid morphine," Catherine whispered back. "Had it for my tooth. It's done the trick. Anyway, she was exhausted."

"Good thinking." I got up and fetched a blanket, and folded it over Zara's small frame. She was out for the count. I sank back into the sofa opposite. "Sorry for being grumpy," I said. "I guess I picked the wrong week to give up smoking."

Catherine smiled and shrugged. She held up the brandy bottle. "So. Is this half full or half empty?"

"I don't know," I said. I held out my glass. "Let's make it easy. Let's just drink it all."

16

WHEN I WOKE AT FOUR the next morning, Zara was still curled up on the sofa. She was so still that I started to worry that something had happened to her in the night, but when I bent down next to her I could feel her breath gently tickling my cheek and I realised that my worry was irrational. People didn't just die like that, in the night, for no reason. All the same, I poked my head around Catherine's door. She too was asleep on her back, snoring gently.

I showered and dressed and headed off to work.

I was producing the Breakfast Programme that week. Sandy, my boss, looked around the studio door. He was a kind, tired, grey-haired man in his early sixties. He was of the old school that still believed in life after work and thought that people who wanted to take a lunch break or go home after an eight hour shift had a point. "You here again?" he said. "I must sort those rotas out."

"That's okay," I said.

"How are you getting on?" he asked.

"Clive's down at Leadenhall Street with Tommy now," I told him. "We've got a piece lined up on the damage to St Ethelburga's and the double hit on the Baltic Exchange. And we've got the Home Secretary on cue after the headlines."

"Well done," said Sandy. "Great work." I gave him a half smile and put my headphones back on. Sandy held the door open. "You okay?" he mouthed at me. I smiled again and nodded.

"Good morning, and welcome to the Breakfast Show," said Jo Castle, the morning presenter, into my headphones.

I waved my arm at Sandy, who stuck his thumb up at me and closed the studio door.

"This last year has been the worst for terrorist attacks," Jo was saying. "In January, the IRA breached security for the second time to strike at Whitehall minutes after the Prime Minister had left. And it's barely more than a year since the City was rocked by the biggest explosion ever on the mainland, which left three people dead and eighty injured."

"Home Secretary on line three," said Nikki Sanders, the show's PA, into my headphones.

"...and finally," said Jo, "The manager of one of London's leading teaching hospitals has resigned less than a fortnight before a report was due to go to the Health Secretary naming his hospital, St Bartholomew's, as one of the four facing closure under the NHS internal market..."

"Back to the bomb," I said to Jo. "Home Secretary on cue."

I flicked the intercom off and sat back. Then I leaned forward and flicked it on again. "Ask him about Barts as well!" I said. "Where will they take the injured next time? Ask him that!" A sea of faces looked up at once and stared at me through the glass from the newsroom. I realised too late that I'd pressed the wrong switch and was loudly and clearly on air.

Sandy poked his head around the door again. "You okay?" he asked again.

I nodded at Sandy, and mouthed the word "sorry".

The phone rang. "It's for you," said Nikki.

Sandy closed the door. I pulled my headphones off and picked up the phone. It was Zara.

"You blame me, don't you?" she said. "You think I was involved."

My heart flipped in surprise at her tone. "In what?"

"The bomb."

"Why would I think that?"

"Because I work at Barts."

"I don't understand."

"I heard you just now," she said. "On the radio. That was meant for me. Why can't you just say it to my face?"

"Say what?" I sat back in my chair, baffled.

"Forget it," said Zara, and put down the phone.

When the programme was over I telephoned Zara back, but there was no reply.

At the end of my shift, Sandy wanted to see me.

"You don't seem yourself," he said kindly. "Is anything bothering you?"

"I don't know," I said. "I think I'm just a bit tired."

"What you witnessed yesterday... well, it was a big thing. You may be suffering from some sort of post-trauma shock."

I considered what he was saying. I didn't want him to think I couldn't handle this sort of pressure: one big story and I collapse. And I was beginning to realise that it wasn't just yesterday's trauma that I was re-living when I closed my eyes. Everything was coming back to me, in waves.

"I'll be fine, Sandy. Honest."

"Well, go home. Get some rest. But if you find yourself feeling low, you come and find me, okay? There are people you can talk to," he said. "It's not a sign of weakness. This sort of thing happens more often than you might think."

"Okay."

Sandy hesitated in the doorway and smiled at me.

"Thanks for being so kind," I added, touched and a little overwhelmed by his compassion.

Sandy saw my discomfort, and simply said: "You're highly valued here, Lizzie. Please come and find me if you want to talk. Any time."

When I got home, I called Zara again. Tim answered the phone.

"Lizzie." He said. "I'm glad you called. I was just about to call you."

"Oh, okay. What's up? And is Zara there?"

"Well that's what I was going to call you about. She's not very well. She's in hospital."

"In hospital?" My heart started thumping. "Has she had an accident?"

"No. Nothing like that. But Shelley took her in around lunchtime." He paused. "She's in Strauss ward."

"What for?" I asked. "What's wrong with her?"

"Lizzie, Strauss is the psychiatric ward," Tim said quietly.

"Oh. I see." Suddenly everything made sense.

"She's a voluntary patient at the moment. But I'm not sure if she is going to stay. Shelley's called her Dad. If she fights it they'll section her."

"Oh, God. I knew something was wrong. She seemed depressed, and I didn't do anything." I started racking my brain for all the warning signs, all the clues, all the times I might have turned my back on her and been too stupid to realise. "I should have been there for her. Looked after her. Maybe it wouldn't have got this bad."

Tim sighed. "It's not your fault, really, Lizzie. We were living with her, and we didn't see it coming. Or at least, I think Shelley did, but she wasn't sure. Anyway, there isn't anything anyone could have done. She needed professional help. She's not... what you have to understand, Lizzie... she's really not very well. At all. And this isn't the first time, apparently."

"Oh," I said. "I see." Although I didn't see, not really, and Tim was frightening me.

"Thank you for letting me know," I said.

"Go and see her," said Tim.

"I don't know if she will want to see me," I said. "She was pretty angry with me earlier."

"That's just the illness," said Tim. "Give it 'til tomorrow. Let the meds kick in, then go and see her. She needs her friends right now."

It was strange, going through the courtyard and past the fountain and up the steps into the ward with the big brick walls looming up around me, just as they had been in my dream. In fact, it felt a bit as though I were in a dream, because I'd been up since four and now this, all this with Zara, had a feel of something quite surreal.

I didn't feel as though I could walk straight in, because the ward Sister was at the reception desk talking on the telephone to someone about picking up a Miss Jenkins' scripts for her and whether or not she was going to need to "come back in and see us again". She kept repeating "come back in and see us", and talked slowly and clearly as if she were talking to a child, although she obviously wasn't. She was wearing a pair of very large thick glasses. I watched her neck moving up and down inside her dark blue collar. Every time she spoke, the white piping round the edge wobbled.

Finally, she put down the receiver and turned and looked at me.

"Can I help?"

"I'm here to visit Zara Lewis," I said.

"Ah, Zara," she said. She pointed to the day room. "You can go on in. She's just having her tea."

Zara wasn't having any tea. She was sitting around a table with four or five other patients, who were all eating in silence. Zara was staring into space, her eyes all red and bulgy from crying, her hands hanging down by her sides. Her food lay untouched in front of her. I walked over and put my arms around her. She turned and clutched hold of me with a frail white hand.

"Who are you?" asked the woman sitting next to her. She turned her sharp beaky face towards me. "What do you want?" she rasped.

"Come on," I whispered. Zara stood up obediently. A man sitting opposite pushed his chair back and stood up too.

"Sit down, Mr Stevens," said one of the auxiliaries, coming into the day room.

"She hasn't finished her tea," she added, to me.

"She doesn't want it," I said, ignoring the look of disapproval from the auxiliary, and took Zara by the hand.

"Where's your room?" I asked her.

It had only been a couple of days since I'd last seen her, but I hadn't realised how much weight she had actually lost. She was wearing a pair of denim dungarees that I'd never seen before. They were draping from her bony shoulders and hanging shapelessly around her as if they were dangling from a broken coat hanger. Underneath, she was wearing a white t-shirt. Her arms were almost the same colour.

She led me down the corridor past the nursing office, where the ward Sister and one of the nurses were sitting down and having a cup of tea. The Sister looked up as we passed, analysing us both through her thick lenses.

Zara stopped, as if she'd been caught doing something wrong. "Is it all right if I take my friend to my room?" she asked, nervously.

"Yes Zara, you can do that," said the Sister, nodding. She smiled at me. I could see she thought I was a good influence. I started planning Zara's escape.

We carried on down the hallway. A good-looking young guy of about twenty wandered past us. He was nicely dressed in a checked shirt and jeans and Nike trainers.

"Hello, Zara," he said, without smiling.

"Hello, Sean," she said. "That's Sean," she told me, after he'd passed us.

"He looks nice," I said.

"He's schizophrenic," said Zara.

She stopped. "This is my room," she said. We entered a small whitewashed single room with a hospital bed set in the middle, and a table and a sink by the window, which overlooked the courtyard below. I sat down on the radiator, which was one of the old big chunky ones, painted hospital green.

"So, have they told you what's wrong?" I asked her.

"Depression," she said. "That's what they say. I'm clinically depressed."

"Well, that's pretty obvious. Do you get to talk to anyone? Are you seeing anyone, a psychiatrist?" I asked her.

She stared at me and shook her head. She picked up a notepad from a table by the window. "How do you spell 'psychiatrist'?" she asked me.

"I'm sure they'll…" I began.

"I forget everything," she said, at the same time. She looked at me. "I can't remember anything from one minute to the next. I can't even read a book, because I keep forgetting what the story's about."

I bit my lip. I could see that planning her escape had been a little dramatic and naive, not to mention premature. She wasn't going to be going anywhere, not for a while yet. She stood there by the table, by the window with her notepad, poised and serious like a badly dressed secretary, her forehead creased up into the old familiar frown.

I spelled "psychiatrist" for her.

"These are my things," said Zara, putting down the pen and notepad and picking up a piece of rose quartz that Catherine had given her for Christmas and a postcard with a Monet flower print on the front. She sat down on the bed.

"Can I?" I sat down next to her.

She nodded. I took the postcard from her and turned it over. It was from her mum. It said, in big childlike print: "Dear Zara, Don't worry, things will get better soon, Love, MUM."

"Why has she written 'Mum' in great big capital letters?" I asked.

"I don't know," said Zara, staring out of the window.

"Is she coming?"

Zara shook her head. "Dad can't get the time off work to drive her."
I looked up at her. "She doesn't want to," she said, her red-rimmed
eyes filling up with tears. "That's all. I phoned yesterday and asked
if they could come and get me, and bring me home. Mum said, 'This
isn't going to be like last time, is it, Zara?' And then she said it wasn't
practical because Aunty Margaret and Uncle John have broken up
and Aunty Margaret's staying, and there's all that to deal with, and
plus my sister's home from Uni, and she said it would be best all
round if I just tried to carry on."

When she finished speaking, she was shaking. I put my arms
around her and stroked her hair. It was wispy and wet, somehow,
and it was sticking to her head. She leaned against my shoulder.

She said, "You think growing up is like — it's like, one day
you're going to wake up with a bowl of cherries and life membership
to the 'Sorted Out Club'." Tears were running down her cheeks. "But
you know," she continued, "it just goes on, and on, and on…"

"I know," I said, because I did.

We sat for a long while without speaking; me holding Zara, her
leaning against my shoulder, and both of us rocking gently back and
forth while the sunlight beamed in through the gaps in the trees and
made small fluttering leaf-shaped patterns on the wall beside us. There
was nothing else to say, because there weren't any more words.

The following day, after my shift, I went straight back to the hospital.
Zara was in her room.

"It's really embarrassing," she said. "Everyone knows me." She
was sitting on her bed wearing a black crocheted top and jeans, which
were bunched in around her waist with a flowery leather belt. Her
hands lay palms upwards on the bed beside her and I could see faint
blue veins trickling down the inside of her pale arms. "With the senior
staff, I've kind of got used to it and they've been really nice to me, but
every time one of the Grade A nurses comes on the ward and sees me,
they give me this look and I want to hang my head in shame."

"They probably just feel for you, Zara. They're nurses. They care.
You've got nothing to be ashamed of," I said.

Zara looked up at me, anxiously. Her eyes were still red and puffy, and weeping slightly. "That's easy for you to say. But people judge you when they find out you've had a breakdown." She wiped at her eyes with the back of her hand. "You wouldn't believe how differently they behave. I know from last time. It's like everyone's sitting around waiting for you to crack up all the time."

I got up and fetched her a tissue from the box on the windowsill. "I didn't know about last time," I said. "You didn't tell me."

"I thought you wouldn't want to know me."

"How could you think that?"

"I didn't know it was going to happen again."

I peered out of the window. "Do you want to go for a walk?" I asked her.

Zara blew her nose. "I don't know if they'll let me."

"They'll let you," I said. "I've already asked. Come on, it'll do you good. Let's go and have a picnic. I've brought some food."

We walked around the courtyard a couple of times and sat on a bench by the fountain. I opened my bag. I'd bought all Zara's favourite food from a deli in Upper Street; there were apples, fresh sardines, hard-boiled eggs, and a packet of Highland oatcakes.

Zara looked disinterested. "I'm not really hungry," she said.

"You have to eat," I coaxed her gently. She stared up at the fountain and said nothing.

When we got back inside, I left Zara in the day room with Sean and went to speak to the Sister. "She's upset," I said. "She's not eating. Are you sure the drugs are working?"

"She's a lot better than she was," said the Sister. She put down a file she was holding and turned to face me. "Much better than she was when she first came in to see us." There it was again: "Came in to see us", as if it were an enjoyable little day trip that lots of people made, just because it was such a nice place to be. I couldn't help but smile.

"So what is it?" I asked her. "What's wrong with her? I mean, apart from being depressed."

"It's called psychosis," explained the Sister.

"What caused it?"

"Well, that's not something that's so easy to establish. But believe me," she said. "There's a lot of strange things that can go through your mind when you haven't slept properly for weeks. Her body's been under tremendous strain," she said. "But she's going to get better." She smiled. "Don't you worry. She's on the mend."

I smiled back at her. I could see why they called them Angels.

I crossed Smithfield and headed up towards Faringdon tube. I turned into St John Street and walked up towards the Angel, then turned right into Essex Road. I realised that I hadn't seen Uncle Silbert for several weeks, and it seemed unlikely that Zara had either. Nor was she going to be visiting him for a while. I would have to take over, I decided, make sure he was okay. I would have to make time for regular visits.

The lift wasn't working, and so I had to walk up all twelve flights of stairs. The stairwell smelled of urine, like the lift had done, only for longer. I reached the top, breathless, and knocked on the door. I stayed away from the railings.

I could see Uncle Silbert shuffling down the hallway through the frosted glass. He didn't have his walking frame and he took a long time to reach the door, which made me feel guilty. He opened the door wide and stood back, breathing heavily and nodding his head at the same time, as if he had been expecting me. "Ah, Elizabeth, come in."

I followed him back down the hallway to the kitchen where the same one ring on the old gas stove was burning. The flat still smelled of dust and pastry. I wondered if he would allow me to have a clean up for him, but decided against asking for fear of offending him.

Uncle Silbert lowered himself into his brown armchair and I sat down on the stool by the stove.

"Shall I put the kettle on?"

Uncle Silbert nodded, coughed, and pointed to the cake tin on the table.

"No. Thank you," I said. "But let me make you some tea. Have you eaten? I could cook for you if you like?"

He shook his head. "No, no. Don't you trouble yourself, my dear. No need."

"Come on. I want to," I insisted. I stood up and looked round the kitchen. "What have you got?"

I opened the small fridge, tucked under the worktop by the door, but it was switched off and smelled of damp and mould. I hastily shut the door again.

"Your fridge isn't working?"

Uncle Silbert waved his long, bony hand. "I switch it off when it's not being used."

"Oh. Okay. Tea and toast, then? Do you have bread?" I made a mental note to do some checks, find out if there were benefits to which he was entitled and not getting. Some way that his bills could be paid for him so that he would have no need to turn his fridge off. So that he would put the heating on instead of living in the kitchen.

Uncle Silbert shook his head. "I don't think so…"

I opened the larder door. Inside was a tin of Campbell's condensed cream of mushroom soup and a packet of stale breadsticks. I opened the can and tipped it into a saucepan, and lit a second ring on the stove. While the soup was warming, I chopped up the breadsticks for croutons and made the tea. A carton of warm milk stood on the work surface by the kettle.

"I'm going to go shopping for you," I said, pouring the soup into bowls. "As soon as we have finished this."

"There's no need," said Uncle Silbert. "The lady who takes me, she's coming tomorrow. This will be enough, for now."

"What about breakfast?" I asked. "At least let me get you some bread, some butter, and some more milk."

"Your company is more to me. Please. Stay."

I smiled and sat down. "Okay. So how are you?" I asked. "Did you hear the bomb?"

"It shook the entire building," he said.

"You must have been worried, wondered what it was?"

"I knew what it was. You never forget what that sound is like. Of course, we were much closer, it was much louder."

"Oh. Of course. I can imagine." I stopped eating. "Well, no. That's silly. Of course I can't."

"Maybe you can."

I put down my soup spoon and looked up at him. "Zara's not well," I said. "She may not come around for a while." I told him what had happened.

He nodded. "She's an angel." he said. "But she's always been this way."

"I didn't know," I told him. "I thought it was just life. Ups and downs. Joy and sorrow, you know? Two sides of the same coin, or so they say."

"For some it is. For others it's too much joy, too much sorrow."

"But how does that happen?"

He smiled. "You're wondering will it happen to you."

"Yes," I agreed. "Could it?"

"I can't see it," he said. "Not in you." He reached out his hand and patted mine across the table. "You know, in the war, the Japanese did some terrible things to their prisoners. Things that you would never believe one human could do to another. Men were tortured, burned and beaten, they had limbs broken. They were used for bayonet practice. Their bodies were cut, they had objects inserted."

"Inserted?"

"Into the cuts. To cause pain. It was horrific. Many died. Many were horribly scarred. But others, others survived and went on to live normal lives. To marry, get jobs, and have children."

I shook my head. "It's hard to know how you could survive something like that. And still live a normal life, that is."

He nodded. "It never really goes away, of course. Not completely." He paused. "The original trauma will often replay like an old tape throughout your life."

"How do you mean?"

"Well. You see," he said, "as humans, we all have to make sense of the world around us and put it into some sort of order in our minds. Our expectations are based on our past experiences. If life has been good to you, you expect it to be good in the future. But if you have suffered some kind of traumatic experience, that's what you are expecting all the time: a random and devastating event that is impossible to predict or control. So you are living in a state of constant anxiety. Until another similar event sets it off."

I nodded. "That makes sense. When the bomb went off, when I saw what had happened, it made me feel things. As if something like that has happened before to me. But I just can't remember anything. Apart from the fact that my father died, suddenly, when I was six," I said. "But I just can't seem to remember anything about that time."

"Well. It's a strange kind of irony. The things that affect us most are the things we can't remember."

"Really? How?"

He shrugged." Well, it is believed that most of our feelings about life, the way that we make sense of it, are formed before we reach the age of five. At that time, our family is the whole world to us, and our relationships within the family form the basis of how we will go on to perceive the real world, the outside world. However, this is before our memories are formed. So we have made a lot of important decisions about life, about the world, about the people in it, but we are unlikely to remember the events that caused us to make those decisions. Then, after that, as we go through life, we find ways to block out events that hurt us too much, that are too painful. Sometimes we don't even know why we are feeling so hurt; we just concentrate our efforts on finding ways to deaden the pain. Drugs. Alcohol. Sex. Work. Anything that makes us feel good instead."

"So how do we know what happened? How do we get that back?" I looked up in alarm, realising that my voice was shaking. I cleared my throat and fought back tears. "I mean…. Well, I just mean that I think that losing my father must have been important to me but I can't remember anything about him!"

Uncle Silbert reached out his hand to me again and I took it. I stroked his long, cold, bony fingers, and then I held them tight. "Trust in it, Elizabeth," he said. "You have the answers. Know your own truths."

I bit my lip and nodded.

After a few moments, Uncle Silbert shifted forward in his chair. He rocked himself back and forth several times and then rose. "I have something for you," he said. He shuffled out of the room. He was gone for so long that I worried something had happened to him and got up to look for him. I collided with him in the doorway as he soundlessly re-entered the room.

"Here. I want you to have this." He handed me some sheets of yellowing paper with small print, bound together with ribbon in one corner.

"Ralph Waldo Emerson," he said. "He was a 19th century American essayist. Also a lecturer and poet. This is his *Essay on Self-Reliance*. I think you will enjoy it."

"Thank you." I took the papers from him. "What is it about?"

"Freedom," he said.

17

ZARA CAME OUT OF HOSPITAL at the beginning of June, the week before my birthday. Catherine and I had planned a party at the flat and Zara said she would come. On the morning of the party, Catherine went out early. I was still in my pyjamas when she returned. She put down her shopping bag and leaned against the sink.

"I've got everything for the punch, four different types of cheeses, nuts, crisps, French bread, napkins, paper plates... oh, and plastic glasses."

She started to unload everything onto the work surface where I was making toast, ripping open the packets and stacking the glasses upside down on top of the washing machine.

"That's a lot of plastic glasses," I said. "How many people have you invited?"

"Not that many. But they were cheap. And anyway, they're always useful."

The telephone rang. Catherine went to answer it. I looked apprehensively at the stacks of plastic glasses. The washing machine went into a spin cycle and they all started shuddering, and then rattling manically, and then bouncing up and down. I leaped forwards to catch them.

"It's for you," Catherine called from the hallway. "It's your mum."

I took the receiver from her.

"Happy Birthday," said my mother. "Are you having a nice day?"

"So far, so good. Thanks."

"Did you get your present?"

"What present?"

"Hasn't it arrived yet? I sent it the day before yesterday. By recorded delivery. I hope it hasn't got lost."

"I'm sure it hasn't. It's just the post being slow. So come on, what is it?"

"You'll see," said my mother, sounding pleased with herself.

As I put down the phone, the doorbell rang. It was the postman with a bundle of cards and a parcel for me that I had to sign for. I unwrapped the parcel. "Oh, my God," I breathed. Inside was the missing doll.

Catherine came out of the kitchen with a glass of purple liquid. "Here try, this," she said. "Tell me if you think it's too strong."

I was still looking at the doll. She was a rag doll with button eyes and black wool hair and an old green and white checked dress and bloomers. It was the doll my mother had talked about, the one she and my dad had given me for my sixth birthday. Seeing her now was the strangest of sensations. I could remember her after all. I remembered holding her, loving her, sleeping with her, never letting her out of my sight. And more, I could remember the day I got her, opened up the parcel — just as I had done minutes earlier — to find her inside. I could suddenly see my father's face, lit with pleasure at my own delight; I could feel his arms around me, his lips kissing my cheek, and his voice saying, "Happy Birthday, Busy Lizzie. Glad you like your doll."

The telephone rang again. This time it was for Catherine. She sat silently for several minutes; her jaw dropped and her face became solemn. All she said was, "Oh no," several times, and then, finally, "Of course I will. Of course."

Catherine put the receiver down. "It's my dad," she said, looking bewildered. "He's in hospital. He's had a stroke. They think it's only a mild one. But my mum needs me. She's in bits. I've got to go home. I'm really sorry, Lizzie. I won't be able to stay for the party."

"Oh, for goodness sakes," I said. "That doesn't matter. I'll take you to the station."

I'd only just got back from Kings Cross when the doorbell rang. It was Zara. She was wearing a see-through chiffon blouse and a denim skirt and knee-high go-go boots. She looked very pretty, although still on the thin side.

"Hi, Zara," I said. "You look nice. Come in. What's happening with Tim and Shelley?"

"Tim can't come. He's had to work. I'm not sure about Shelley. I think she's meeting Gavin from work."

She came in and shut the door.

"How are you feeling?" I asked her.

"Up and down," she said.

"I suppose you feel different from day to day?" I offered.

"Not really," said Zara. "Try from minute to minute."

I hugged her and she clutched hold of the back of my dress. She still felt fragile, as if she could snap at any moment. She followed me into my bedroom, where I was doing my makeup.

"Who's this?" she asked, picking up my doll and stroking her hair.

"She was mine when I was little," I said. "My mum and dad gave her to me for my birthday, when I was six."

Zara sat the doll on a chair. "Little Lizzie," she said.

I smiled and tightened the cap on my mascara bottle. "So are the tablets helping, do you think?"

"I don't know. I think so." Zara sat down on the bed. "When I wake up in the morning, I only feel like killing myself 'til about lunchtime. So I suppose that's something." She saw the look on my face and smiled at me. "Don't worry," she said. "I'd never do anything about it. To tell the truth, I haven't got the courage."

I felt very weak, all of a sudden. I hoped that that was true.

"Usually, I just take my pills and go right back to sleep again," she added. "Then there's just the afternoon to get through."

I zipped up my makeup bag and sat down on the bed next to her. "Maybe you shouldn't be sleeping that much," I told her. "Maybe it doesn't help."

She shrugged. "Tim and Shelley have been waking me, and making me get up. But mornings are difficult. It just doesn't feel like there's anything to get out of bed for."

I said, "I wish there was something I could do."

Zara smiled and touched my arm. "You're already doing it." She paused. "Really. You are. Just by being my friend."

"Well, of course I'm your friend! Now more than ever!"

She shrugged again. "Most people can't cope with any sign of weakness. They see tramps on the street," she said. "And they feel sorry for them. But they wouldn't want to know them, be their friend. They want to be needed, but not that much. I'm scared you'll feel like that too, before long."

"I won't," I protested. "I promise. That's not how I feel."

"I keep thinking I'm going to end up like that, a bag lady, begging from shop doorways."

"Don't be silly," I said. "That's not going to happen."

"Why not?" she insisted. "They're just ordinary people who are down on their luck. One false move and you're under. Go to jail, do not pass go, do not collect two hundred pounds. It could happen to anyone. It could happen to me."

"I won't let it," I said, firmly.

"What if I made you crack up too?"

I turned to face her. We sat for a moment, looking into each other's eyes. Hers were weak and desperate, but there was something else there as well. It was as if she were challenging me and begging me at the same time.

"You won't," I said, finally. "I'm stronger than that."

It was the right answer.

I decided to cancel the party.

"Please don't, not on my account," pleaded Zara.

"It's okay, really. What with Tim and Catherine not being here and you… well, I can easily get hold of people from work, tell them not to come."

Catherine rang a short while later to say that everything was fine, her dad was stable, but she was going to stay for a few days. "I can't get hold of Martin," she said. "He was supposed to be coming over later."

"We're not having the party now, anyway," I said. "There's been a change of plan."

"Oh. Okay. Well look, the numbers for my friends from college are in my address book. Just ring Sally and she'll call everyone else. And if I can't get hold of Martin and he turns up, can you just tell him what's happened and where I am? We're going back to the hospital now."

"Of course."

I made several phone calls while Zara sat and stared out of the window. Then we sat down to watch a movie. I noticed Zara was drifting off, so I switched off the TV and made her a cup of tea.

"Sorry," said Zara, taking the cup. "It's hard to focus still." She grinned. "I really *am* losing the plot."

I smiled. "You're better than you were a few weeks ago. And that's the main thing."

"You know the funny thing," said Zara. "I knew I was talking rubbish, even while I was doing it. But I had no other thoughts to replace it with, if that makes any sense."

I nodded. "Yeah. It does, actually. It sounds like those dreams when you're doing strange things. Running around naked or something. But you know you're doing it and it's only a dream."

"Except it isn't," said Zara. "More like a living nightmare."

"Yeah. Of course. I'm sorry." I sipped my tea. "So what's it like, the illness?"

"Well, in the manic stage you think you can do anything. You can get any job, or become famous, do anything you want, so there are no worries about money. The ego's out, and you can get any man you want. But then you will slowly come down over a few days or even hours, and start to feel cut off from everyone, frightened. You don't want to go out, you can't face anything. You lose your inner world. You have no stability, no trust in anything or anybody. You're watching out for any negativity, you're hyper-sensitive to any comment by anyone. I thought you were angry with me for dating a terrorist." She paused. "And then I stopped defending it and became it, if you see what I mean. When they put me in hospital, I thought it was because I was bad. I started to identify with James, or what I thought he was. I thought I was ruthless and had a murderous mind, that I was on the same frequency as these people."

"You were thinking all of that?"

She nodded. "I was dating a bad guy. Guilty by association. And you start to read into things to prove your own point: if there was a yellow car outside it meant another bomb was coming. If an alarm went off in the hospital, it meant they knew I was involved and they were trying to shake me up. And then even with normal thoughts, things that were real, I would doubt and second guess myself so much…"

"So what started it? The psychosis? Did they tell you that, at the hospital?"

"Yeah. That's just my brain. It's how it's wired. But it's triggered by the mania, by getting too high… So now I take drugs in the morning to stop me going too high. And, inevitably, they make me feel really low. Until around this time of day. I don't feel too bad at the minute."

I squeezed her hand. "That's good."

She said, "It was triggered by the stress of studying. My exams, of course. Like last time. But it goes deeper than that. I think it was also triggered by what happened when I was a child. It's like I had to re-create the old feelings of rejection from when I was a kid and re-live them."

I nodded. "I'm sure that would have something to do with it. Did you talk to them about it?"

"They don't really talk to you, psychiatrists. They just give you drugs."

"Really?"

"Really." She shrugged. "Anyway, I suppose it's always been there with me, since I was a kid, just bubbling away under the surface, 'til the pressure just set it off. I suppose that's what happens to feelings. They've got to go somewhere."

I nodded. "Or come out in different ways. Ways you don't expect."

"Like depression," said Zara. "Either that or you kill someone."

"Mad, bad, or sad," I said.

"Yeah," said Zara. "Only I was all three."

I laughed and hugged her tight. She clung to me again and put her head on my shoulder.

I said, "You weren't bad. And James isn't a terrorist."

"I know that now," she said. "But I don't think he's ever going to want to see me again."

"But why?"

"I scared him," she said. And then she said, "He's not like you."

There was a knock at the door. I looked out of the window. There were four strange men standing on my doorstep."

When I opened the door, Shelley popped up from the midst of the crowd on the pavement like a fairy out of a cake. "Hi!" she shrieked. "Party time!"

I stood on the doorstep with my mouth open. I looked back over my shoulder.

"It's okay," said Zara from behind me. "Really."

Shelley introduced everyone. They were Gavin, and friends of Gavin, all wearing suits and short haircuts. They all looked exactly the same — one amorphous mass of grey pin-stripe and garish ties.

"You don't mind?" Shelley asked me.

"No," I lied. "I don't mind." Someone had to eat all the food, and drink the punch, I supposed.

I opened the door dutifully and they all poured in. Gavin's friend Giles hung back in the hallway.

"So." There was a pregnant pause and a slight raising of one eyebrow; Giles was evidently a Roger Moore aficionado. "This is your pad."

He eyed the decor with seeming approval.

"Well, yes," I said, hesitantly. "In a manner of speaking." Giles was now eyeing me up in the same way he'd been looking at the Gauguin prints a minute earlier. One of them was of a naked woman reclining under a tree. He looked from me to the painting and back again, and smiled.

I sidestepped him into the already crowded kitchen. I looked for Zara, and spotted her leaning up against the fridge behind Shelley and Gavin and Gavin's friend, Anthon. Malcolm handed me a glass of punch, and gave one to Giles, who had come up behind me.

"Good stuff, this," said Malcolm.

"Yes, well," I said. "I'm not quite sure what's in it, to be honest. My friend made it. Vodka, I think."

"Ah," said Giles. "But it's the fruity bits that make all the difference, wouldn't you say?" He winked at me as if this was supposed to mean something.

Shelley was handing around bowls of nibbles.

"Nuts?" she said.

"Over here," said Zara, and actually smiled. I caught her eye and winked at her.

Malcolm took a peanut from the bowl in Shelley's hand and popped it into Zara's mouth. I smiled at her and raised my eyebrows. Zara giggled, and I felt relieved. Maybe this was what she needed after all, to lift her spirits.

Giles took my glass out of my hand and topped it up again with punch, before handing it back to me.

"So, what do you do?" I asked generically, from where I stood in the middle of the kitchen. I was feeling like some stage had been missed out in the bonding process.

Malcolm chose to answer me. "Gavin's a rep for Gateway Pharmaceuticals," he said. "The rest of us are bankers."

I started to giggle, suddenly, and found I couldn't stop. Something went the wrong way down my windpipe and I started to cough.

"It's not that funny," said Malcolm.

Shelley thumped me on the back. "Everyone listen. It's Lizzie's birthday," she announced.

"Happy Birthday," everyone chorused.

"Shall we sing?" asked Malcolm.

"Please don't," I said, putting my hands over my ears.

"I know," said Giles. "Let's play some party games instead."

The party games — which were actually drinking games— ended somewhere around midnight. I had fallen over backwards into the punch bowl, which had been placed on the floor. Zara had gone to bed in Catherine's room. Shelley was running around with a tea towel and sprinkling salt onto the carpet when the doorbell rang. I tried to get up but failed, and landed up somehow sprawled in a beanbag with Giles on top of me. Someone went to the door, and a minute later Martin walked into the living room.

"Hello Martin," I heard Shelley say. "Catherine's not here. Would you like a drink?"

Martin came nearer and glanced around the room, at Malcolm and at Anthon on the sofa, at Shelley and Gavin on the floor, and at me lying in the beanbag with Giles on top of me. We all watched him in silence; it was like a scene from a Western. He looked as though he were about to draw a pair of pistols from his pockets and turn the room into a bloodbath.

After what seemed like a very long time, Martin said to Shelley, "A beer would be nice." Then he smiled and sat down.

Some time passed by, or maybe it was only minutes; it was hard to tell. I was lying in the beanbag still and the lights were way too bright. I tried to sit up, but only in my head, it seemed. Then people's legs were walking past me and I heard the front door slam.

"Hey," I said. "Where are you all going?"

"Shhh," said a voice beside me and then a mouth descended on mine and began to kiss me. I gave my brain a second or two to engage, but it was all too blurry and too much like hard work, so I closed my eyes instead.

And then something woke me again, but this time I was in my bed and there was daylight seeping through a gap in the curtains.

Something wasn't right. I turned my head and saw that there was someone next to me, sleeping. I lay there for a moment, trying to work out who he was and how he had got into my bed, and also how I'd got into my bed, come to think of it. And then I realised that I was naked. And that the body of the man next to me was naked too. And just as the enormity of the whole situation was beginning to hit me and bring me smack bang back to my senses, he stretched, and yawned, and turned towards me.

"Morning," said Martin, and smiled.

18

MARTIN MOVED CLOSER and put his arm round my waist. I froze, involuntarily then shifted slightly and pulled away.

"What's wrong?" he asked.

"I don't understand," I said. "What are you doing in my bed?"

"Oh, come on," he said, half laughing, half annoyed. He held out his arm. "Come here."

"Don't." I pushed him away. "Don't touch me."

I wanted to get up and get dressed but I didn't want him to see me naked. Although I was guessing that that part had already happened.

Martin sighed. "Oh come on," he said again. "Don't play the innocent."

"What do you mean?" I pulled the covers up to my chin and tried to sit up. My head swam, and I immediately lay back down again.

"You know you wanted it," he added. "You were up for it."

"Up for *what*?" I cast my mind back to the previous evening but I couldn't remember anything at all after around midnight apart from laying in a beanbag with Giles. "What exactly happened last night? And how did I... did *we* get in here?"

Martin snorted and sat up. "Right. We're going down that road, are we?"

Fear began to prickle inside me. Martin was staring down at me, looking directly into my eyes, in a searching but menacing manner, and I knew with a jolt to the stomach this was not going to end up well.

"I need you to go," I said, quietly. My mouth was so dry, I could barely speak. My stomach was in knots. "I need to get dressed."

"Right!" Martin threw back the bedclothes and stood up. I caught a glimpse of his broad, lean back as he rose, and hastily shut my eyes.

I slunk down further under the bedclothes and waited. I could hear him silently moving around, picking up his clothes and zipping up his jeans.

Suddenly, I heard my chair screech across the parquet floor. There was an audible thump against the wall, followed a split second later by a thud landing heavily on the pillow next to my head. My head bounced slightly and I opened my eyes, startled. Martin thumped the pillow again and I jumped.

"You bitch," he snarled. "You led me on."

I shrunk back under the bedclothes. I noticed fleetingly that my doll was no longer on the chair where Zara had put her the previous day. I glanced down and saw her face down on the floor near Martin's feet, her raggedy checked skirt tipped up over her head. Martin followed my gaze and with one swift kick sent the doll flying across the room.

"Please," I said. "Don't. My dad gave me that."

Martin turned and kicked the bed, and I jumped again.

"Zara's in Catherine's room, you know," I added, hastily. I hoped desperately that that was still true.

Martin stopped moving around and glared at me. "What are you on about?" he said, nastily, but more quietly.

"She stayed the night," I muttered.

Martin looked uncomprehendingly at the adjoining wall to Catherine's room, looked back at me again and then sat down on the bed and put his head in his hands. He clearly hadn't planned on there being a witness. He leaned forward slightly and didn't move. I could see he was plotting his next move. Finally, he picked up his shoes and put them on.

He turned and looked at me.

"You say anything to Catherine, about this," he said. "And I'll tell her you seduced me. I'll tell her it was all you. And you won't see her for dust."

"Martin, I was legless!" I objected. "How could I lead you on?"

"How? For months. From the start. You were at it the day I met you."

I started to laugh, then stopped myself.

"Just try it," he hissed, leaning over the bed. He grabbed my jaw with his thumb and forefinger and pushed my head sharply back, so that my mouth was all squashed up and my lips pursed stupidly. "You just try it. Say a word to her — and see what happens next."

It felt as if I had frozen into a block of ice, except that my face was burning and my heart was pounding heavily against my ribcage. Martin's face was right up close to mine. Then he let me go, suddenly, and pushed me sharply at the same time, so that I fell back and hit my head hard against the wall. I closed my eyes again and waited for the ringing in my ears to stop.

I heard the front door slam and realised he was gone.

I opened my eyes and let the room come back into focus. I lay where I was for several minutes. My head felt sore, but the coolness of the wall felt good against my cheek.

"Lizzie? Who was that?" said Zara, poking her head sleepily round the bedroom door. "I thought everyone had gone?" I sensed her stop in her tracks when she saw me lying at a funny angle on the bed, my cheek still pressed up against the wall.

"Do me a favour Zara," I asked, shakily. "Get me a drink?"

Zara nodded. "Sure." She disappeared, unquestioningly, and came back a moment later with a glass of water, which she placed carefully on my bedside table.

"Are you all right, Lizzie?" she said, softly, and knelt down beside me. I shook my head, bit my lip, and tried very hard not to cry.

"I'll be okay, sweetie," I said. "Just give me a minute, would you?"

"Okay." Zara bent down, picked up the doll, and put her on the bed next to me. Then she left the room. I could hear her moving around. Eventually I got up, picked up my clothes from the floor, showered, and dressed shakily and wandered into the lounge.

Zara was sitting on the sofa, looking at a magazine. She had emptied the ashtrays and cleaned and washed up all the dishes, and all traces of the party had been more or less wiped away. All that remained in the kitchen were a couple of French sticks, a pile of napkins, and most of the plastic glasses, still stacked upside down on top of the washing machine.

Zara followed me into the kitchen and paused in the doorway. "Whatever's happened," she said. "You can be upset. I'm okay."

I turned and forced a smile. "It's okay," I said. "I'll be all right."

"I'm not going to crack up," she persisted.

"Ditto," I smiled again. "I promised, right?"

"I know," she said. "I *know*. And it's okay to be upset."

I put my hands palms down on the worktop and breathed steadily for a moment. Zara was still standing silently in the doorway. I walked over, picked up the napkins and opened a drawer, then paused, changed my mind and dropped them into the bin instead. Something strange was happening inside me; my legs felt weak and my skin was prickling, and I had butterflies in my chest. I opened the window to let in some air, and before I really knew what I'd done, I'd picked up the remaining two French sticks and hurled them out in the direction Martin had just gone. And then I stood in the middle of the kitchen and screamed.

It wasn't a high-pitched piercing frightened-type scream, but a deep, angry, throaty roar. I picked up a stack of plastic glasses from the washing machine and hurled one across the kitchen at the window. The plastic glass shattered on impact and splinters flew off in all directions. I threw another, and it hit the wall and bounced off the cupboards and smashed against the floor. I threw another, and another. Something inside me took over and soon the whole pile had gone and there were splinters of plastic glass all over the worktops and the floor and in the sink. One by one, I worked my way through stack after stack of glasses until there were no more left. The kitchen was a sea of broken plastic. I sank to my knees on the floor in the midst of it all and put my head in my hands and cried.

Time seemed to stand still, then; I seemed to be locked on my hands and knees on the kitchen floor with a vague impression of Zara hovering uncertainly in the doorway. After a while, she took my arm and lifted me up out of the pile of broken plastic and took me into the lounge. I was still crying; I couldn't stop — I just went on and on, weeping gently one minute, and then sobbing violently the next. All the while, Zara sat next to me, holding my hand.

"It was Martin," I said eventually, my voice hoarse. "I slept with him. Or so he says. I don't remember a thing."

"Martin? *Catherine*'s Martin? I didn't even know he was here. Was that him who just left?"

I nodded.

Zara looked angry, and I was scared for a split second that her anger was directed at me. She put her hand on my arm and I breathed out. "Did he hurt you?"

"A bit," I admitted. "Not much. He just frightened me mostly. He made me promise not to tell."

"*What?*"

"He said I led him on. Maybe I did, somehow. I don't know. But I let it happen. With *him*. What does that make me?"

"You didn't," said Zara.

"Didn't what?"

"Lead him on. Let it happen."

"That's what he says. He says I've been coming on to him for months."

"You haven't! I've never seen you. He's bound to say that. He's just trying to justify what he's done. Please don't blame yourself."

"How can I not blame myself? I've slept with my best friend's boyfriend!"

"Oh, Lizzie, I think it was the punch. Giles kept topping up your glass and giving it to you. I saw him do it. But I don't think anyone realised it was that strong."

"But I didn't have to drink it. I didn't have to let him near me." My words began to tumble out so fast that I barely stopped for breath. "This has all happened because of me. Because I'm lonely. Because I'm empty. Because I miss Larsen so fucking much that I sometimes can't bear it, can't bear to be alone for one more second. But no one compares, Zara. No one compares. And I'm terrified! I'm absolutely terrified. Because I don't know if they ever will!"

Zara nodded and continued to hold my hand.

"I know," she said. "I know. And I think you're really brave."

"Brave? Or stupid?"

"Brave. If it was me… well, I know I would have taken the easy option. I would never have let him go."

I looked down at my knees and sighed. "Look where it's got me."

"It's got you your independence. You're your own person," said Zara. "You're so capable and strong. You don't need a man to feel whole. Not like me. I really admire you for that."

"I need love too," I said. "That's why this happened."

"No, it's not. You were out of it and he took advantage of you. That's what happened. I admire your self-honesty, Lizzie, I really do, but you take too much responsibility for things that are not your fault — and people like him, they can see it. They know that's your weakness, and they take advantage of that."

"You think?"

"I *know*," said Zara. "I know. And the reason I know is because I'm the same. When someone falls out with Shelley, she turns around and she tells herself, 'What's their fucking problem?' But me, I always think it's me."

"I know. Me too. It's *shit*," I said.

"Shit," repeated Zara.

We sat that way for a long time, me curled up in a corner of the sofa and Zara just holding my hand. Eventually, she stirred beside me.

"Don't go!" I said.

"I won't," she said. "I promise. I'll be back in a minute. Tea," she added. "We need tea, at a time like this."

I lay back on the sofa, exhausted. Behind the humming in my ears I could vaguely hear the sounds in the background of Zara filling the kettle and clearing up in the kitchen, sweeping up the broken plastic and dropping it into the bin. I was aware of her coming back in with my duvet and putting it over me. After that, I must have fallen asleep.

When I woke, it was late afternoon. Zara was sitting on the arm of the chair, hugging her knees and staring out of the window. The weather had turned bad and streaks of rain were making runny broken lines down the window pane. Raindrops pattered gently against the sill.

"Hi. How're you feeling?" Zara said, seeing my eyes open. I thought about it for a moment.

"Better," I said.

The phone started ringing.

"It's okay," said Zara. "I'll get it." And then, "It's Catherine," she said.

My heart stopped in my chest and a wave of guilt washed over me. Catherine. What on earth was I going to say to her?

Zara passed me the phone.

"Hi, Catherine," I said, as brightly as I could muster.

"Hi," she said. "It's all okay, everything is fine. Dad's on the mend. He can talk, and move, and he's already giving my mum a hard time." She laughed. "I'm going to stay another day or two, though. It's been quite nice spending time with my mum again."

I took a deep breath. "I'm so glad, so pleased that everything's all right."

"You okay?"

"Yes. Yes, I'm fine." I looked up at the ceiling and screwed my eyes up tight. All I wanted was to see her, to fling my arms around her and tell her that she meant the world to me and that I would never in a million years have deliberately done anything to hurt her. And yet, I knew that this would kill her. There would always be a wedge between us, whatever way you looked at it. Even if she understood. Even if I ignored Martin, and told her. She would be so hurt. And then it would always be there, simmering away between us.

"Come on, Lizzie. It's me you're talking to. What's wrong?"

I took another deep breath. "Oh, nothing. Just drank a bit too much of your punch last night."

"You had the party!" Catherine sounded pleased.

"Sort of."

"Did all the food get eaten? Did Martin come? I still haven't been able to get hold of him."

I paused. "No," I said.

"Oh. Right. That's strange."

I tried to think of something to say, but was lost for words.

"Oh well, I'll try him again later," said Catherine. "I hope you feel better, honey. I'll see you in a couple of days."

I put the receiver down and put my head in my hands.

"What sort of a friend am I?" I asked Zara, through my fingers. "I sleep with her boyfriend and lie to her."

"I told you. It wasn't your fault. Any of this."

I looked at her and shook my head. "I doubt Catherine would see it that way."

"She would if she was a real friend. Maybe you should just tell her."

I shook my head again. "I can't."

"Why?"

"Because he told me not to. And if I do, he'll twist it so that it *was* my fault, and she'll believe him."

"How do you know that?"

"Oh, I know that."

"But how can you be so sure?"

"Because," I said. "She loves him."

Zara shrugged. "The truth will out," she said. "It always does."

"Only in the movies," I told her.

Zara was silent.

"Look," she said, eventually. "I was thinking about going over to see Uncle Silbert."

"When?"

"Now. Do you want to come?"

I realised that it was very much what I wanted. I nodded and got up off the sofa and went into the bedroom and sat down in front of the mirror. I stared at my reflection; my eyes were swollen and red. There was a slight lump at the back of my head where I had fallen against the wall. I ran my finger over it. It was tender to the touch and I bit my lip to stop myself from crying again.

Then I remembered Uncle Silbert's words to me: *know your own truths*. And I realised with sudden clarity that what Zara had said was the truth, *my* truth. The way I was feeling right now, this was evidence that it *did* happen the way that Zara said. I hadn't invited this. I hadn't invited any of it. Any decent bloke, like Larsen, or Tim, would never have done what Martin had done and then tried to pass the blame onto me. I realised that the only way in which I had let myself down was by not trusting myself, by being so hard on myself.

Zara came into the bedroom behind me and sat down on the bed.

"You know," I said, looking up at her. "It's not just Larsen. I think I miss my dad."

Zara nodded. She bent down and picked up my doll and placed it into my arms. I hugged the doll and smiled up at Zara's reflection in the mirror.

"Don't worry," said Zara from behind me. She put her arms around me. "You mustn't worry. Everything's going to be all right."

19

THE LIFT STILL WASN'T WORKING and we had to walk up the stairs again. When we got to the top, I walked up to the edge of the railings and peered over. It was such a long way down. The cars in the road below all looked so tiny, like matchbox ones. It made my head spin to look at them. I flattened myself against the wall while Zara banged on the door.

"Uncle Silbert!" she called through the letterbox. We waited for a few minutes, and then she tried again. She turned to face me. "It's awfully quiet in there," she said.

Five minutes later, we decided we would have to break the lock, but neither of us knew how to do it. In the end we found a brick and smashed a window into one of the unused rooms, and Zara climbed through. A few minutes later the front door opened and she was standing in the hallway. All the blood was drained from her face.

"Call an ambulance," she said and skidded off back down the hallway.

I raced downstairs to find a neighbour with a telephone, then ran back up again, and into the kitchen. Uncle Silbert was hunched over in a chair by the gas stove, his head hanging forward and his eyes closed. He was wearing Zara's red jumper over his pyjamas and a dressing gown over the top. His face was chalky white and his lips were blue. His bony fingers were twisted together in his lap.

"Is he... all right?" I asked, stupidly.

"No," said Zara. "He's not all right, at all. He's breathing, but only just."

She crouched on the floor in front of him and grabbed his hands. "Uncle Silbert. Can you hear me?" she shouted.

Fear crept up inside me. My heart started thumping in my chest and I felt my legs starting to give way from underneath me. I grabbed at the wall and propped myself up. "Oh God, no," I whispered. "Please don't let anything happen to him."

"Uncle Silbert," shouted Zara again. "Can you hear me? Can you hear me?" she repeated over and over again. She stood up and slapped his cheeks, pushed his head back and reached into his mouth.

"What are you doing?" I asked her, as she whipped out his teeth and plonked them on the table beside him.

"See if you can find another blanket," said Zara. "Go and have a look in the bedroom."

There was only a sheet and one blanket on the unmade bed. It didn't look as though it had been slept in.

"Good," said Zara when I came back in. "Now wrap it around him. Keep his arms away from his body." She was holding a lighted match over the gas stove but nothing was happening. "Damn, no gas," she said. She looked up at me in astonishment. "He must have been cut off."

Just at that moment Uncle Silbert's neighbour came in through the front door with two paramedics. They covered his face with an oxygen mask and lifted him onto a stretcher while we watched in silence. As they lifted him up, I touched his shoulder. It felt hard and shell-like through the thin layers of clothing. Then they were gone, out of the door, and down the steps.

The journey down was fraught with difficulty as the stairwell wasn't wide enough and turned at funny angles. Zara and I hung back anxiously as they manoeuvred the stretcher up and down and around the corners; it all seemed to be going on forever. Finally we got to the bottom and they put him into the ambulance. Zara jumped in after him.

"See you there," she said.

The rain was still dribbling down dismally as I drove to the hospital. I parked the car and hurried across the car park to the now familiar entrance to Saint Barts' Accident and Emergency department. The waiting room, as usual, was packed.

Zara and Shelley met me in the corridor. Shelley had just finished her shift. Two elderly ladies and a young man were pushed up against the wall on trolley-beds.

"Which way?" I asked.

"He's in there," said Zara, pointing to a curtained-off room further down the corridor. "We have to wait."

"What's happening?" I asked.

"It's pneumonia," said Zara. "They've got him on a drip." She wiped at her eyes with the back of her hand. "Anyway. They're doing everything they can."

"Zara?" A doctor was walking towards us. He nodded to us, took Zara by the arm and led her into the room behind the curtain. Shelley and I sat down and waited. The corridor was brightly lit, as if they were trying to keep everyone awake. My eyes felt tight and weary despite the fact that I'd slept all afternoon.

"What happened to you lot, last night?" I asked Shelley. "Why did you all just disappear?"

She shook her head and frowned. "Don't you know? Martin kicked us out."

"What! Why?"

"I thought you realised," she said. "You saw the way he was acting, right? Mind you," she added. "You were pretty well gone. I think he thought Giles was trying to take advantage of you. Which," she added. "He probably was, knowing Giles. So I suppose he was just doing the right thing."

"Who?"

"Martin. Your knight in shining armour."

I heaved a big sigh and said nothing.

"Although," said Shelley. "He was a bit out of order, the way he went about it, ordering us all around. Gavin wanted to clock him one." Shelley paused and looked at me out of the corner of her eye. "No offence to Catherine, but I would definitely say he fancies you."

I looked at my feet.

"So you were okay, then?" Shelley persisted. "After?"

"Yeah," I lied, still looking at my feet. "I was okay. Just, you know, went to bed. Slept it off."

We seemed to sit there for a very long time.

"It's a good sign, isn't it, don't you think?" I said, eventually.

"What is?"

"That they've been in there so long."

Shelley shook her head. "That's just the consultation room," she said. "He's not out of the woods yet."

Zara lifted the curtain and came out.

"What's happening?" I asked her.

"They've got nowhere to put him. They want to take him to Homerton," she said.

"What? He's got pneumonia... how can they?" I asked.

The doctor appeared behind her. "I'm afraid we simply don't have a bed for him here. It's the nearest hospital with beds," he said. "An ambulance will be arranged."

I went to fetch the car. Shelley and I followed the ambulance through the now pouring rain, which was battering against the roof of the car in torrents and flooding the road ahead of us. I switched my wipers onto the fastest setting.

"Jesus Christ," said Shelley, and shook her head.

We drove up past the Barbican towards Old Street and into Hackney, all the time staring at the tail lights of the ambulance ahead of us. They were just a few hundred yards in front of us, but the back doors were obscured by the lights and the rain. It felt strange to be so close yet so far away.

We passed London Fields and pulled into Homerton High Street. Finally, the lights of the hospital shone out like a beacon through the darkness.

I pulled up outside the entrance. Zara was getting out of the ambulance in front of us and standing in the rain watching as they brought out the stretcher, her hair plastered to her head and the wind whipping at her flimsy top - which was now wet through, and even more see through — and flapping the edges of Uncle Silbert's blankets. I pressed my face up to the windscreen and squinted as they passed through the beam of my headlights but the respirator was over his face and they moved quickly away and through the double doors into the hospital.

I turned to Shelley. "Go on in," I said. "I'll park the car and come and find you."

"I'll wait for you in the entrance," she promised.

I drove around the car park several times. The rain was coming down in huge sheets, the droplets dancing in the light from my headlamps. Every time I thought I'd found a space, the bumper of another car reared up before me, and I had to keep stopping and reversing, and driving around again. Finally, I rounded a corner to find a car backing out from a space. I slammed on my brakes, skidded to a halt and edged hurriedly into the gap. I ran across the car park with my bag over my head, rain soaking through my shoes and splashing up my jeans. I met Shelley at the entrance and we hurried down the corridor in the direction Zara had gone. As we rounded the corner we saw her sitting on a chair in an empty corridor, her hair still wet and clinging to her head.

"Where is he?" asked Shelley, as we ran up to her. Zara lifted her head and looked at us, her face blank.

"In there," she said, nodding towards a room opposite.

"Can we go in and see him?" I moved towards the door. Zara didn't say anything. I stopped. "Zara?"

"You can if you want to," she murmured.

"Of course we want to," I said, turning the handle. I stopped again. "He's going to be okay, right?"

Zara looked up at me, as if seeing me for the first time. "You don't understand," she said, shaking her head, her voice fading to a barely audible whisper. "Uncle Silbert... well, he's in there still. But he died a few minutes ago."

I stayed at Zara's, the two of us huddled up in her bed, and we both slept until lunchtime the following day. When Zara woke she sat up and said, "I'm going to be sick," before running off to the bathroom.

"You okay?" I asked when she returned.

She nodded and climbed back into bed. "It's probably just the upset," she said. "Or tiredness. I feel so amazingly tired."

"Well, you just get some rest. I'll make some tea and toast."

I went down into the kitchen. When I came back up again with a tray, Zara had fallen back to sleep. I climbed back into bed beside her and drank my tea and nibbled on a piece of toast and then I lay back down and drifted back to sleep as well. It was late afternoon when I woke again. Zara was still asleep. I decided in the circumstances to leave her in bed. I couldn't see the point in insisting she get up when I didn't feel much like facing the world myself.

"I've got to go," I whispered into her ear. "But I'll call you later. And I'll come around after work tomorrow."

"Okay," Zara nodded without opening her eyes.

I got dressed and went downstairs. The house was quiet. Shelley and Tim must still have been at work. I didn't want to leave Zara alone, but I was due back at work the next day, and there was still some clearing up to do back at the flat before Catherine came home. I shut the front door behind me and walked down the road to where I had parked my car.

The flat felt empty and strange. I instantly regretted having returned on my own. It was as if time had stopped still since I had woken the previous morning and found Martin in my bed. I wandered around the flat. Every room reminded me of him and what had happened. I stripped the bedclothes and threw everything into the washing machine and tipped all of the remaining party food into the bin. I picked up my doll and held her tight, but the comfort I had found in Uncle Silbert's words to me the day before had gone, now that he himself was no longer here to share his wisdom and his love.

I found myself standing staring out of the window for what seemed like hours, immobile with fear and hurt and guilt and grief. My stomach was churning but I couldn't eat, or sit down, or clear up, or do anything at all, except stare out of the window and wish that I could turn back time.

Suddenly, I spotted Catherine crossing the mews, her rucksack slung over one shoulder. My spirits immediately lifted. I watched with relief as she walked up the path, fishing around in her handbag for her keys. I moved out from under the curtain, and went to open the door for her, but then stopped as I caught sight of Martin's car, which was turning into the garages and reversing around.

As the key turned in the lock and the front door opened I saw the look on Catherine's face and knew instantly that she knew. She looked back at me as she closed the door, and said nothing.

"Hi," I said, weakly.

"Hi," she said. "I've come to get my things. I'm moving out."

"Why?" I asked pointlessly.

She stopped and looked at me, her chest rising and falling heavily. Her eyes had a misty, far away look, which made her appear as though she was at peace, like a Buddha, but actually meant she had been crying. Catherine wasn't the kind of person to lash out. She wasn't the kind of person to punish me either. She was simply hurt. And so she was going to leave.

"Look, I'm not going to do this now," she said. "Martin's waiting for me in the car. I understand why you did it. I know you're lonely. But you've hurt me more than you will ever know."

"Look, Catherine," I said. "I don't know what he's told you…"

"Only the truth," she said. "Which is why I just can't look at you right now."

She turned her back on me and walked into her bedroom. I followed her. I stood in the doorway and watched as she opened up her rucksack, which I now realised was empty. She pulled her suitcase down from on top of the wardrobe and began scooping up her makeup and her jewellery and putting things into bags.

"Catherine, please," I begged her. I held my hand out towards her. "Go if you want, leave if you have to. But first please, *please* give me a chance to explain."

"What is there to say?" she said, with her back to me. "You wanted my man, and now you've had him. It's almost ruined things between us. And now me and him have got a lot of sorting out to do."

"Look," I said. "I don't know what he's told you, but has it occurred to you that it might not be the truth?"

"Martin wouldn't lie to me," she said, looking up at me with a saintly expression, almost as if she were proud of him. "Whatever he has done, he wouldn't lie. He said that's why he had to tell me. He didn't want any secrets between us." She didn't have to say "unlike you" because it was written all over her face.

"He told me not to tell you," I muttered, but I knew it was futile.

"He told me you'd say that. He didn't want me hurt. He wanted to wait until he knew I was okay, until he knew my Dad was all right."

It occurred to me that when I had last seen him, Martin had not even mentioned Catherine's father, nor had he appeared to be even remotely concerned about him. He had clearly known she wasn't coming home that night, third hand from Shelley, perhaps. But he hadn't even asked me where Catherine was, what was wrong with her dad, or which hospital he was in.

"He told you not to say anything because he didn't want me upset," Catherine continued. "And he thought it would be better coming from him."

I shook my head. "I bet he did."

Catherine folded the last of her clothes, the pink, white and blue floral sundress that we had bought together back last autumn and a navy blue chenille shirt that I loved and had borrowed many times. She placed them in the suitcase and folded down the lid. I leaned over and put my hand on the top.

"Please, Catherine," I begged her. "Don't go back to him. I don't care if you hate me, but please don't go back to him. He's lying to you. He doesn't care about anyone but himself. He's not safe to be around."

Catherine picked up my hand and removed it from her suitcase. I started to cry. She looked at me for a moment, then turned away and pushed the bulging lid down and zipped it up. "Funny," she said. "That's what he said about you."

"I don't hit people!" I sobbed. "I don't threaten them!"

"Oh Lizzie, get over that, will you. That was a long time ago. He's not that person anymore."

"He is!" I pleaded. "He hasn't changed! What happened with me and him, that was his doing, not mine. He hurt me!"

Catherine turned to look at me. "What do you mean, he hurt you?"

"He was angry," I said. "When I wanted him to go. He grabbed me. Pushed me."

She stood still, looking at me for a moment. Then she shook her head. "I don't believe you. Why would I? I can't trust anything you say anymore." She picked up her handbag and turned to face me. "And it doesn't matter what you say, Lizzie. Nothing you say can change what's happened. I just can't be around you right now, that's all."

She staggered past me with her arms full of bags and opened the front door.

I wiped my eyes and followed her with her suitcase. As Catherine walked down the path she said something to Martin, and he got out of the car and came to the front door and took her suitcase from me. I tried to look him in the eye but he glanced away. He avoided looking at me until Catherine was in the car. And then he turned, as he drove away, and he looked directly at me, and he smiled.

20

THEY BURIED UNCLE SILBERT two weeks later, a sunny Tuesday morning in late June, "they" being the vicar and a taciturn but ostentatious middle-aged man whom I suspected to be his grandson. He was dressed in a long suede jacket with a fur collar, and had a portly stomach and a long shiny black car. I thought his car was the hearse when it first arrived but that came along afterwards, rolling reverently over the gravel towards us. When it stopped he got out and stood by the car door and waited without saying a word, and it seemed as if there was going to be no one else; so we three girls led the way inside, followed awkwardly by the small crowd in the porch.

All in all there were fewer than a dozen people: us, a handful of neighbours, two district nurses, and the man in the suede jacket, who had to keep going outside to answer his mobile phone. It would have been more if you'd counted the six pallbearers, but they didn't stay for the service. I found myself feeling glad for the first time that Uncle Silbert had died with nothing; nothing, at least, that his family could get their undeserving hands on. I hoped that the funeral had been expensive.

We took the front row and stood and watched as they lowered the coffin down solemnly onto the empty grating before the altar. The nurses were in the middle somewhere behind us, the neighbours huddled apologetically into a pew at the back, mumbling into their prayer books. Shelley, Zara, and I sang out loudly, to compensate, our voices echoing plaintively around the empty chapel.

When the service was over, we tramped over the springy mounds of grass that covered the graveyard and watched as they lowered the coffin into the ground. Zara was standing next to me, crying softly, while the vicar talked a lot about Jesus and only very abstractly about Silbert and it even made me wonder for a split second if they'd got the right person, if anyone really knew who it was laying there anonymously in the coffin in the ground.

"I can't remember what he looks like," I burst out in a loud whisper to Zara, then looked up, worried that I had interrupted the vicar's monologue. I felt a sudden surge of fear, fear that he would slip away and I'd make myself forget him and that then I wouldn't be able to grieve again for another twenty years.

I felt Zara slip her hand into mine. "Just close your eyes," she whispered.

So I did. I stood there holding Zara's hand and wobbling slightly on the uneven ground, the brim of my hat shading my face from the already warm morning sun. I closed my eyes and then I saw him quite clearly, lying there with his pale face and his thin lips and his aquiline nose, dressed in Zara's red jumper with his bony arms sticking out at the sleeves.

When I opened my eyes again, Tim was standing opposite. He was wearing a long dark coat and black boots despite the heat, and his head was bent down. It struck me how handsome he looked, like some hero from a period drama. Sensing my eyes on him, maybe, he glanced up briefly and I smiled at him. He smiled back and winked at me, and I felt such a warm glow inside that in that moment I wondered if I loved him, maybe, after all. Tim's eyes continued to meet mine. I blushed and looked back down again into the ground.

"...and Jesus said unto them," said the vicar, "this is the gateway to heaven. And therein will you find your salvation."

Then he added something about holy washing and I had to let go of Zara's hand and turn away under the pretence of a coughing fit, but really I was trying to stop myself from laughing because all I could see when I closed my eyes was a row of mine and Catherine's knickers hanging over a radiator in some heavenly bathroom, glowing ethereally in the everlasting light — which in turn triggered a knot of pain in my chest, because Catherine wasn't here, and I was pretty certain that I would never see her underwear draped over the towel rail in my bathroom again. Heaven only knew if I would ever see her again, at all.

When the service was over, Zara and Shelley stopped to talk to the vicar and I headed off with Tim through the gravestones and through the trees until we reached a stile crossing a fence into the car park beyond. My high heels were sinking into the soft turf. We stopped for a moment and I pulled off each shoe in turn, and scraped off the moss and earth with a finger.

"Here," said Tim, as I wobbled, and offered me his arm. I grabbed hold of the sleeve of his coat, and Tim steadied me, with an arm around my waist. I glanced back briefly towards the church entrance where the girls were waiting. Zara was standing on the path, shading her eyes with her hands. She nodded towards the car park, then pointed to the church, and she and Shelley wandered off up the path towards the vestry.

Tim was climbing over the stile, his coat sweeping the fence.

"Sit a minute," he said, pulling me down next to him on the stile. We sat silently for a moment, watching as Zara and Shelley disappeared round the corner.

"Zara seems well, given what's happened," I commented. "I thought this might set her back, losing Uncle Silbert. But it doesn't seem to have done."

"She's been good," said Tim. "She seems to be on the mend."

"She certainly looks happy."

"How about you? Are you okay?" asked Tim.

"Not really," I said. "I feel like some kind of rug has been pulled from underneath me. Everything's falling apart."

Tim took my hand and held it tight. "You mean Uncle Silbert?"

"Partly, yes."

I paused. And then I told him about Martin. I wasn't sure how he would react, but I owed him an explanation, or something. Or maybe I just needed to connect with him, with my remaining friends. I needed to not feel so alone. But when I'd told him, Tim looked hurt and angry, and he let go of my hand. I realised that I'd done the wrong thing and isolated him instead.

"The bastard," he said.

"It's really hurt Catherine. And now she's gone."

"She'll get over it," he said.

"I doubt it."

Tim stared away up into the trees. I knew that he was angry with me as well as Martin. I knew that he felt betrayed. I knew that he was secretly wondering whether I really wanted Martin. I now regretted having told him.

"I never wanted it to happen," I said. "If that's what you're thinking. I knew he liked me, it's true, I could sense that. But it was all one way. I swear. And even if it wasn't, do you seriously think I would have risked hurting Catherine, risked my friendship with her? Apart from Zara, she was the best friend I ever had."

"I'd like to punch his face in," said Tim.

I sighed. Tim was no different from any other bloke in this respect. His pride was hurt because he felt that I was his. And that was all that he could think about.

Tim sat and looked at the church in silence. I turned away and put my head in my hands.

"It's not just about him," I said. "It's triggered things. Other things. I just can't stop feeling frightened. I feel like something terrible is about to happen, every minute of the day."

Tim didn't say anything for a moment. Then he said, "Let me look after you."

I swallowed hard and wiped my eyes on the back of my hand. Tim put his hands on my shoulders and turned me around to face him. "I love you, Lizzie," he said. "I've loved you from the very first moment I set eyes on you."

I looked up at him and smiled, briefly. For a few moments we just sat there, the air around us warm and still, the sweet, sickly smell of cow parsley, clover, and knapweed mingling and rising up from the hedgerows.

Then Tim said, quietly, so that I almost didn't hear him, "But you don't love me."

I looked up again. "I do..." I began, but I was too slow.

Tim got up and looked me squarely in the eye. I could see he was angry again.

"Bullshit," he said, and jumped off the fence and into the car park.

"Tim!" I yelled after him, but he was gone.

Back at the house we sat in the living room, where we ordinarily never sat, and surveyed each other in gloomy silence. It was a big room. There were a couple of paintings propped up on the floor against the wall and dustsheets over the furniture. The room, which was cold and never got enough light anyway, was suitably funereal. It looked like the front room in an American horror movie.

Zara kept getting up and making tea. Every time she got up and went out to the kitchen I jumped, thinking there had been a knock on the door and that she was going to answer it.

"He's got a key," said Shelley, after a while.

"I know," I said. "I just feel bad, that's all."

Zara came back in with the teapot.

"He'll come back," said Shelley. "When he's ready."

Zara put down the teapot and stared at her, her tear-stained face illuminated with hope.

"Do you really think so?" she said in a whisper.

"She doesn't mean Uncle Silbert," I told her. "She's talking about Tim."

"Oh," said Zara. "I see." She sat by the window and stared out onto the front lawn. "I can't believe he's gone," she said.

"Who are we talking about now?" asked Shelley.

"Uncle Silbert," I offered. "And maybe he will. That's what Catherine would say. Maybe he's here with us now."

"He is," said Zara. "I know it. I can feel him around us."

"You're spinning me out now," said Shelley. "I'll go and make some more tea."

When Shelley was out of earshot, Zara grinned and said, "I've got something to tell you."

I felt something tighten inside my chest, a fluttering of my heart. I seemed to have been in this semi-permanent state of anxiety since the day after the party, since Uncle Silbert died. It felt as though I was waiting for something bad to happen at every turn.

"What is it?" I asked. "Are you okay?"

"You bet," said Zara. "I'm more than okay."

"More than okay?" I said. "Doesn't that mean 'not okay', for you?"

"No," laughed Zara. "It doesn't. It means I'm pregnant."

"What? Are you sure?"

"I'm certain. I've been to the doctor. I thought it was just what with being ill and everything that I was so late. It didn't even occur to me that that was what it was. But the doctor confirmed it. I'm ten weeks gone."

"Oh my God! That's… incredible."

"I know." Zara grinned happily.

I hesitated. "So… well, you're having it?"

"Of course I'm having it Lizzie!" Zara looked at me as if I was stupid. "This is what I've always wanted, all my life! You know that. You know I always regretted not having the baby before, Doug's baby. Now I've got a chance to get over that."

"But… what did the doctor say?"

"He said I'm having a baby." Zara was starting to look cross.

"But… what about the illness? And the drugs?"

"He's taken me off the mood stabiliser and put me on a different anti-depressant."

"So, the doctor said it's okay?"

"Yes."

"I mean, did he say you should have it?"

Zara hesitated. "Yes. Of course. You don't kill a baby just because you're depressed."

"I know that. But you weren't just depressed, Zara, you were psychotic."

"It's my choice. He said it was my choice."

"But what did he advise?"

Zara was silent. I looked across at her, sitting curled up in the armchair in the corner, her legs underneath her, her hands in her lap and her golden hair tumbling over her shoulders. She looked calm and peaceful, more so than I'd seen her in a long time. "He said it wasn't going to be easy," she admitted. "But that it was my choice."

I sighed. "Well, of course. That's true."

"Life changes direction," said Zara. "You just have to go with it. You have to 'Feel the Fear and do it anyway'."

I said, "That book's not for people with manic depression, Zara."

Zara grinned back at me and we both burst out laughing.

"See? I'm well now," said Zara. "I *feel* well. I'll be fine."

"Okay," I said.

"Okay?"

"Okay." I paused. "Are you going to tell James?" I asked her. "I assume it's his?"

"No. I mean, yes, it's his. But I'm not going to tell him. He doesn't want me. And I can tell you right now, he won't want the baby. He'll think it's a trap. And he'll pressure me to get rid of it. Like Doug did. I'm not having that."

"You don't know that!"

"Oh, yes I do. He's young. He's ambitious. He doesn't want a family. And if he did, he certainly wouldn't want a baby with me. Not with my genes. The last time I saw him he looked at me like I was crazy."

"You were," I smiled. "A bit."

Zara smiled. "I know. But I'm not anymore. My nurse said that I may not have another episode for years."

"Was that really what she said?"

"Okay. She said I could also have one again next week."

"And coming off the medication?"

"She said that it was a possibility that the pregnancy hormones would keep me 'buoyant'."

"But?"

"But that I could get ill again."

"So, about James… well, I just thought, if you get ill again then… maybe you could do with the help."

"No. He won't help. He won't want it." Zara's face suddenly lit up. "Hey, though. Here's an idea. You could help me. We could do it together. Didn't you say that you'd have to move out of Lynne's at some point? You could move in here, have Clare's room. We could bring it up together!"

As Zara turned away from the window to face me, her golden hair caught the light and glowed like a buttercup, and for a second I could see her aura spread out all around her. I watched her little chin jut out and her big blue eyes wrinkle up the way they did whenever she asked a question. I thought about Tim. And I thought about how safe and secure it would be, the four of us living here like a family, with Zara's baby.

And then I thought about Larsen, about Catherine, and Uncle Silbert, and the fear came creeping back again. It was like a sick feeling that just kept rising up in my chest like bile, and never really going away. But I couldn't talk about how I was feeling because I knew that Zara would try and reassure me, and there was simply nothing

anyone could say to make it go away. So I sat there on the sofa in the
dusky living room, which smelled of joss sticks and dust and Zara's
oil paints which were spread out across the table, and I just smiled
and said, "Maybe we could," because I didn't know how to tell anyone
that I was terrified that they'd gone — Larsen, Catherine, Uncle Silbert —
and that it could happen to anyone at any time; that it could happen
to me, and to Zara and to Tim too, and that eventually it would, to
all of us; it would happen to all the people that you cared about and
the more you cared the worse it would be, when one day they just
weren't there anymore.

"Lizzie? So what do you think?"

"It sounds like a plan," I said. "But quite a big one. Let me think
about it for a bit."

"Okay, okay," Zara laughed.

I stood up and looked around the room. "You're painting. Those
are yours," I said to Zara, realising suddenly. "You're painting again.
That's what the dustsheets are for. "

Zara grinned at me coyly. "Well... I'm giving it a go."

I threw a cushion across the room at her.

"Okay, okay," she smiled. "I'm painting again."

"These are really good," I said, getting up and taking a closer look
at the ones against the wall. They were all of flowers again, but they
were different from the still-lifes I'd seen in her room before. These
were abstracts, and really atmospheric. There was one of a row of
daffodils on a hill, with a big white cloud floating up above.

"Wordsworth," said Zara. "'I wandered lonely as cloud…'. I'm
experimenting with poems about flowers."

"That's great. Really great." I picked up a gloomy canvas with a
single blood red velvety rose, wilting against a black background.

"William Blake?" I smiled. "Oh rose, thou art sick…"

"Yes!" said Zara, excitedly. "That's it!"

I turned to face her. "Maybe this *is* the right thing for you," I said.
"You seem really happy."

"I am," said Zara. "I really am."

I caught the tube home. When I got to Baker Street it was already dark. I
hurried through the empty back streets, glancing over my shoulder
all the while. I'd never been nervous about walking home on my

own late at night, and yet tonight I was alert to every sight, every stranger, every sound. I couldn't shake off the feeling of fear and vulnerability that had been with me all day.

As I reached my front door, someone moved out of the shadows and up the steps behind me. I stifled a scream, then realised who it was.

"Oh Tim," I gasped. "It's you."

Tim put his arms around me. "Who did you think it was?"

"It doesn't matter," I said. "Come on in."

Tim stood in my kitchen in his long black coat and boots while I made hot chocolate for us both. He watched me as I opened cupboards and moved around fetching mugs and teaspoons from the sink. I spotted one or two bits of broken plastic that Zara had missed, on the floor below the cooker. As I bent down to pick them up, I had to steady myself with one hand on the floor.

"You're shaking," Tim observed.

"I know. But I'm okay, honest."

Tim looked at me suspiciously. I handed him a mug and he followed me into the living room.

He took off his coat and sat down. "I'm sorry about today," he said. "What I said."

"What did you say?" I smiled.

Tim put down his mug and smiled back at me. "Are you sure you haven't got anything stronger?"

I got up and fetched two glasses and a bottle of wine from the kitchen.

When I returned, Tim was standing by the window with his back to me, misting up the glass with his breath. I stood and looked at him for a moment, at the familiar tall lean back, the muscled forearms, the black curls at the nape of his neck. I walked up behind him and put my arms around him.

"You're wrong," I whispered. "I do love you, you know."

"But not in the right way," said Tim.

"I don't know if I can love anyone in that way right now," I told him. "There's too much I have to sort out."

"Is that an excuse?"

I shook my head. "This isn't about you, Tim, this is about me. I've always depended on someone else for my happiness, and blamed them for my misery. I need to take control of my own life. I need to know I can survive on my own."

"No man is an island," said Tim.

"I know that. And that's true. But... this may sound crazy, but I don't feel I can be really free to let anyone love me properly until I don't need them to anymore."

Tim turned to face me. "I can't help it," he said. "I still want you."

I sighed. "I don't know, Tim. I don't know if I can promise you anything."

"It doesn't matter," he said and put his arms around me. And as I kissed him and as he unbuttoned my blouse I wondered if I were the one that was crazy and if I was giving up the securest thing I'd ever had for the freedom to face the world alone.

The radio was playing softly in the background. Tim was making a rollup with one hand, his other arm around me. He lit it and settled back against the pillows. I leaned forward and kissed him on the stomach.

"What did you think of the funeral?" I asked him.

"Gateway to heaven," he said disdainfully. "Looked like a hole in the ground to me."

I didn't say anything. "When I go," he continued, "I want them to chuck me in the sea." He took a puff of his rollup. I craved a puff myself, but took a deep breath instead.

"Not a bad place to end up," I agreed. "In the sea, your soul free and floating around with all the fish."

"Lizzie, what happened to your father?" asked Tim. He asked this hesitantly, as people always did, because they weren't sure that they should be asking. I only minded that they might not really want to know.

"He died," I said. "He was hit by a car. I was six. He collapsed, as he was crossing the road, and a car hit him. I was there outside our house, waiting for him on the pavement. I saw it happen."

"Oh, God," said Tim. "I'm sorry. You've never really mentioned him before." He squeezed my hand.

I said, "I suppose the subject just never came up. Until you asked, that is. I've never known how to talk about it without worrying that I'm upsetting someone else."

"Someone *else*?"

I nodded. "No one ever seemed to want to talk to me about it. It's as if they think you're going to crack up if they do. I just got used to shutting up about it. Until I met Catherine and Zara, that is. That's the first time anyone wanted to talk about me. Before that… well, I got attracted to other people's problems and tried to solve them instead. It's like some kind of self-nurturing by proxy. But it doesn't really work."

Tim nodded, so I carried on.

"It's like everyone else's pain was always out there needing attention. You seek out people who are the same as you, the walking wounded, because that's what you know, what you're comfortable with. But then, they are so wounded too that they can never give you what you need. Larsen's father left when he was six, the same age as I was when I lost mine. When I told him about my father, he dismissed it. Told me that having a dead father was preferable to having an absent one, in that a dead one was rejection only by default. I accepted what he said; I could see his point. But in the end, it doesn't really matter who does the leaving. You still have to learn to live without them just the same. And if that's too painful…"

"What?"

"You just convince yourself you never cared about them in the first place. Forget them. Replace them. Only, of course, that doesn't quite work. Not in the end, because there'll always be one day when you end up alone, when you have to face your ghosts."

Tim looked up. "Is that what's happening now?"

"I think so. Everything's started coming back to me. Things that I had forgotten. Or if I did remember, it was just in a factual, anecdotal way. I'd lost the associated feelings. I could remember standing outside our house, the trees that lined the street, the sun shining down, even the dress that I was wearing that day, my favourite pink dress. But I couldn't remember how frightened I was when the ambulance came, or what happened in the days and weeks that followed. It's a bit like freeze framing scenes from a movie with no sound. "

"So what did happen, to you, I mean, when your dad collapsed?"

"A neighbour called an ambulance, and I stood there on the pavement and watched as they were both taken away."

"Both?"

"My mother went with him. Pete, my brother, was at school. I was taken into a neighbour's house. Then the police came and told me my dad was dead and my mum was staying at the hospital. They said she had had an asthma attack. She never really told me what happened. I stayed at the neighbour's house for a few days with Pete. And then my mum came and took us home. But it wasn't mentioned, wasn't talked about. I suppose my mother just couldn't."

"So how did it feel, losing your dad like that?"

"Frightening. I know that we had to move. We couldn't stay in the house, my mother told me that later. But all I remember at the time is we left suddenly with no warning. I still can't remember anything much about it. Except feeling frightened. The whole time. Feeling… just scared. Pretty much what I'm feeling now, as it happens. I think my dad dying so suddenly like that… I think I must have thought that it was going to happen to my mother, and then to me too. I've always had these nightmares, about ghosts. I think that's what they were about. Death. Ghosts coming to claim me, just like they claimed my dad."

Tim hugged me to him. "That makes sense."

"But that wasn't the end of it. My mother then met the man who became my step-dad. He hated us, me and Pete. His pleasure came from making us unhappy. It wasn't just the random, unpredictable violence, the times he hit us, pushed us from behind, so that we stumbled and fell, the times he kicked us up the backside, humiliated us, smacked our heads into walls…" Tim looked shocked, aghast. "It was the bullying, the teasing, the way he belittled us, called us names. It just erodes your self-confidence. Eats at the essence of you. It was as if he was trying to destroy me as a person. If I complained, tried to tell my mother, he would just say I was weak, couldn't take a joke. My mum couldn't cope with it, any of it. Nobody talked about what was going on. I think Pete felt so humiliated and angry that he didn't want an ally in me; he just alienated himself from the whole family. Who could blame him? Nobody could acknowledge it. But that made it even more isolating. Sometimes I would watch my mother, I would know she wasn't happy, and I would wonder if she would have it in her to leave. But then along came Keri. So we stayed. I just went to school to get away. Then Pete left, went to live with friends, and I realised that I could do the same. On my sixteenth birthday, I packed my bags and left home."

Tim was silent, taking it all in. He held me tighter. "What a bastard," he said.

"I know," I agreed. "But it wasn't until Martin came along that I allowed myself to remember, relive it. How bad it had all been, you know? It's not just the actual violence. It's living with that permanent threat of it hanging in the air; that's worse in so many ways. I spent most of my childhood treading on eggshells, trying not to upset him, trying to make him like me. It's like those people you hear about who are kidnapped and then start to identify with their kidnappers. Violence, the threat of it — it makes you stop being yourself and start being what you think they want you to be."

"You were just a kid," said Tim, shaking his head. "I want to kill him."

I nodded. "I know Pete felt that way. For a long time. Probably still does. He did the right thing, allowed himself to be angry, to hate him. Me, I just adapted, tried to be good, blamed myself when I wasn't, when I made a mistake, got things wrong. My mother left him eventually. And I escaped it all, in the end, before then. I moved in with my boyfriend, David. I lived with him and his family for three years and realised for the first time what a normal family was like. Then I got a grant and went away to college and had the confidence to leave David behind.

"But the past crept back in. I was scared of being alone, facing myself. Until I met Larsen that was, and then it felt like I had finally found what I had always been looking for. That bond. That indescribable closeness. The thing that I had never had with a man, with a father, the thing that I had been missing all my life. That person who loved me so deeply, so passionately, that he could never let me out of his sight. We were inseparable from the very start. It felt as though he was what had been missing all my life."

Tim took his arm from around my shoulder. "So why did it end? With Larsen, I mean?" He picked up his Rizla papers and started to roll another cigarette.

"I think that what attracted us to each other was the thing that destroyed us in the end: we needed each other too much, to fill a void.

We were literally each other's 'other half' when what we needed to be was whole. Neither of us had faced our ghosts."

Tim was silent for a moment. He finished rolling his cigarette and turned to face me. "And now?"

I pushed back the bedclothes and stood up. I pulled on my dressing gown, drew back the curtain, and stood for a few moments by the window, looking out at the black chimney tops over the fire escape and at the bright, white full moon that sat alone in a vast and empty indigo sky. "I think now it's time to face the truth about what's happened and be who I really am again. And it's something I need to do alone. Being with you is…" I paused. "You make me feel…"

"Brand new?" suggested Tim, with a smile.

"Brand new," I smiled. "Like a movie star." I turned to face him. "But I'm sorry, Tim. I mean it when I say it. I've got to do this alone."

21

I MADE MY DECISION to leave England on the night of Uncle Silbert's funeral, as Tim slept, as I lay in his arms and looked out of the open curtains at the moon, full and bright and beckoning, like another planet waiting to be explored. I hadn't yet formulated a plan, but I realised now that this was what I wanted — to go to France, first of all, and then maybe to travel for a while. As strong as my desire to stay with my friends, to feel safe and secure, was the need to begin the process of self-definition, away from everything and everyone who wanted me to be something that I wasn't at all sure that I was anymore. But there was something I had to do first.

The following day I waited until the lunchtime show was over and then knocked on Sandy's door.

"Lizzie, come in," said Sandy. He immediately put down his pen and papers and jumped up, as if he had been expecting me. He ushered me into a sofa next to his desk, and sat down in an armchair opposite me. He folded his hands in his lap and waited for me to speak.

"I need to leave," I said. "I am so sorry. But I have to go away."

Sandy's face fell. He clearly hadn't been expecting this. "Really?"

"Yes. I'm sorry," I said again.

"Is there anything I can do? Anything to persuade you to change your mind? You are a great asset to us, Lizzie. You are very talented. In fact, I had had in mind that you might be interested in taking on the role of News Editor."

"News Editor? Really?" I was astonished, overwhelmed. I contemplated this for a moment, then shook my head, sadly. "I'm sorry," I said, for the third time. "And I am really very grateful. But I can't accept. I've made up my mind. I have to go."

"I'm the one who is sorry," said Sandy. "Sorry to lose you."

"Thank you. That means a lot."

Sandy smiled, and shifted a little uncomfortably in his chair. "You know, you could take some leave. And then think about it. Take a holiday, take a sabbatical. If that would help."

I considered this for a moment, then nodded. "It would."

"All right," said Sandy, looking relieved. "Good. That's settled then. When do you want to go?"

"Well, my contract says three months…"

"We won't hold you to that. Not if you need to go sooner."

"Is eight weeks enough notice?"

"That will be just fine."

I hesitated. "Actually, there was something else. Something else that I think would help, that is. You mentioned, once before... I was wondering if you could, in fact, put me in touch with someone. You know. To talk to."

Sandy nodded and stood up. "Of course." He went over to his desk, thumbed through a book and wrote a name and number on a piece of paper.

"There," said Sandy. "It's a man. Is that alright?"

I thought about this for a moment. "Yes."

"I'll call and let him know you'll be in touch."

"Okay." I stood up and started to walk out of the door, then turned back, walked over to his desk and kissed him on the cheek. Sandy looked a little taken aback.

"Thank you for everything," I said. "And, I'm sorry."

"You don't have to apologise," said Sandy. "Not for anything."

He stood up and took my hands and held them for a moment.

"Thank you," I said, again.

In mid-July, Lynne phoned to tell me that her contract was ending early. I put most of my belongings in storage and moved into the house with Zara, Shelley, and Tim. I had researched and found a list of guest houses in Paris and was ready to find a flight and book my ticket. But something strange was going on. Gradually, I noticed that I couldn't eat or drink certain things, things that I had always liked before. I couldn't face my dinner in the evening, or the smells of Shelley's cooking in the kitchen, wafting into the hallway and up the stairs. I found that I was getting home from work each afternoon and going straight up to bed, exhausted, where I'd sleep for ten or eleven hours. And then one morning, a few weeks after I had moved into the house, and just as Zara had finally stopped throwing her guts up, I started throwing up myself.

I knew immediately whose baby it was. I also knew immediately what I was going to do; I was going to keep it. Lord knows it wasn't what I had planned. I was supposed to be travelling, leaving England with no ties, no anchor, with nothing to stop me making and amending my plans from one moment to the next. Having children wasn't even on my radar. But as Zara said, life changes direction and you just have to go with it. I knew that there was no other option for me.

Zara was over the moon when I told her.

"Now you can't go travelling," she said, excitedly. "You'll have to stay. We can bring them up together. They could be sisters! Or brothers! Or brother and sister!"

I smiled, and said, "We'll see."

After the initial shock had worn off, Tim too was pleased. "I know this wasn't what you planned. And I know I wasn't part of your plan. But I want to be there for you and the baby. We can do this together," he said. "I'll be there for you every step of the way."

"I don't know, Tim," I told him. "I just can't think beyond the next five minutes. We'll have to talk about this another time."

The sickness floored me. I was unable to think about anything for several weeks, except for how to stave it off. By then, fortunately, I had left the radio station, and I had the luxury of being able to crawl back to bed in the daytime and stay there for most of the day. I still had the money from Jude's parents, sitting in my investment account, but I didn't want to start dipping into that just yet. I put an advertisement in the paper to sell my car.

Zara went out for bananas and Weetabix — they were all I could stomach, along with the mashed potatoes Tim made me each evening, or at different times of the day, depending on his shift. Zara sat on my bed and held my hand and chatted happily, and made plans for us both and our babies, while she flicked half-heartedly through the daytime TV channels on an old portable black and white TV that Clare had left behind.

Once a week, I dragged myself out of bed to see my counsellor. I had had been seeing him since the start of the summer and it was helping beyond belief. When the session was over, I was both physically and mentally exhausted. I would walk back to the house, climb back into bed, and intermittently cry and throw up, but I was happy in a strange, sad, and ironic way. I knew that the counselling was necessary, not just for me, but for the baby too. I had come to believe firmly in the principle that what you don't hand back, you hand on. I soon realised that I wanted this child more than anything, and that I didn't want its legacy to be one of anything but love.

In contrast to me, Zara was full of energy. I had noticed how bubbly she was, how happy and how many plans she had for us and the babies. It had vaguely crossed my mind that it could be mania setting in, but I had dismissed that as cynical. For the first time in her life, she had everything she wanted. She was feeling well for the first time in weeks, now that the hormones had settled down. Why wouldn't she be happy?

But one morning, when she hadn't come in to see me as she usually did and I had got sick of the sight of my bedroom walls, I dragged myself downstairs to find her sitting in the living room drinking tea alone. I poured myself a cup, sweetened it, and sat down opposite her. I noticed she had dark shadows under her eyes.

"You okay?" I asked her.

Zara nodded, and said nothing.

I looked around the room. The dust sheets had been cleared away, a carpet had been laid and the room was now habitable. Zara's canvases were now tacked to the walls.

I looked at the Rose and said, "I know how you feel."

"What?" said Zara. "What do you mean?"

"Not you, the Rose. Wilting. Sick."

"Oh."

Someone outside the window caught my attention, a man with a bald head, wearing a beige Macintosh. Zara had spotted him too. I heard Shelley running down the stairs and opening the front door.

"Who was that?" said Zara, jumping up and pulling back the curtain.

The front door slammed shut and there was a male voice in the hallway. Shelley poked her head around the door. "Lizzie, there's a man here to see you. He says he's come about your car."

Zara frowned. "Who?" she said. "Who is it?"

"Oh okay," I said. "Tell him to come in."

The man in the Macintosh walked in and I waved him into a chair. "Sorry," I said. "I'm not feeling the best. You saw it outside, right? I'll get you the keys."

I stood up and went to find my handbag.

The next thing I heard was Zara's voice, screaming, "Get out!"

I rushed back into the hallway and collided with the man, who was backing out of the living room with his palms up in front of him. I noticed that the back of his head was red and wrinkled and then I saw that so was his face. He looked astonished.

"What's going on?" I asked him.

The man shook his head and pointed at Zara. "Her," he said, in a thick cockney accent, his chin wobbling. "She's barking."

I poked my head around the living room door to see Zara, crouched in her armchair as if she were about to pounce. She was scowling, and her eyes were dark.

"What is it?" I said to Zara. "What's wrong? What did he do?"

"He shouldn't be here," said Zara, defiantly, glaring at the doorway.

"What do you mean? What did he do?" I asked. "Did he hurt you?"

"What are you talking about?" said the man from behind me. "I never went anywhere near her. She just started shouting at me. She's off her head."

"Get out!" screamed Zara again. "Get him out of here!"

Shelley came thundering down the stairs. "What's going on?" she said.

"I don't know." I turned to the man in the Macintosh. "I'm sorry, I think you had better leave."

"You have got to be joking!" said the man indignantly. "I ain't done nothing. I've just come all the way from Enfield. I'm a busy man. You ain't even gonna let me look at it?"

"Here," I said, spotting my car keys lying on the telephone table in the hallway. I picked them up and thrust them at him. "Help yourself. Front nearside brake light's out, handbrake needs attention, rear bumper slightly scratched. Other than that it's in good nick."

"No!" yelled Zara. "Don't. You can't!"

"Can't what?" said Shelley, and ran to Zara and put her arm around her. Zara shrugged her away.

"Don't let him near your car. He'll bomb it!"

"No, Zara, listen," I said, grabbing her hands, and bending down in front of her. "He's a dealer. I told you, I'm selling my car. He answered my ad. I knew he was coming. And quite frankly, he can do what he likes to it once he's given me two grand."

"Don't take his money," said Zara. "Please. I'm begging you. It's blood money."

I heard my car engine revving outside and then quietening as it went off up the street.

"Listen," said Zara. "He's taken it."

"He's gone for a test drive," I said.

"He's evil," said Zara. "Don't you see? Didn't you see his eyes?"

"Oh, God," I said, and looked at Shelley, who gave a vague nod of the head.

"What's that supposed to mean?" Zara swung round and glared at Shelley.

"What?"

"I saw you."

Nausea started to creep over me again. My mouth filled with water. I sat down next to Zara and rested my elbow on the arm of the chair, my chin on my thumb and my face cradled in my forefingers. Zara turned and looked at me for a moment as if I was a ghost, then jumped up and headed for the door.

"Where are you going?" I lifted my head.

"Zara!" called Shelley, at the same time.

Zara turned in the doorway. "You're supposed to be my friends," she said. "I saw that, Lizzie. Sticking your fingers up at me, trying to hide it. Don't think I don't know that's what you were doing." She turned and bolted out of the door.

I looked down at my fingers, confused, and then moved to get up.

Shelley put her hand on my arm. "I'll go," she said. "You're in no fit state."

She jumped up and sprinted after Zara. I lay back in the chair, fighting back the bile that was rising in my throat.

A few minutes later, I heard shouting in the street outside. I lifted the curtain and looked out. Zara was on the pavement, grappling at Shelley, who was trying to catch hold of her and calm her down. I watched as my car came round the corner. At the same moment Shelley and Zara tipped into the road. My car screeched to a halt in front of them.

I leaped up and ran outside. The man in the Macintosh was getting out of the driver's side.

"What the bloody hell…?" he said.

"Sorry," said Shelley, bending over Zara, who had fallen over, and was sitting in the road.

"Is she okay?" I asked Shelley.

"She's fine," said Shelley. "No harm done."

"No harm done!" said the Macintosh man. "What about me? She nearly killed me."

"Don't exaggerate," I said, and added, weakly, "and anyway, at least you know the brakes work."

"She's pregnant," explained Shelley. The man looked at Zara, who was being helped up by Shelley, then turned and looked at me.

"Which one?" he said.

"Both of them," said Shelley.

"That explains a lot," he said, and walked round the car to where I was standing. I was leaning against the driver's side window. Saliva was filling my mouth. I couldn't move, or speak.

"Okay. I'll take it. Two grand, right?"

I nodded. The man took out his wallet.

"No!" screamed Zara, shrugging Shelley's hand from her arm.

"Oh, God. Excuse me," I said, suddenly, and, steadying myself with one hand on the roof of my car, I leaned over the kerb and was violently sick. The man jumped backwards as vomit splashed his shoes. Zara saw her opportunity and made a run for it.

"For crying out loud," said the Macintosh man, emphasising all his vowels far more than was really necessary.

Shelley called the police. We didn't know what else to do.

"She's a danger to herself," insisted Shelley. "And to her baby. She nearly got us both run over."

"Okay," I agreed, reluctantly, as I stuffed a bundle of fifty pound notes into a drawer in the kitchen. I hated the thought of Zara being arrested, being grabbed and held against her will. "If there's nothing else we can do."

An hour later the phone rang. Zara had got as far as Faringdon Tube station when the police arrived. They had arrested her under the Mental Health Act and she was once again a patient on Strauss Ward at St Barts.

Zara wasn't allowed visitors until the following day. When I arrived at the ward with a big bunch of flowers, I noticed that the same staff nurse was at the reception desk. She smiled at me in recognition but clearly couldn't place me. I was just another worried face to her. Whereas to me, it looked as though she lived here. I wondered what it felt like, working here every day, sleeping here at nights, permanently breathing in this hospital smell, this stench of disinfectant and broken lives.

Zara was in bed, curled up in a ball and staring at the wall.

"I got you these," I said, waving the flowers around. "And I brought your pencils, and your pad. I thought you could draw them. Look at the lilies. They're really something."

Zara continued staring at the wall. A tear trickled out of the corner of her eye.

"Zara? Come on, sweetie, talk to me."

Slowly, she pulled herself up and looked at me. Her hair was matted and sticking up like a halo round her head. Her eyes looked red and wild. She picked at a fingernail and chewed it.

"You tricked me," she said. "You sent the police to get me. I thought I was helping them. I thought they'd come to catch that man. The one who took your car."

"I'm sorry, Zara. We didn't know what else to do. And he didn't take my car," I said gently. "He came to buy it. He took it for a test drive."

Zara looked up at me, and started to cry. She sat up and held her arms out to me. "Help me, Lizzie. I don't know what I'm going to do. I can't take this anymore."

"Oh, sweetheart, come here." I put the flowers down on a table and wrapped my arms around her. I sat down on the bed beside her. Zara clung to me and sobbed into my shoulder.

"I can't do this anymore. I've had enough. It's the baby, that's what it is."

"Zara, they've examined you. The baby is fine."

Zara looked up, her face pale and blotchy and tear-streaked. "No! You don't understand. It's not fine at all. It's the baby that's done this to me. I don't want it. They've got to get it out of me. It feels like I've got an alien inside me!"

"Oh, come on honey, that's just the illness talking…"

"No!" Zara started to thump her stomach with her small pale fist. "You've got to help me, it's got to go, it's got to go, it's got to go!"

I grabbed her hand and held it firmly. "Stop, Zara. Stop it. Otherwise I'm going to have to call the nurse."

"So call her. Tell her they've got to get me a termination. I don't want it, I don't want it anymore." Zara started to scream.

I held her tight. "Shh, Zara, please. You're upsetting yourself."

"Then tell them, tell them!"

I got up and stuck my head out of the room, and looked down the hallway. Zara was scaring me and I couldn't see anyone around to help. Zara's voice got louder and louder behind me. I wondered if I should go and find a nurse or whether Zara would calm down again in a minute or two. I didn't want her to start telling the nurses to give her a termination; I knew that couldn't be what she really wanted. I wondered if I should maybe go and try and find Shelley, who was at work on the cancer ward. She would know what to do.

Finally, a nurse came walking down the corridor towards us. She spoke gently but firmly to Zara, and then a consultant came in too. Zara was alternately screaming and then sobbing and biting her hand. But within minutes she had been sedated and was soon drifting off to sleep.

I watched her for a moment and stroked her hair. Then I bent and whispered into her ear, "It's all going to be okay, honey, I promise. We're going to get you better."

I followed the consultant out of her room. He was a small-framed man, in his early sixties, I guessed. His head was virtually bald, all bar a few patches of white hair, and he had kind eyes behind big thick glasses. I couldn't help but notice with irony that he had hair growing out of his ears.

"We can't locate her parents," he said. "I wonder if you can help? Do you have another contact number for them?"

"No," I told him. "Only the one she has given you. To be honest, they don't have much contact with her. I've never even met or spoken to them. Please talk to me. I'm her closest friend. I need to know what you're going to do to help her. You must be able to see that she's desperate."

"Come with me." The consultant took my arm and moved me into a side room off the main corridor. The room had beige plastic sofas with beige plastic cushions to match. A pot of plastic flowers sat on a side table along with a pile of magazines. "We need to stabilise her mood," he said. "The anti-depressants aren't enough on their own. What she really needs is a mood stabiliser and an anti-psychotic too."

"Okay," I nodded. "That's great. So that was the problem then? She was on the wrong drugs?"

The doctor looked uncomfortable. He blinked hard with each eye alternately and his glasses moved up and down on his nose. "I'm afraid it's not as simple as that. We stabilised her mood initially, the last time she left the ward. We prescribed Lithium, and it seemed to be working well. But then when she discovered that she was expecting, we had to stop the medication. Lithium can't be taken during pregnancy. All the research shows that it can be harmful to the developing foetus. There is no alternative drug that's effective and safe in pregnancy. So we are in a bit of a predicament. I'm afraid that there is no other way to put this. Zara has a rather difficult choice to make. It's either her mental health, or the baby."

"What?" I whispered. "You're kidding, right?" Even as I heard my voice, I knew that I sounded stupid, that this was no joke.

"She's a little over eighteen weeks pregnant," the Consultant continued. "So a termination carries some risks, but it's not unusual to carry out the procedure at this stage. And in her situation... well, I simply don't believe that her mental state is going to improve by itself."

I backed into the sofa and sat down heavily onto one of the plastic cushions.

"This can't be right," I said. "There must be another way."

The consultant shook his head. "I'm sorry."

"This baby, it's everything she has always wanted," I protested. "She's in a bad way right now, but you should have seen her a week ago. A few days ago, even. She was on Cloud Nine." I stopped and realised how that sounded. Cloud Nine was a dangerous cloud for Zara to be on. "She was so happy," I corrected myself, as if trying to alter Zara's mood with my words. "About the baby, I mean. Look, she's lost one before, and she can't lose this one too. Please. There must be something you can do."

"I'm sorry." The Consultant scratched his head and took off his glasses. His eyes were big and a little bloodshot. He blinked hard several times. "You know she's saying she doesn't want it?"

"But that's just the illness…" I protested. I stopped. "Isn't it?"

"It's hard to say." The Consultant blinked again and I saw that in fact he had a tic. For some reason it made me want to put my arms around him.

Then I realised, suddenly and with alarm, how futile this situation was. I didn't know which bit of her was in fact the real Zara: the high, happy Zara, or the low, tearful, depressed Zara. I cast my mind back to try and remember a time when she had been just somewhere in between, so that I had something to go on. I remembered her sitting in the King's Arms the previous summer, the day we met up again. I remembered her telling me how much she had regretted aborting Doug's baby. I knew that this could not possibly be what she would choose, if choice was really something that was open to her. But was she well then? Or was that the illness talking too? She had terminated her first baby, after all. I remembered Doug saying that she had been ill, and I realised now what he had meant. He hadn't meant physically. Zara had been unwell long before I had known her.

But even if a baby *was* what she really wanted, how could she be a mother, how could she raise a child, like this? They had to stabilise her, there was no other way. And to do that, they would have to kill her baby. Once she was stable again, I had no doubt that she would be in pieces over what she had lost. But right now, what other options were there? She could never be a mother to her child, not like this. And she couldn't stay like this for the next five months, biting herself and crying.

"I get what you're saying," I said. "And I know she'll agree. Right now, she just wants to feel okay again."

The Consultant nodded. "I know this is difficult," he said. "We'll talk to her in the morning."

Then he was gone.

The operation was carried out two days later. Zara gave her consent immediately and without hesitation. And, as I'd predicted, once she was stable and realised what she had lost, she was heartbroken and her grief was hard to bear. I sat on the ward on and off for days, and held her hand while she cried, and I wondered briefly if she would soon begin to hate me for now having what she had lost.

I left for Paris in the autumn. I had just had my twenty week scan, and was told that the baby was a girl. I was over the moon. "I'm so happy! It's a girl!" I told Tim, on the phone, as if I would have felt any differently if it had been a boy. "Hurrah! It's a baby!" said Tim. I had called Sandy and told him that I wouldn't be coming back to work. I packed and finally booked my ticket.

I knew that Shelley thought I was crazy.

"Do you really want to give birth in a foreign country where you know no one and have no support?" she asked me.

"Yes," I said. "That's exactly what I want to do. It may be hard to understand. But I want this new start. And besides, I'll make friends."

Both Zara and Tim knew that there were deeper reasons why I needed to go, and both of them accepted my decision. Zara was stable, and Tim and Shelley had promised to look out for her.

"Don't worry about me," said Zara. She had recovered surprisingly well and appeared to be accepting with grace that this was her fate and the fate of her unborn child. "I'm going to make it, you know," she told me.

I held her tight. "I know," I said. "I could have told you that."

Tim had borrowed a car from a friend at work and he took me to the airport.

"So," he said, after I'd checked in, and we were stood at the gates to the departure lounge. "You'll keep in touch? Let me know when the baby's born?"

"Of course."

"You know I will be there for you. Be a proper dad to her. If you change your mind. You know?"

"I know," I said.

"Call me. Anytime. Night or day." He looked at me, blinking back tears.

I looked back at him and nodded. "Thanks."

"So," he said. "How does it feel?"

I smiled. "It's like the feeling you get in the pit of your stomach when you jump out of an aeroplane."

"Never done that," said Tim.

"Me neither," I said, and shuddered. "But I can imagine."

"And…. Don't do that, by the way," said Tim. I smiled. "You don't have to go," he added, one last time. "It's not too late to change your mind."

I didn't reply. I didn't say, "You could come with me." Because we both knew that this was a journey I had to make alone. For a moment we stood by the gate, looking at each other and smiling. Then I kissed him, and took hold of my trolley and said, "Goodbye, Tim."

"Just you?" said the flight attendant, taking my passport and boarding pass.

"Just me," I smiled, and walked through the gate. Just me and my baby.

22

WE LIVE IN A TOWN CALLED EAUBONNE, just to the North of Paris. It has everything we need, including the forest where we run, and walk the dog by the lake and, in summer, have lazy picnics. There is a modern competition-sized swimming pool right by the rail station, from where it is only a twenty minute hop into the Gare du Nord.

Like me, my daughter, Helena, is a keen swimmer — in fact she is a much stronger swimmer than I, and an able all-round athlete. She attends the Association Sportif, a sports college nearby where she is studying for the International Baccalaureate, but is also in training in earnest for the Pentathlon Moderne. She gets up at five each morning to run and then swim, and I join her at least twice a week. The pool is quiet most of the time. There is just one diving board in the middle, at the end, and the lanes are marked out. Along the other side is a wall of windows with doors opening out onto a terrace. I have never swum in a lovelier pool.

Eaubonne is our home now, and has been for many years. I moved out of Paris when Helena was a baby, seeking a bigger house for less money along with the beauty and tranquillity of the countryside. I never went travelling; I had no need. I found what I was looking for in Paris, in Helena, in myself. I found a job translating journals and publications for a small agency located in the tenth arrondissement, and I have been there ever since. The nature of what I do for a living means that I can work from home, and it is a life that suits me well.

The town is really friendly; I can't go to the market without meeting friends on the way, and a few more while I'm there. There is a stall which sells olives and tapanade, candied fruit, and nuts. There is an Arabic couple who make their own patisseries. They are beautiful and delicious, made of honey, nuts and "brick" (I can't find a word for this in English). The lady is incredibly fat but absolutely beautiful. Her skin is smooth and glowing like honey and her eyes sparkle. She always serves mint tea free of charge to anyone who buys her cakes.

There is a beautiful forest nearby: the Foret de Montmorency. It is busy at weekends, but less so during the week. Early in the morning, or indeed whenever we get the chance, Helena and I take off with Lily, our dog, running through the forest and alongside the lake, then up the hill to a prairie with a big oak tree in the middle. It is rare to see anyone there. We run up a big hill onto a shingle road with chestnut trees on both sides. In the winter, there are big Alexander beetles and big red slugs on the road. In the summer, there is pale coloured sand. The forest floor is very leafy and there are lots of chestnuts and mushrooms. There are wild purple foxgloves growing there and soft springy leaf mould which then becomes sand. There are snakes in the banks, which scare me, and my fear makes Helena laugh.

She is an audacious girl, and there is not much that fazes her. She has the indulgent and entitled air of many of her generation; she is a normal eighteen-year-old, in fact. I am happy to see that she is so confident and headstrong and, although it's true that I also envy her this, I am pleased that she is so comfortable in her own skin, that she feels she has the intrinsic right to be here, in this world, in our house, in the lives of those around her. I am glad she challenges me and demands to be heard. I am glad that she feels safe enough to do so.

For the first time in many years, though, she has been asking about her father. She wants to know everything about him, and I don't know where to begin. How much do I tell her? How much does she need to know? The whole truth? Or a half truth, a white lie? What, I am wondering, is the right thing to do? When she was little it somehow wasn't an issue. Along with Father Christmas or the Tooth Fairy, it wasn't that difficult to pass him off as a creature of myth. And later, as she grew older, she just seemed to accept without question that he was to remain remote and invisible, not entirely unlike the one up in heaven. ("My Father, who art in England," she used to joke irreverently during the Lord's Prayer). But now she is eighteen, a student of the International Baccalaureate, and she is being taught to enquire. Her mind is opening up to new possibilities and it is right that, before she ventures out into the world, she should want to know where she came from. How can I blame her for that?

When I first moved to Paris, I took with me the copy of Ralph Waldo Emerson's *Essay on Self-Reliance* that Uncle Silbert had given me. Heavily pregnant with Helena, I spent a long time in the Bibliotheque Nationale searching through dictionaries, study notes and archives, and preparing my own translation of the essay into modern English. I have found a lot of comfort and guidance from it over the years. Its inherent irony, however, is not lost on Helena, for whom I dug it out last night.

"He wants us to think for ourselves, to be original, to refuse to follow the crowd. So why should we listen to him?" she asked.

We were sitting in the kitchen drinking coffee with my friend, Suzanne.

"C'est vrai, c'est un paradoxe," laughed Suzanne. "Comme toi. Like you," she said. Helena responded by sitting down heavily on Suzanne's lap and wrapping her arms tightly around her neck. Helena is tall, and way too heavy for Suzanne's petite frame.

"Stop it, Helena, you're suffocating her," I reprimanded.

Suzanne laughed and waved her hand. "Ça va."

"But isn't it selfish?" Helena persisted. "To put your needs before others, in the way that he recommends?"

"Au contraire," said Suzanne. "It is by having respect for yourself and your own feelings that empathy for others is born."

Helena thought about that for a moment. "What are you like if you have no empathy?"

"Antisocial," said Suzanne.

"You mean like people who commit crimes, hurt other people?"

"Yes, that's right. They can be very charming, give the outward appearance of being interested in you. But in reality, they don't have that capacity. These people are cut off, disconnected from their own feelings, and if they don't know how to feel for themselves, they can't feel for anyone else either. In the extreme, they are psychopaths."

"So why don't we just teach them how to feel instead of locking them up?"

Suzanne smiled. "Have you ever thought about running for President?"

"No," said Helena. "I have only thought about running."

I smiled at my daughter and went to the stove, poured more coffee. Suzanne patted Helena's knee. "You are a true philosopher, mademoiselle."

"I think his essay is like anything else you read," I said, setting the coffee cups down on the table. "You have to take the parts that resonate with you and leave the rest."

Helena nodded. "Okay. Well, I certainly agree with him that you have to be who you really are. And you must tell the truth, even if it hurts, absolutely. Living a lie, living in denial, it's not fair to anyone, least of all yourself."

I turned to face her. "You really believe that?" I asked.

"Of course" she said. "Don't you?"

Today has been one of the first real days of autumn after a few hot weeks of summer, and there was that chill in the morning air which always stirs something inside me, reminding me of new school books and new beginnings; of childhood walks in the forest and crunching fallen leaves followed by hot cocoa, drop scones and chilblains by the fireside. I got up at dawn with Helena and we ran with Lily, through the forest and past the lake, where Lily always goes for a dip before running on to catch us up. The lake is beautiful. It is grey-blue and glistens white. From a distance, the seagulls look as if they are part of the sparkle, until Lily arrives and the birds get frightened and suddenly fly off. There are bulrushes and tall soft grasses near a little castle, with ducks and their babies nesting amongst them. In the summer, there are a few coots and lots of little turtles, which come out of the water to lie in the sun.

I watched Helena as she ran ahead of me around the lake, dipping through the bulrushes and up the hill, and I came to a decision: I must tell her the truth. She may despise me. She might not understand. But it's a risk that I must take.

It's now evening, cool and dark. It's Friday night and we are at home in the kitchen, preparing a supper of the food that we both love: salad with endives and avocado and garlic vinaigrette, goat's cheese, fat juicy olives, and delicious crusty baguettes from the Boulangerie on the corner at Place Aristide. Helena is setting out glasses and cutlery on the table, pouring thick red wine and telling me about her day. I watch her from where I am standing near the stove. She is very beautiful. Of course, I would say that. I'm her mother. But it's true, and I can never quite believe that she is mine.

"What?" Helena asks, churlishly. "Why are you looking at me like that?" She shrugs a pile of ironing off the kitchen chair and onto the sofa, sinks down onto it, and picks up her fork.

So where to begin? I contemplate this as Helena tips a pile of dripping leaves onto her plate and pushes a piece of bread into her mouth. I sit down at the table beside her and fiddle with the stem of my wine glass.

"I've got something to tell you," I hear myself say.

So now it's late, and I've told her the whole story. The bread, cheese, and wine are gone, and the salad bowl is empty. The blinds in the kitchen are still open, and the empty blackness of the sky framed by the window above the stove reminds me of a photograph that is yet to develop.

It seemed right to begin that day, that wet spring day in 1992, the day that Catherine walked back into my life. That was the point, it seems, that my life began to unravel. And that, of course, is the day that I met him for the very first time. I wonder briefly, for the millionth time, how different things might have been if the pool had been shut, say, that day. A power failure. Heaters, or something. Or if, on the way home, I had crossed the road at the traffic lights as I should have done, instead of running into the road. But then I would be living in a world without her in it, and my imagination stops right there. I can't see my past, or my future, without Helena. It just isn't a place that I would ever want to be.

Helena is sitting still, looking at the table. She is silent for several minutes. Finally, she says, "So he raped you." Her voice cracks slightly as she speaks.

"Yes. In law, he did. If you believe that, of course. That I didn't give consent. Remember that this is my story. He may tell it differently."

"How? How could he tell it differently? How could you have given consent? You were knocked out by that punch. The punch that Catherine made. Everybody saw that — Zara, Shelley, everyone, including him. That's why he did what he did. He took advantage. It's obvious." She shakes her head.

I nod and look up at her, both grateful and full of admiration for her certainty, her lack of doubt. I study her face. She has the same tall, athletic body as her father, and has inherited his hazel eyes and sandy hair. Other than that, there has never been any obvious connection between the two of them, and I have never felt his presence in her at all.

"So, that's it?" asks Helena sadly. "I'm the product of a rape?"

"A gift. The one good thing to come out of it," I tell her. "You know how much I love you. You changed my life."

Helena is silent again.

"Look, I considered telling him," I say. "But I knew that if I did it would be irreversible. I just didn't know what would happen — to me, to you, to Catherine."

"I didn't say that you should have told him." Helena fiddles with the stem of her empty wine glass, rolling it between her thumb and forefinger, twisting it first one way, then the other so that its base rolls in a heavy semi-circle across the table top, threatening to topple over and break.

She hesitates. "So, what was he like?"

Of course, I didn't know him well. So all I can tell Helena is the little about him that I do know — snippets that had mostly come from Catherine. I know that he liked cars, he liked sport, and that he had had to give up his swimming career because of a sports injury. He was bright, interested in politics. And he had a good sense of fun. It's hard to explain the nice things about him in terms that don't contradict what I have just told her. But nothing will alter what I know to be true: that my life, and Helena's, and Catherine's too, would all have been altered immeasurably by his knowledge of her existence —and not for the better, I am sure of that.

"So that's why you left England?"

I nod. "The main reason, yes, in the end. I could have stayed. With Zara and Tim. But I was never sure if Catherine would try and get in touch. Or him. I couldn't live like that, never knowing when I was pushing your pram down the street, or leaving the house, if he was going to pull up outside or knock on the door and put two and two together."

Helena sets her wine glass down on the table and looks up at me in silence.

"But you're an adult now," I continue. "It's your call." I take a deep breath. "So, do you want to find him? Do you want to meet him?"

Helena pauses, looks at me, then shakes her head. "Non," she says. "Ça ne vaut pas la peine." *It's not worth it.*

Or, as it translates literally, *it's not worth the pain.*

I heard once that all stories end with one of three things: forgiveness, revenge, or tragedy. I have spent some time lately pondering which my ending is, or will be.

Forgiveness, so it's said, is the Christian thing to do. But I don't believe you have to forgive to be happy. Why forgive, just for the sake of it? That seems like a cop out to me, a betrayal of the self. Not forgiving changes things forever. But not necessarily for the worse. Non-forgiveness is my shield against the loss of self. It is something that I will carry with me always.

Revenge? Not necessary. I have learned to live with injustice. I have wondered, in passing, if my revenge has been my absence, my stand, my decision to deny Martin his child. But I know that if that were true, then it is only a small strand of what happened; my primary motivation has always been the desire to protect my child, and, yes, to protect myself, too. As Uncle Silbert said, it's all about knowing your own truths, and not needing a defence, or a second opinion.

Tragedy? On the contrary. Mine is certainly not an unhappy ending. And, in spite of the losses that both Zara and I have endured, we have been left with our friendship. That is something I will always cherish.

We see her often. Sometimes when she is well, she will get herself to Waterloo and onto the Eurostar and she will stay for weeks at a time. Other times when she can't face the journey we will go to her. She still lives in London, in Clerkenwell, in a supported housing scheme just off Goswell Road. It's a little crowded when we are all there together but none of us mind and Helena is used to Zara's ups and downs.

The illness is there for life, it seems, and Zara is unlikely to work again, although she remains somewhat skeptical about the theory of a chemical imbalance that can't be cured with diet, sunlight, and exercise, and that still remains her dream. For now, though, she is still dependent on the drugs that keep her mood stable. She's not bitter, although at times she says that she feels as though life is passing her by. Mostly, she just feels relief at being allowed to avoid the battlefield that is the real world, and to be able to take things at her own pace. She has her paintings. She can afford new clothes and makeup every now and again, and she doesn't have to sell her soul and her sanity to get them. I remain hopeful for her. She may be vulnerable, but she is not a victim; on the contrary, she is determined, courageous, and strong. It seems we all have to find our own medium between security on the one hand and freedom on the other, and for some, like Zara, the balance must be more finely tuned. I have come to realise, though, that we can't have hope without a degree of uncertainty in our lives; and that those things that induce fear and discomfort in me are the very same things that make me feel truly alive.

Now, after all that's happened, I am inclined to agree that everything was meant to be. Catherine would be pleased. Do I believe in fate? Possibly. Maybe there is no such thing. Or perhaps the way our life unfolds is a complex equation, made up of many things: a pre-destined trajectory combined with our own character, plus a smattering of random, accidental happenings. No one can possibly know for sure.

But this is my story. These are my truths. This is what happened. Of that, I am certain.

THE END

FROM THE AUTHOR

Thank you so much for reading my debut novel. Please visit my website RuthMancini.com for information about my upcoming books. I'm also on Facebook and Twitter as @RuthMancini1. I hope to see you there.

MORE GREAT READS FROM BOOKTROPE

A Medical Affair by **Anne Strauss** (Fiction) A woman has an affair with her doctor. Flattered, she has no idea his behavior violates medical ethics and state law. The novel is based on solid research of which most patients are unaware.

Thank You For Flying Air Zoe by **Erik Atwell** (Contemporary Women's Fiction) Realizing she needs to awaken her life's tired refrains, Zoe vows to recapture the one chapter of her life that truly mattered—her days as drummer for an all-girl garage band. Will Zoe bring the band back together and give The Flip-Flops a second chance at stardom?

A State of Jane by **Meredith Schorr** (Contemporary Women's Fiction) Jane is ready to have it all: great friends, partner at her father's law firm and a happily-ever-after love. But her life plan veers off track when every guy she dates flakes out on her. As other aspects of Jane's life begin to spiral out of control, Jane will discover that having it all isn't all that easy.

Riversong by **Tess Thompson** (Contemporary Romance) Sometimes we must face our deepest fears to find hope again. A redemptive story of forgiveness and friendship.

Just Friends with Benefits by **Meredith Schorr** (Contemporary Romance) When a friend urges Stephanie Cohen not to put all her eggs in one bastard, the advice falls on deaf ears. Stephanie's college crush on Craig Hille has been awakened 13 years later as if soaked in a can of Red Bull and she is determined not to let the guy who got away once, get away twice.

Unsettled Spirits by **Sophie Weeks** (Contemporary Romance) As Sarah grapples with questions of faith, love, and identity, she must learn to embrace not just the spirits of the present, but the haunting pain of the past. Can she accept her past in order to let love in?

Discover more books and learn about our
new approach to publishing at **booktrope.com**.

Lightning Source UK Ltd.
Milton Keynes UK
UKOW05f0140080114

224115UK00002B/13/P